The Research Results

Book III

Sarah Fawcett

To my children
Who encourage me to write every day and
leave me alone when I am.
It still amazes me how I raised such
fantastic kids.
I'm a proud mom.

Acknowledgements

To my amazing super fans: lil Sarah, Monique, Laurie, Marjorie and Laura. Thanks for all the pep talks, advice, listening ears and making me believe that what I'm writing is worth reading.

To Josie, my new editor and fitness friend. Thanks for your precision and speediness.

The Research Results

Book III

1.

Mr. Baker is staring at me, motionless from the sidewalk. I can't help but stare back at him through the slit in the curtain on my front door. What's he doing here? Why is he just standing there? Even from this distance, I can see that his eyes are black and menacing. I need to call the police. I blindly find the strap of my purse on my shoulder and follow it down, finding the zipper and tearing at it to get it open. I dig through it, searching for my cell phone and finally grasping it in my shaking hands. I look down momentarily and dial 911, quickly focusing my eyes on Mr. Baker once again. He hasn't moved.

Suddenly, the shrill of my alarm echoes through the house and I almost drop the phone. It doesn't even faze Mr. Baker. He shifts his position slightly and takes a swig of his flask. I think he's smiling. My stomach churns.

"911. What's your emergency?"

I can barely hear the woman over the alarm. "I need the police," I yell into the phone.

"Hold, please."

What? I put all my weight against the door, but my shoes slip on the spilled wine. I can't get any leverage. He could get through if he wanted. Did she tell me to hold?

"Police. How can I help you?"

"My name is Colleen Cousineau. Send the police quickly to 58 Seaton Street. A man that I've had trouble with in the past is outside my house. His name is Martin Baker." I continue to babble, but stop when Mr. Baker steps forward onto my walkway. "He's coming closer!"

"Colleen, try to remain calm. The police are on their way. Go to your bedroom and hide in the closet."

"The closet?" I look at Mr. Baker and then look towards the stairs. It's a long way. I shake my head. "I can't move."

"What is this Martin Baker doing now?"

"He's standing on my property, drinking from his flask."

"Is he coming closer?"

"No, he only took one step."

"Is that your house alarm?"

"Yes." I can't believe that my neighbours haven't raced over to see what all of the ruckus is about. Thanks, Henry! Next time you cut your grass in your speedo, I'm taking pictures and posting them online!

"Keep the alarm on, it may scare him away."

Mr. Baker adjusts his stance, but it doesn't look like he's going anywhere. He doesn't seem to care about the alarm.

"Colleen, you'll be fine. The police are minutes away."

Minutes? Any other time I call, they get here so fast. Where's Officer Nicholl's? I liked him. He was nice. I'd even take the mean one. What was his name?

Mr. Baker takes another long drink and spits it out onto my lawn. Then, he abruptly turns and starts walking down the street.

"He's leaving! He's leaving!"

"Which direction is he travelling?"

"Left! I mean, north! He's travelling north on Seaton Street." Where's he going? They won't be able to catch him.

He's gone from my view at the front door, so I move to the living room, but I can't see him there either, so I move back and open the door a crack, peeking out. He's gone. I open the door completely and step out, getting up on the balls of my feet. I can't see him.

"He's gone! You won't find him! He's gone!" I shout into the phone.

"But you're safe now. Please stay on the line until the police arrive."

"Fine." I'm so angry. The alarm seems louder than before, but I don't shut it off. Officer Leeds. That's his name. Where is he?

"Are you ok now, Colleen?"

"No, not really."

"The police should be—

"I see them!" I drop the phone, run out of the house and flag down the police car.

Officer Nicholls steps out of the car. "He went that way!" I point down the street. Officer Leeds nods and drives down the street with his lights flashing.

"What happened?" Officer Nicholls escorts me back up my walkway and allows me to go into the house first. I didn't shut the door.

I step over the glass and try to avoid the wine, but it's everywhere. "Well, Mr. Baker—

"Could you turn off your alarm, please?" He yells and looks at the floor, stepping carefully around the mess.

"Right. Sorry." I key in the code and turn back to him. "Mr. Baker just showed up at my house. I had just gotten home and when I turned to close the door, I saw him standing on the sidewalk."

"Did he do anything?" He picks up my cell phone, wipes it on a towel and places it on the counter. Then, he pulls out his notebook and starts scribbling in it.

"No, he just stood there staring at me."

"Did he touch you?"

"No."

"Talk to you?"

I avert my eyes, "Well, no…" I'm starting to feel embarrassed. "He just stood on the sidewalk and stared at me and the house. I'm sorry. I thought he was going to attack me or hurt me."

"You were right to call us." He looks down to the floor. "What happened here?"

"Oh, I dropped two bottles of wine when he startled me." I kneel down to pick up some glass and immediately cut my finger. "Ouch!"

"Hey!" He bends down and touches my arm. "Don't do that. Where's your dustpan? I'll do it."

"No, I'm fine. It's just a small cut."

"Just sit down and tell me where I can find something to clean this up," he says gently.

I nod and point to the sink. "It's under there." I clean up my wound and sit down, watching him pick up all of the glass. I need that wine right about now. Why did he want to scare me like that?

"The glass is all picked up. How do you want me to clean up the wine?"

"You've done enough. I can wipe that up quickly."

He nods and walks to the middle of the kitchen, while I grab paper towels and a sponge. Bent over, reaching for all of the wine, I realize that on my hands and knees in my dress I'm pretty sure I'm giving him a good show. I move quickly, knowing I can give it a better cleaning later.

When I stand up, I see that Officer Nicholls is writing in his notebook. Maybe he wasn't watching me. "Do you want some coffee or tea?" I start putting water in the kettle.

"No, thank you. Is this about the fifth incident with Martin Baker? Not including the actual abduction?"

"Sounds about right."

"You're holding up pretty well."

"Thanks, but it's all just a front." I smile and he comes to stand beside me. I see the large handgun in his holster and I instantly feel safe. How am I going to feel when he leaves? I need a gun or better, I need to date a policeman.

There's a knock at the door and I jump, almost dropping a mug that I just took down from the cupboard. Officer Nicholls reaches to catch the mug in my hands, but I already have it secured, so his hands just wrap around mine.

"I got it," I smile, feeling uncomfortable. I don't want to date this policeman.

7

Officer Leeds steps inside my house at exactly that moment and looks at our hands. Officer Nicholls releases his hands from mine and Officer Leeds rolls his eyes. "I couldn't find Martin Baker."

I'm stunned and infuriated. Of course you didn't find him! You took too long getting here. I turn to face the counter and busy myself with wiping the countertop. I scour one spot over and over again, cursing Officer Leeds under my breath.

"Pardon me?" Officer Leeds questions me?

"Can't get the damn wine stain out." I throw down the sponge. "What were you saying?"

"Mr. Baker was long gone by the time we got here. I drove around and shone the spotlight onto some properties, but it was too dark and I didn't have enough man-power. I couldn't see him." He throws up his hands in irritation.

"Oh," is all can manage. I'm angry. I'm so glad that he took his time. What if Mr. Baker comes back? I have to rely on these guys?

"If he comes back, we'll be on the street all night."

I look at them blankly. What about for the rest of my life?

"Don't worry. We'll catch him."

"I'm sure you will." I try not to sound sarcastic or disbelieving. They don't realize who they're dealing with. Mr. Baker doesn't seem like a smart man, but he's proven to be cold and calculating. There's a reason why he just stood outside waiting and doing nothing. Was it to prove that he's not afraid of me? Of the police? He wants something. There's no doubt that he's out for revenge.

2.

After the officers leave, I change into sweats and get down on my hands and knees again to scrub the wine off the baseboards. Then, I vacuum the entire kitchen, making sure that all of the glass is gone. Of course, now I have to mop the floor.

As I wait for the kitchen floor to dry, so I can put the kitchen table back where it belongs, I go through the mail and flyers that have piled up on the table. I notice my Sex Project notebook, but the pile of invoices that I haven't paid lately gets my full attention. How did I not pay my credit card bill? How much interest am I going to have to pay? I sit down in the living room and use my phone to transfer money from my bank to pay my bills. When I'm done, I place the whole stack in my office that I'll organize and file later.

Back in the living room, I scrunch up my nose as I survey it. Yuck! Look how dusty everything is. Oh no! I hope that mark comes off the coffee table! I scratch at it with my fingernail. It looks permanent. I rush to grab my cleaning supplies and dig deep, vacuuming and dusting. When did I become such a slob? Jack had hinted at that once and he was absolutely right.

A red vase sits in my hand as I stop mid-dust. Jack was right about a lot of things. I slowly go over the shapely red glass and remember running by the water with Jack. That was the last time I saw him and had he told me again that I should move on and forget about Steve. *'Steve's always been a pathetic cheater. He's a little boy and he couldn't deal with your success and your strength. God, your strength! I love that about you. He could never be the man you deserve.'*

I remember his words so vividly. Why didn't I listen to him? He had also told me that he loves me. Flip flop. There it is again. The good old flip flop. I shake my head and put the vase down, moving onto the picture frames.

Why do I still have pictures of Steve in my house? I look at our wedding day lovey dovey photo and the really old one of us wearing our volleyball uniforms. Ugh! I put down my dust rag, grab a heavy duty garbage bag from under the sink and walk around the house throwing out every reminder of Steve. I have no sentimental reason to keep anything that associates to him. Everything has to go! The photos, including their frames, our collection of movie stubs and other paraphernalia from our date nights and especially our photo albums all go in the garbage. I tie up the bag and throw it by the front door.

Jack should feel better coming into my house now with everything gone. When he professed his love, it was the wrong time for me. He had such hurt in his eyes when I told him that I didn't want anything from him. I hurt him. I don't know how deeply, though. Maybe he's over it and has moved on? Flip flop. I hope he hasn't moved on. What if he has?

The blankets that Jack had used when he slept on the couch are on the floor, so I pick them up and bring them close to my nose, breathing deeply. I'm not quite sure if I can smell him on them. I fluff them up and smell them again. Nope.

I can feel the tears welling up in my eyes. *Come on, Colleen! You're fine!* It's just all the excitement and anxiety from today. I'm just being too emotional. Maybe I should call Jack and tell him what happened. He'd probably rush right over... No! I can handle this. I don't want to drag him into another crisis. I still want him to think I'm strong. I refold the blankets harshly and put them in the closet down the hall.

"Done!" I say aloud. The living room is spotless and somewhat bare without all of the knickknacks, but I can always collect more. I drag the kitchen table back and stand with my hands on my hips looking around, nodding to myself. The kitchen is perfect, too. Shoot! I'm not done down here. The main floor bathroom and spare room still need to be cleaned, vacuumed and dusted. I look into my office on the way to the bathroom and decide that it can wait until tomorrow.

With the main floor spick-and-span, I look out the living room window to check if the police car is there. I see the head of one officer in the dim light of his cruiser. I sigh softly and start heading upstairs, grabbing the books, socks and other odds and ends that have accumulated there over the last few weeks. My arms are overflowing when I get to the top of the stairs and I drop it all onto my bed.

"Oh my..." I can't believe how disgusting my room looks. My bed's not made, my clothes are scattered everywhere and I can see dust bunnies under the bed on the hardwood floors. "Ugh!" One of my favourite purple fitness bras is lying on my suede jacket. I hope it wasn't sweaty when I put it there! I pick up the jacket and rub the soft material. There's no damage thankfully. I crumble up the bra in my both my hands. How have I been living this way?

I drag my laundry basket to the middle of the room and scoop up all of the clothes, finding more on the floor of my closet and in the bathroom. There's even a pair of pants in the bathtub!

The laundry basket is heavy, but I'm able to get it downstairs and start the washing machine. I know I'm not going to bed anytime soon. I'm too wound up. I start the wash and check out my front window again, to see the police car parked there. I can't help myself. I need that security.

As I walk upstairs, Jack's face flashes in my mind. Flip flop. His sexy face with the blonde hair that always falls in his eyes...and his rugged, unshaven face...with those lips that I've kissed—

What am I doing? How could I think that way about him all of a sudden? I've been rejecting him for weeks and all of a sudden I have feelings for him? I have the emotional stability of a three year old! I don't like him...I like him... *Grow up!*

I need to calm down and figure out my life. I definitely don't need a man. Look how well that turned out with Steve. My world has been revolving around getting Steve back and now, there is no Steve. I need to get back on track with me and my needs. I've done enough with my libido to last me awhile.

Since my bedroom is tidied, I feel I need to go all the way and change my sheets. I pull off all the bedding and throw it out the door. I'll wash that tomorrow. I go into the linen closet and carefully take out what I call my fall comforter. It's the most luxurious, beige silk shell, filled with Canadian White Goose Down. I splurged on it last winter, but never used it because Steve said it was too bulky. I bury my face in it and close my eyes. So soft!

I make my bed quickly, but decide to shower first, knowing that I still have to put my clothes into the dryer. No sense getting all comfy and then getting up when the timer goes off.

The shower is a welcoming consolation. I turn up the heat slightly, close my eyes and let the spray wash down my neck and over my shoulders. I immediately notice my muscles relaxing and my busy mind shuts off. I've not been myself lately and I feel things are returning back to normal, but there are some things needed to be changed. Taking time for showers is one of them. It's not only about soothing and washing my body, it's about me and my state of mind. I've always worried about everyone else's. I smile and put my hands up on the walls of the shower. The water can take away my stress down the drain along with the dirt of the day.

After I get out and dry myself off, I clean up the entire bathroom, losing my towel numerous times. Finally, I put on flannel pajamas and run downstairs to put the clothes in the dryer, checking one last time for the police car. The sight of it reassures me and I fly up the stairs, jumping into bed. I hope that the weight of the comforter will feel like I'm lying with someone. It's heavy on my body, but I know I'm alone. It's soothing, in any case.

I turn off the lamp on my bedside table and see that the clock reads 2:48 a.m. What a night! There's never a dull moment in my life. Knowing that the police are outside, gives me enough confidence to make jokes like that. I turn over, but can't seem to get comfortable. It's so hot! I don't need jammies. I tear them off, remaining naked. I hope the cops don't barge in here for any reason.

It's funny that over four months ago, my life was completely normal. I was happily married and I loved going to work every day, but raced home to spend time with Steve. Now, I've dated and slept with… How many? I count on my fingers… Twelve? Twelve! I shake my head. My life is not normal at all. I've slept with twelve different men and will officially separate with Steve as soon as I can. Twelve?

Does logical, methodical and robot-like Colleen exist anymore? I still like things neat and my practice will run a tight ship, but personally, I feel like I'm open to more excitement and experiences. The run-ins with criminals and dealing with the police could be eliminated—I wouldn't miss those at all. Despite all of the angst and danger, I feel great! I can handle anything!

Losing Steve wasn't the worst thing to ever happen to me. I can get over Steve. Actually, I may already be over him. The abduction was the wickedest experience in my life, but I endured it and know with trepidation that there's more to come if they don't catch Mr. Baker. He proved that tonight. Hopefully, it won't be another aggressive act of violence, but I'm sure something will happen and I'll be ready.

"Bring it on," I say aloud, but with slight anxiety.

3.

The police are not in front of the house when I go downstairs in the morning and I panic. When did they leave? Did they leave when I was getting dressed? Or when I was sleeping? I wasn't safe in my room? How could they do this? I pace back and forth and check to see if my house alarm is still on. It is, but I'm sure Mr. Baker could somehow cut the wires or something. Breathe. Just breathe. I'm fine.

I fill up the kettle with water for tea and tear off last week's grocery list to start a new list to take my mind off things.

To Do:
Call Christine
Bring Margie Flowers
Go to yoga 3x/week
Start running again
Reschedule flying lessons
Schedule appointment with Dr. Wylie
Email Ann-Marie—takeover book club

I hesitate to write the next bullet. Can I do this? Is this too soon? I think I want to, but I don't know if it'll ever happen.

Go on a date with Jack

The kettle starts to gurgle, but I'm too worked up to wait for it. I'll get a latte at the corner café. Maybe Jack will be there. That thought gets me moving. I stuff the list into my purse, grab my coat and almost forget to reset the alarm before I leave.

It's dark outside for seven o'clock, but winter *is* just around the corner. My heels click on the sidewalk and echo in the neighbourhood. The black sky is slowly lightening and I see a hint of blue. I let my car heat up a few minutes before I pull away and race to my office.

I park and walk briskly to the café, taking a deep breath before I open the door. I scan the café and the line for Jack. I have butterflies! I rub my belly and smile. I haven't even seen him yet and I'm getting the flip flop feeling. I'm nervous and excited to see him.

The door opens behind me and I turn to see if it's Jack. It's a blonde man, but not Jack. He smiles at me, but I just nod and turn back around. I'm disappointed. I order and while I wait, I keep watch. When my name is called, I slowly pick up my latte and step to the side where the cream and sugar station is set up. I fiddle with the sweetener packets and take a few sips of my chai tea latte.

I'm being silly. It's super early and I can't wait here all day. I can call him later. Flip flop. Can I?

I've done such a one-eighty in only one day. For weeks it's been Steve, Steve, Steve. Now it's Jack? Why couldn't I see Steve for the man he really is? How was I so blind to his vulgarity and over-inflated ego? He was so gross at his apartment last night. He put his hand down his pants and scratched his ass! Ewww! I laugh to myself as I walk back to my office.

Steve was disgusting, dirty, crude and obnoxious. He's always been that way. I stop walking. He always checked out girls when we were out, he picked his nose and flicked his boogers in the house, and he always talked about blowjobs and getting 'some'. Why did I love him? He didn't treat me well. He never bought me flowers or opened the door for me and asking him to take me to dinner was always met with excuses.

I'm floored, but start walking again. Not only did I ignore those signs, but when we did separate, everyone had a negative story to tell about Steve and I wouldn't believe them. Colleen and Margie both told me to move on and Jack had the most damaging information about Steve. I didn't listen to any of them!

I pushed Jack away and made excuses as to why I couldn't be with him. I'm proud of myself for fighting for my marriage, but sickened at my reasoning and what I may have lost in the process. I was awful to Jack, but he has to understand about loyalty and devotion.

At one of the numerous dinner parties that we had held at our home, Jack had invited a voluptuous redhead as his date and I couldn't take my eyes off her cleavage. Anytime I had tried to engage in conversation with her, which was difficult because she wasn't very intelligent, I had to stop myself from eyeing her breasts.

"So, Georgette, what do you do for a living?" Steve had asked.

"I do nails."

"You're in aesthetics?" I tried to help.

Georgette shrugs and her breasts heave, "No, I just file, shape and paint nails."

I wasn't able to keep the conversation going, so I had left the room to finish making dinner and Jack had followed me into the kitchen, as he always did.

"Georgette seems really nice."

"She's ok. Can I help with anything?"

"Could you get the boobs, I mean buns out of the oven? I had blushed furiously and turned away from him, vigorously mashing the potatoes.

Jack had laughed while attending to the hot popovers, then he came up to me touching my arm. "It's ok, don't be embarrassed."

"I'm sorry! I didn't mean anything by that. It's just that they're so...so...in your face!" I couldn't even look at him.

"Come on. It was funny. She's got a body, that's for sure, but no—

"Brain!" I stated boldly, looking at Jack. He had just stared at me and immediately I was mortified. He wasn't going to say that! "I'm so sorry. I didn't mean it that way. She's lovely—

"You're absolutely right." He had started laughing. "I was going to say personality, but no, she doesn't have a brain either."

I had smirked at him. "Why do you go for women like that? I'm sure there are much better choices out there."

"There's no one like you, Colleen."

I had thought he was kidding, so I laughed and offered him advice on dating. I don't know why I had thought I was the authority on dating, but it was nice to have company in the kitchen and Jack assisted me in any way possible. He had even let me teach him how to fold the napkins into ducks.

Jack was always there, I just didn't see it.

4.

I purposely woke up early to get to my practice. If my house was any indication of how upturned or chaotic my life was, I'm sure my office needs some tender loving care too. I don't remember the last time I stayed to tidy it up. I'm kicking myself now for firing the cleaning company just because they didn't clean the mold from the crevices of the window panes. I was such a neat freak. I hurry up the walkway, sipping my latte and open the office door.

Margie's desk looks fine, as does the reception area, but I balance my belongings and straighten the magazines anyway, noting the dust on the tops of the curtains and the stains and bits of debris on the carpet. It definitely needs a deep cleaning. I'm sure I can find other cleaning services for hire in this area.

At my office doorway, I stop and survey the room. Wow. What a disgrace. Why didn't Margie say anything? I place my coat and purse in the closet, finish off my latte and begin to clean up the toys and books that are still on the kids table. I've always thrown out broken crayons, but a heap of them sit in the middle of the table, along with used colouring pages. How could I let this pile up?

When the mess is gone, I attend to the multicoloured play dough bits that are all over the table and the floor. I use a larger blob of dough and dab the small bits, picking them up, but it doesn't get all of them, so I grab the hand vacuum from the closet and go to work on my hands and knees. I should've worn pants today. The black pin skirt I'm wearing isn't very flexible. I can feel it riding up with every movement.

"Colleen!"

My heart leaps into my throat and I turn and fall onto the side of my hip, holding the vacuum up in defense. It's only Officer Nicholls.

"You scared me!" I put the vacuum on the floor and try to catch my breath. What's he doing here?

"I'm sorry, but I knocked first. Your car was outside, so I knew you were here. I let myself in and called your name a couple of times."

I notice that my skirt is revealing way too much leg and who knows what else, so I scramble to stand up, somewhat clumsily and try to compose myself. "I didn't hear you." Even my blouse is askew. I cover my bra strap again. God, I always seem to be in compromising positions when he's around.

"I know. I'm sorry for startling you. You were really engrossed in your vacuuming," he smiles slyly.

Oh no. "Um, why are you here so early?"

"I wanted to tell you in person that we caught Martin Baker."

"What?" Surprise and relief washes over me.

"We apprehended him early this morning."

That's why they weren't there when I woke up. "How did you find him?" I feel awful. I thought they were both bumbling idiots.

"At around four o'clock, we started to drive away to get coffee and we saw a man, fitting Baker's description coming out of your neighbour's garage. We quickly circled the block and found him at the side of your house, with a knife in his hand."

A knife? My heart's beating furiously. What if the police weren't there? Would I be dead?

"He was trying to get your basement window open."

Oh my God. I don't have alarm monitors on that window. It would've been so easy for him to get in without me knowing. "You have him in custody?"

"Yes, he was arrested and is being held at the Toronto South Detention Centre. Baker will appear in court today and we have requested a show cause hearing to keep him in custody."

"Thank you! Thank you so much!" I shake Officer Nicholls hand. "And thank you for coming here to tell me right away."

"Well, I know that you were afraid and I wanted to be able to put your mind at ease." He covers his hand with mine and caresses my knuckles.

I look up at him and smile nervously. "I appreciate it."

He's eyeing me. Uh oh, I know that look. Please don't ask me out.

I pull my hand away slowly and take a step back. "I can't thank you enough. Both you *and* Officer Leeds have been great. Where is he? I'd like to thank him too." I walk out into the reception area and he follows. Please don't ask me out.

"Officer Leeds is waiting in the car. He's giving me time to ask you out."

Dammit! "Oh?" How do I get out of this?

"Yes, would you like to go to dinner with me tomorrow night?"

"I think a celebratory dinner would be great," I start rambling. "Dinner to thank you and Officer Leeds—

His laughter cuts me off. "No, just me. I'd like to take you out on a date."

"Oh?" I don't even remember his first name. I need to let him down gently. I don't need a pissed off cop in my life.

"I know this great Italian place down the street. They have the best pasta."

"I know the place and it sounds great, but I don't think I should."

"It's not unprofessional, if that's what you're thinking. I wouldn't do anything unethical." He looks angry.

16

"No! It's not that," I say and think hastily. "I'm just recently separated and I'm really not ready to date." If only he knew the truth.

"I didn't know that. I'm sorry about your circumstances, but you're a beautiful woman, I couldn't help but ask." He smiles and places his hand on the doorknob. "I'm not surprised that you were married, but separated? Who would let you go?"

I smile and nod, feeling uncomfortable. "Please thank Officer Leeds for me."

"You still have my card, right?"

"Yes."

"Call me if you change your mind about a date."

"Sure. Have a good day."

"You too." He opens the door and walks out.

That was completely awkward and borderline unprofessional, but I don't need to dwell on it. I can't believe the news. Mr. Baker is behind bars! I jump up and down, hugging myself. He's in jail! I have to call Jack!

I rush to my desk and dial his number on the phone. "Dammit!" I say in frustration when Jack's phone goes directly to voicemail. I wait for the tone, "Hi, Jack. It's Colleen. Could you please call me when you get this message? Thanks."

"Well, hello there!" Margie's at the door with a big smile on her face. I rush over to hug her. She holds me tightly. "What's all this about?"

"Great news!" I release my affectionate hold on her, "The police caught Mr. Baker! He's in jail!"

"Really?"

I quickly give her the details about last night's events and this morning's capture and her smile gets wider and wider.

"That's great, Colleen. What a relief."

"No more rocks through windows or disturbing phone calls."

"No more stress or being afraid."

We hug again and laugh like school girls.

"Enough of this lovey-dovey stuff. When's my first appointment."

A giggle escapes Margie as she sits down at her desk. "Lovey-dovey? My husband says that all the time, but coming from you, it seems very strange." She fiddles with her computer. "You don't strike me as the lovey-dovey type."

"You have no idea how lovey-dovey I actually am," I taunt.

"Sure you are," she laughs, shaking her head. "Shayla will be here at nine."

"Perfect. I can finish cleaning."

"Cleaning?" Margie follows me into my office.

"Why didn't you tell me that I was a slob?" I start cleaning my desk and putting psychology journals back on the bookshelf.

"You would've bit my head off."

I cringe and look at her sheepishly. She's right.

"Sorry, but you haven't been the best version of yourself lately."

"I know and I want to apologize for that. I haven't been the best boss or friend. A new me starts now, I promise!"

"Has something else happened? You seem very different. Back to normal…but better."

"I feel different. My mind is so clear. Clearer than it has been in a long time."

"Mr. Baker behind bars puts a whole new perspective on things."

"It sure does, but it's more than that."

We hear the front door open and Margie peeks out, "Hi, Shayla. Have a seat and we'll be right with you." Margie turns back to me. "We'll have to discuss this change later."

"Definitely. If Jack calls, please let him know that I need to talk to him."

Margie smiles and gives me a knowing look, "Of course."

How does she do that? "Thanks. Please tell Shayla to come in."

5.

After my last appointment, I press the intercom, "Has Jack called?"

Margie replies, "No, for the hundredth time." I can hear her laughing and then she walks into my office. "Why do you keep asking?"

"I need to tell him about Mr. Baker."

"Is that all?" She raises her eyebrows.

"I'm... I'm just excited to tell him."

"Sure you are." She clicks her tongue and walks away.

"He's just a friend!" I call out after her. I don't know why I'm being so defensive.

"I'll see you tomorrow, Colleen!"

"Good bye, Margie!"

When I hear the door close and I know she's gone, I call him again and again it goes to voicemail immediately. "Hi, Jack. It's Colleen again. Sorry to keep bothering you, but I really need to talk to you. Call me back please," I sound desperate.

I don't even know what I'm going to say to him when I do talk to him. Obviously, I want to tell him about Mr. Baker, but is that all? I guess I have to wait and see how he is towards me before I ask him out. He could still be mad and ignoring my calls on purpose. I feel sick. I hope not.

Just then, I can hear my cell phone ringing from the closet. Jack? I hurry to open the door and rip the contents out of my purse to find it. When I get my hands on it, I drop the purse and yell into the phone, "Hello?"

"Ci-Ci? Are you ok? Why are you screaming into the phone?"

I'm a little disappointed, but happy to hear from Christine. "Sorry! I was just rushing to answer it. Hey? You're still talking to me?"

"Well, yeah. I know that you're going through some shit, but I'm not about to ditch you, even if you did yell at me and tell me to stay out of your life."

"Oh no...I'm so sorry, Christine. You're such a good friend. I didn't mean any of it. Please, I need to make it up to you. Are you free tonight?"

"Absolutely! Can you come get me at work now?"

"I can be there in twenty minutes."

"I'll wait outside for you. I'll be the hot blonde in the black suede jacket."

"You're the best," I laugh, loving her positive and sassy character.

I place my cell phone in my purse and pick up everything that I threw out of my purse and put it back in. I stop when I see my name badge from the Psychology Symposium that I attended on Monday. It seems so long ago… How could I have been so stupid to go to a hotel room with a university student? Was that my lowest point? I think Jackhammer John from the car dealership was pretty demoralizing, too. I could name a few more, but I don't want to rehash the negative. I throw the name badge into the trash.

The Sex Project was a solid study. It taught me so many things. I can't bash it, but I can't dwell on it either. Where's that notebook anyway? I saw it when I was cleaning up my house. Forget it! I can't think about it now. I have to meet Christine.

I throw on my coat, rush to my car and head to Bloor Street. Christine's insurance office is between Spadina and Bathurst and traffic will be a bit hectic. I pass by the high-end stores, like Gucci and Louis Vuitton and remember that Steve had pressured me to buy him clothes there. He had made me return the lower-end clothes from the Bay, telling me that he had an image to uphold. I had spent my hard-earned money on Burberry ties and shirts for him and what did he do in return? He had taken off his Frigo one hundred dollar boxers for other women. I'm an idiot. I growl under my breath. No need to get angry. What's done is done.

Then, I pass by the university and the Varsity Centre and I'm bombarded with memories of meeting Steve, losing my virginity to him and being hopelessly in love with him. By the time Christine opens my car door to get in, I'm livid.

"How are—

"You were so right about Steve!" I interrupt. "He's an asshole and always has been an asshole."

"It's going to be that kind of night is it? Let's go get some drinks. Turn right," she points.

I jabber on about meeting Steve last night and how disgusting he was, all the while following her directions. We end up on John Street and snag a parking spot right on the street. When we get out of the car, I realize that I've been ranting non-stop and haven't let Christine say a word.

"I'm sorry that you had to listen to all that."

She grabs my arm and pulls me towards Milestones, an upscale chain restaurant. "Don't you worry, I'm here to listen and I'll tell you my opinion after I get a few cocktails in me."

We smile at each other and head straight for the pretty, young hostess who directs us to the bar.

"Two peach Bellinis, please," Christine barks to the bartender.

The young bartender nods, but does a double take when Christine takes off her jacket. She's wearing a form-fitting pale blue dress and her breasts are busting out of the scoop neck. He watches her climb up onto the bar stool and I can't help staring too.

"You look amazing. Did you wear that to work?"

"Of course, but I wore a conservative scarf all day. It held the dogs at bay, but now it's time to let 'em loose."

The bartender drops off two light orange drinks with a peach garnish and doesn't even notice me. He's probably in his early twenties and adorable, but too young to think twice about him.

Christine holds out money for him and he takes it, but she doesn't let go. She grips his hand tightly. "Keep the change, and if you don't let my glass get empty, there'll be more of that for you later." She winks at him and turns her attention to me.

I watch him look at the money in his hand, look at Christine and beam from ear to ear almost skipping away. She's got it down to a science.

"I haven't forgotten about you, Ci-Ci. Just give me a second." She downs half the Bellini and sighs, "What a day!"

"I'm sorry for being so selfish. I didn't even ask how you are or anything. I'm sorry I've been such a horrible friend."

"Forget about it. If you haven't realized it by now, you're never getting rid of me." She takes another sip. "You *have* realized though that Steve is a douchebag. No one could tell you that, you had to figure it out for yourself. I'm so glad." She holds up her glass, "Cheers! Onto better and bigger things!"

I clink her glass, "Cheers to that!"

"What's next for you?"

"What do you mean?"

"Come on, Ci-Ci, you always have a plan."

"Not this time. I need to clean up my life and figure out what makes me happy."

"Are you done with the Sex Project?"

"Yes, I don't need to do that anymore."

"Will you still dabble?"

"Dabble?" I laugh. "I don't know. I'll admit that it was fun and exciting, but those bad experiences are just as common as good ones." I tell her about Zach and how aggressive he was in the airplane hangar.

"I've had a few close calls too, but I carry pepper spray and use my heels as weapons."

"Christine! Why didn't you warn me or give me *that* kind of advice."

"You're a big girl and it was *your* Sex Project. You needed to learn a thing or two for yourself."

The bartender sets down two more Bellinis and Christine slides money toward him. "Come here," she beckons to him. He leans over and as she whispers in his ear, I watch him stare at her cleavage. Then he walks away.

"What was that all about?"

"You'll see."

"Oh no." It's either tequila shots or she asked him to meet her later.

"Have you talked to Jack?"

"No, I've been trying to call him all day... Wait... Why do ask?"

"You're going to sit there again and deny that there's nothing between you two?"

"There *is* nothing. I mean, he likes me and there's an attraction, but I think I blew it last week. I kept pushing him away and now, I think he's never going forgive me. I didn't figure out that I *like him* like him until recently."

Christine giggles. "You're so cute. He's got it bad for you. Just give it a little time and don't stop trying."

She does know men and her words pacify me, but I'm still confused. "Isn't it too soon to pursue him?"

"Not at all. However, do you want a relationship or just sex?"

"I don't know. I think I want a relationship, but I can't wait to get him in bed."

"I expected you to ask what the difference was. You really did learn a lot from your Sex Project."

"Sure, I learned a lot, but I didn't learn how to read a man's feelings."

"I've never bothered to learn about them. I know the basics: if he's interested and if I can get him in the sack."

"If that's all you know, how can you say to give Jack time?"

"He's interested. Plain and simple. He told me and I think he's told you a few times. He might be a bit miffed because you deflated his ego when you pushed him away, but just give him time and try to stay in his thoughts." She takes a bite of the peach garnish. "You take the time too and find out if you want more than sex. Sometimes when you jump into bed with a man, things can change rapidly. You might not share the connection you want or he may show his true colours."

"Here you go. Two tequila shots." The bartender places each shot on the table with slices of lime and salt.

"Ugh. I knew it."

She licks her hand and pours salt on it. "Bottoms up!" She holds a shot glass up to her lips, waiting for me to take mine. "Ci-Ci! Ci-Ci!" She chants.

The bartender chimes in, "Ci-Ci! Ci-Ci!"

"Ok! Ok!" I salt my hand and get my lime ready. "Go!"

We down the shots and suck on our limes, laughing and this time I pay the bartender.

Christine gasps, "Look at that handsome hunk of a man!"

"Where?" I look where she's motioning with her eyes and at a table behind me I see Darren the self-defense instructor being seated beside us with two other men. I whip my head back to Christine. "You don't mean that buff guy in the blue tee shirt, do you?"

"Yeah! Do you know him?"

"That's who we would call dim-witted Darren. I'm ashamed to say that he was one of my samples for my Sex Project."

"Why are you ashamed? He's gorgeous!"

"Darren's dumb, egotistical and did I mention dumb?"

Christine laughs loudly and tosses her hair back. "Was he good in bed?"

"That's the only positive thing that I'd say about him. If you could muzzle him, he'd be perfect."

"It wouldn't be the first time I've gagged someone during sex. Introduce me!"

"Really? Even after I've slept with him?"

She looks at me seriously. "I'm sorry. Would that be weird for you if I slept with him?"

"No, not at all."

"Do you have feelings for him?"

"No! It wouldn't affect me one bit. I just thought you might rethink it, now that I've told you about his lack of intellect."

"That kind of thing intrigues me. Dumb, but good in bed. He's perfect."

"Well, I should tell you something else about him."

"What?"

I whisper, "He's extremely endowed."

"Ooooh," she croons. "That intrigues me even more." She stands up and smooths down her dress, pushing up her breasts. "I'm going to walk by him to use the washroom. See how he reacts and then get his attention, so you can talk me up a bit."

"I thought we finished university!" I can't count how many times she made me do stuff like this, but it's Christine. God love her.

She fluffs her hair and pulls her shoulders back. "I'll be right back."

I move my chair over and watch her leave. She walks past their table and Darren's reaction, as well as the reactions of the men he's with, is not surprising. Darren actually leans out into the walkway and ogles her behind for a little longer. When he turns back to his friends, they act like undersexed teenagers, using their hands to describe Christine's body. I see him glance at me and I nonchalantly look away, but he stares for a few seconds and walks up to my barstool.

"Colleen?"

"Yes?"

"Don't you remember me? I'm Darren. We went out last Saturday."

"Darren?" I pause a second, trying to look confused.

"We went to a Halloween party and I gave you a gi to wear." He looks stunned that I might not remember him.

"Oh, Darren. Right. How are you?"

"You scared me. I mean, how could you forget me?" He laughs quietly, but seems insecure. "How come you never returned my texts?"

"Work has been very busy lately."

"Do you want to hook up later?"

I quickly shake my head. "Did you see my friend? She was the one in the blue dress who just went to the ladies room?"

"She's your friend?"

"Yes and she's very interested in you."

"Really?" He's impressed. "You don't mind?"

"Not at all."

"You really are a cool chick."

Christine comes back to the table and I look around while they chat. I hear the same stuff he told me about how he's the best instructor in Toronto and how he makes a lot of money. Good luck, Christine.

Darren's words repeat in my mind. *'You really are a cool chick.'* I *am* a cool chick. I'm giving and unselfish. I'm hard-working and driven. I'm faithful and devoted. I deserve better. I deserve the best.

After a few minutes, Darren leaves and Christine leans in, "Are you sure he's good in bed?"

"Yes, you can basically tell him what to do and he'll do it."

"That's great because you're right. He's as dumb as a stump!"

We giggle uncontrollably and finish our Bellinis. Her plan is to go home with him when I leave.

"Thanks for meeting me tonight. I had fun."

"Me too."

We both stand up and hug each other tightly.

"Be safe," I say.

"Always."

6.

With my coat still on, I dig around my office for the Sex Project notebook and find it under a pile of flyers. I take it with me upstairs to my room and after I get ready for bed, I scan the pages and read all of my data collection.

Reading the details of some of my samples, I smile and get a few flip flops, like with my Latin lover from the nightclub. The reminders of other samples give me angst and regret, as with Kevin the sex therapist and of course, Zach the pilot. It was all for research. I shake away the negativity. The biggest learning outcome was that I need to like the person that I'm intimate with to thoroughly enjoy the experience. It's not enough that they're athletic, sexy or have a great job. They have to be intelligent, caring and emotionally present. Sex is sex, but when there's a connection it can be amazing and I'm sure that as the relationship grows, the sex gets better.

Sex with Steve was fantastic, but I somehow saw him as a God in my mind. I'm such an idiot. I really would've done anything he asked, but he settled for…what did he call it? Pity sex. Asshole.

For fun, and a little spitefulness, I include Sample #13 to my notes:

Data Collection

Sample #13:

Seek persons who understand study & are willing to express inner feelings & experiences
- *Man, aged 35.*
- *Pharmaceutical rep.*
- *Slightly balding, overweight disgusting pig.*

Describe experiences of phenomenon
- *Met him at his apartment.*
- *I tried to seduce him and performed fellatio, but was interrupted by a football game on TV.*
- *Convinced him to move it into the bedroom, but there was no spark or willingness on my part.*
- *It ended badly, with me kneeing him in the groin.*

Direct observation
- *I was attracted to him because of the past.*

- *I ignored all signs that I should move on.*
- *How did I think I was to blame?*

Audio or videotape *Never. Never. Never!*

Data analysis

Classify & rank data
- *-10 out 5*

Sense of wholeness
- *I pursued this sample due to my history and past with him. I loved him at one point, but I can't see how that ever happened. He's an egotistical, narcissistic, disgusting adulterer.*

Examine experiences beyond human awareness/ or cannot be communicated
- *I felt stupid and unfulfilled.*
- *I will never let a man make me feel unloved and unworthy again.*
- *I'm a sexual being. I don't need a man to tell me that.*
- *I deserve the best.*

    I don't need to summarize or examine all the data in this book or resolve anything concrete. It's already in my mind. I'm a stronger woman than what I used to be. I close the notebook and put it in my bedside table.

7.

I'm lying in bed, looking up at the stars through a skylight. The stars are bright and seem so close. I feel like I can reach out and touch them.

When I raise my hand up and Charlie's face blocks my view. I haven't seen Charlie since the night at the strip club. He's still pretty cute. I remember how soft his facial hair was when he kissed me.

"Charlie?" Why is here? And where is here? This isn't my bed.

"Take my hat off. I want to make love to you." He caresses my face and kisses my forehead. His beard tickles my skin.

Shivers run up my body. Flip flop. I pull off his hat and toss it to the side. Why not? I don't know how he got here, but he was a wonderful lover and one of my very first samples. I'm so much more experienced now that I want to see if I can impress him.

I look under the blankets and see that I'm already naked. "Do you like what you see?"

"Yes, I do," a muffled voice comes from beneath the blankets and a tongue immediately starts lapping up my sex.

It feels amazing and I don't want it to stop, but I'm confused. How did Charlie get under the blankets so fast? I rip off the blankets and recognize Shawn the artist's wavy brown hair.

"Shawn?"

He looks up at me from between my legs and his hazel eyes twinkle. He pauses a moment and says, "You were my most promising student." His tongue delves deep and my back arches involuntarily, pushing my hips into his face. "I could've taught you so much."

"Yes!" I growl. I need more.

"You want more?" That's not Shawn's voice. My head snaps up. I see Ryan kneeling buck naked, stroking his rock hard erection. Flip flop. He looks the same, muscular and sexy, but his…it's just so big. Where did Shawn go?

"Make love to me, Superstar."

I close my eyes and open my legs wider, feeling the intense pressure of Ryan's hardness entering me and brutalizing my tender insides. I wrap my legs around his waist, wanting it all, both pain and sensuality. He thrusts slowly a few times and I feel myself on the edge of an orgasm. This can't be happening already.

Ryan suddenly withdraws, picks me up and sits me on the edge of my bed. I smile, remembering his acrobatics. I don't cover up, I want him to look at me and want me. I'm ready for anything he wants to give me.

"We could've had a second date, Colleen."

I look up and Dave the orthodontist is standing completely nude with his hands on his hips, staring at me. Number one is drawn on his chest, down to his belly button. I grab the blankets and try to cover myself up, but he pulls them away. I scoot off the bed.

"Why can't we go out again?"

"No second dates!" Christine's voice echoes in the room and I see her in the corner. She's straddling Darren the self-defense instructor on a chair. They're having sex!

I turn away and shake my head. "Christine, what are you doing here?" This is getting weird.

"No second dates, Ci-Ci!"

Suddenly, the room is full with all of my samples. They're naked with numbers written on their chests. Ryan has the number three, Charlie has a two, and Shawn has a four.

"I'm sample five," my Latin lover says. "Don't talk, just make love to me again."

He reaches out toward me and I squirm away, but bump into Mark the doctor. Why do they have their sample numbers? Why are they all here?

"No, I'm next," Mark says. He has the number seven written with thick black marker. "You left in the middle of the night." He pulls my naked body towards him. "I'm not done with you."

I struggle to get away and break free from his grip, but I run into Zach. He's scowling at me, scratching at the bright red number ten on his chest.

"I get *my* turn with you next. You owe me, you little cock tease."

"No! Get out of here! All of you!" I start crying. Everywhere I turn, the men are pawing at me, trying to pull me near them.

The door opens and all I can see is the shadow of another man. I don't know who it is, but I don't care. "Please go away! I don't want any of you! I don't want any of this!"

"Colleen, it's me."

"Jack?"

"Yes. Come here." He places a blanket around me and I collapse into his arms.

"Jack, is it really you?"

"Yes, I sent everyone away."

I look around and my samples have all disappeared. We're now in my bedroom and he's lying with me on my bed. Just like the night I had a bad dream. I'm even wearing the same flimsy nightgown and he's naked from the chest up. "You keep saving me."

He wipes the tears from my eyes and holds me tighter. I recognize the delicious scent that epitomizes him and I breathe it in.

"It's always been you, Jack." I press my body against his.

"How could you do this to me, Colleen?" He suddenly bursts out, throwing me off of him and standing up. He's holding my notebook.

"What?"

"I can't believe that you slept with all of those men! You had one night stands with them! You're just as disgusting as Steve!" He throws the notebook down.

"No! No, it was a project!" I run to stand next him and place my hands on his chest. "Please don't be mad!"

He lifts my hands off of him and pushes me away. "You're a whore!"

"No!" I scream and sit up straight in bed, bathed in sweat with my heart racing. What? Where did Jack go? I look around and it quickly dawns on me that it was all just a nightmare.

I fall back onto my bed and when my head hits the headboard hard, I cradle it as it throbs and yell, "Fuck!"

8.

The next morning, I dress with the same hope of running into Jack at the café. I put on a pretty pink sweater and tan skirt with my brown wedge boots and short suede jacket. I woke up with a feeling of uneasiness and still have it walking into the coffee shop. That stupid dream keeps replaying in my mind.

I look around and feel dejected when I don't see him. I order my latte and wait, staring at my boots. Why do I feel so juvenile and desperate?

"Colleen?"

Flip flop. I know that voice. My heart beats wildly. I look up and swish my hair back over my shoulders. "Hi, Jack," I breathe, as I look up through my lashes. He looks so handsome.

He takes a sharp breath in and doesn't say anything. What's wrong? Was that too much? Shit. I went overboard.

"How are you?" I look down again and then to the barista, trying to look casual.

"I'm good. Did you get my message?"

He called? I zip open my purse, but he places his hand on mine. Flip flop. And sparks! I feel magnetized by him. I look at him and he's just staring at me. Does he feel it too?

"Um..." He slowly takes his hand away. "I called your house last night around eight and left a message."

Dammit! I scream to myself. "Did you? I didn't check my messages last night," I say softly.

"I received your voicemails yesterday, but I couldn't call you back because I was out of town. I just got back early this morning. Is everything ok?"

"Yes," I say, not being able to take my eyes away from his. The bright blue of his jacket reflects brilliantly in his eyes. They're mesmerizing.

"Then why did you need to talk to me?"

I snap out of it. "Oh! They caught Mr. Baker!"

"They did?"

I beam, "Yes! He's in custody awaiting a show cause hearing."

"Oh."

"That's good, isn't it? I thought you'd be happier."

"I'm happy. Do you feel better now that they caught him?"

"Of course! You have no idea what he did before they caught him."

He frowns. "Really? Do you have time to tell me?"

"Yes." Oh yes.

I give Jack the details of the parking garage, my slashed tires and everything from how Mr. Baker was on my front yard leading up to how the police found him with a knife. Jack's face remains grim throughout my entire account and doesn't say a word.

"I'm finally safe, right?" I place my hands on the table, wanting reassurance.

He pauses and smiles slowly, "Of course you are." He takes my hands in his and squeezes them.

There's something about how he says it that troubles me, but I brush it off quickly. He's touching my hands and the sparks are overwhelming.

"What time do you have to be at work?" He releases my hands to look at his watch.

A wave of disappointment washes over me. "What time is it?" I want to stay here with him.

"It's a quarter to nine."

"I really should get going."

"I'll walk you there."

Flip flop. "You don't have to do that. I'll be fine."

"No, I want to."

"Ok, thank you."

We begin walking to my office in silence. I ponder the idea of telling him about Steve, but there's not a lot of time and I don't want to bring up negativity or bad feelings. It's a good sign that he still wants to be with me or maybe he's just making sure that I'm safe. Whatever the reason, I shouldn't push it. I probably shouldn't ever talk about Steve again, if I want anything to happen with Jack. My stomach turns. And I'll never mention my so-called project either. So, what should I talk about?

"You said you were out of town? Where were you?"

"Calgary. I was at a seminar for physiotherapists."

"Calgary? I've never been there. Did you get to do any sightseeing?"

"Not much, just a football game. Calgary against Edmonton. There wasn't much time for anything else."

"The game must've been cool. I'm jealous. Business must be good for you to leave."

"I needed the certification, but yeah, business has been fantastic."

"That's great. I'm so happy for you."

We're facing each other now, at the walkway of my office, looking at each other.

"You seem different, Colleen. You're happy, more relaxed."

"I feel different." Flip flop. Should I ask him out now?

He averts his eyes and looks behind him for a second. "I should go. I have a client coming in at nine-fifteen and my receptionist will be wondering where I am."

"Talk to you later?"

He cocks his head to the side and lowers his eyes, nodding at me. "Yes. Definitely." He begins to smile.

What a great smile. I giggle nervously. "Ok… Goodbye, Jack."

"See you soon."

I wait until he turns to leave and I head up the walkway, watching him saunter away. He's got a nice bum. When I get to my office door, I catch him looking back, but I quickly open the door, catching my foot on the outside and tripping into the office. That was graceful.

"Watch your step!" Margie calls out. "What are you smiling about?"

"Nothing." Everything!

"Oh, it's something, missy, and its name is Jack."

"Jack? Sure. I just ran into him at the café. It was nothing."

"Nothing? That was surely something," she teases.

I walk into my office, scolding myself. I'm acting like a love struck teenager. Jack was last on my 'to do' list. He's not a priority. I need to focus on my other interests. I hug myself quickly and get down to business.

"I'm ready to roll, Margie! Send in my first patient when she gets here."

9.

"Any plans tonight?" Margie steps into my office, already wearing her coat and carrying her purse.

I'm half-sitting, half-lying on the couch. "No, I'm too tired."

"Why don't you call Jack?"

I sit up and stare at her. "Why? He's just a friend."

She smirks, "Friends can go out together, Colleen."

I stand up and start busying myself with the files on my desk, not really doing anything with them. "I know."

Margie comes over and takes the files from me. "Just call him."

I roll my eyes. "Good night, Margie. Have a great weekend."

"You too."

I wait until I hear the front door close and I reach for the phone, but I pull my hand away.

"No!" I can't call him. There's no need to rush or seem desperate.

I pull out my 'to do' list and scan it quickly, crossing off the first one:

To Do:
~~Call Christine~~
Bring Margie Flowers
Go to yoga 3x/week
Start running again
Reschedule flying lessons
Schedule appointment with Dr. Wylie
Email Ann-Marie—takeover book club

I do pick up the phone and call my florist, ordering flowers for Margie, to be delivered on Monday morning. I cross that one off, too.

What can I do tonight? I'm tired, so yoga and running are out. I'll have time tomorrow to get back into exercising regularly. The other points can wait until Monday.

Again, what can I do? Today's Friday... I can head to the deli, grab a salad and sit by the window to people watch. Didn't I do that last Friday? I did. That was the night I ran into Jack *and* Chris from cooking class. Oh, that was awkward. Chris had whispered how he and his wife loved whipped cream. So very awkward.

But Jack came in... maybe that's a normal Friday night routine for him. I grab my coat and purse and head outside.

It's a chilly night. It's almost too cold to walk, but I decide quickly to brave the temperature and hurry to the deli. I'll never find parking and it's not that far. Halfway there, I realize that I'm not dressed for the weather, but I trudge on. Everyone is wearing heavy coats and those that aren't look like me, with their hands stuffed deep in their pockets and their shoulders up to their ears, trying to keep the wind off their necks. My nose is in the collar of my coat and I start to jog slightly. The wind is also going up my skirt.

The door to the deli opens just as I get to it and I rudely slide through, immediately feeling the warmth on every part of my body, especially my bare legs. I rub my hands together and blow into them. Wow. We barely had a fall season and now it's right into winter.

I step into line and stay close to a couple in front of me. They're arms are around each other and they're giving off some heat. I move up, not caring about personal space.

"Colleen?"

I turn around and my heart jumps out of my throat. It's Jack. I'm so happy to see him. "Are you following me?" I joke.

"Why would you say that?" He says with a frown.

"I'm kidding. It's just that I saw you this morning and..." What did I say wrong?

"I come here pretty much every Friday after work. You look like you're freezing. Did you walk here?"

"Yes. I thought it was warmer than it is." I blow into my hands again and pat myself on the back for being right about guessing his Friday night routine.

Jack steps closer to me and rubs my arms, pulling me close to rub my back. "Is that better?"

I start shivering more. "Yes," I can barely speak.

"You're trembling. Here, take my coat." He takes his blue coat off and wraps it around me. "What do you want to eat? I'll get it while you sit down at the back of the restaurant."

"No, I can't let you—

"What do you want?" He smiles, but only partially.

"The kale and chickpea salad, please."

"Go sit down at the back." He points and steps up to order.

His demeanour puzzles me, but I obey and walk to the very back of the restaurant to find a booth. I slide in beside the wall and huddle against it, feeling warmer with his coat on. I keep it hugged tight to me and cover my nose with it, breathing it in. Mmmm... It's Jack. I close my eyes and breathe deeply.

"You're not sleeping, are you?"

My eyes flip open. "No, just resting."

"I got you a kale and bean soup and a turkey sandwich on whole wheat. The salad won't make you warm and you're getting too thin."

"Thank you?" I think he's being nice, but there's a hint of bossiness. I take off his jacket and hand it to him.

He takes it and stuffs it beside him. "Are you getting warmer now?" He blows on a spoonful of his own soup. It looks like chicken noodle.

I nod and start to eat my soup. It's really tasty and I finish it without saying a word.

"I knew you were hungry. You're not eating, are you?"

"Jack, I came to the deli because I'm hungry. I eat like any normal person." I'm not sure why I have to defend myself.

"You're a tiny girl. You need to eat."

"Please don't boss me around. I'm a big girl," I say softly.

He looks me in the eyes and then slowly starts nodding. "Sorry." He tilts his bowl on the side to get the last spoonful of broth and swallows it.

What have I done? I don't know why he's treating me like this. We were fine this morning in the café. He seemed to have gotten over or forgotten my rejection from a few days ago. What changed? I don't feel like eating my sandwich at all. I pick up half of the sandwich and bring it to my mouth, but the smell of it nauseates me and I put it back down.

"Eat your sandwich."

"Don't tell me what to do."

"Colleen," he states slowly. "Eat."

"You eat it." With that I get up and head out of the store, bumping into a few patrons and apologizing inaudibly. I push open the door, not caring to hold it open for anybody and when I get a few feet away from the restaurant, I feel someone grab my arm.

"Colleen, come back inside." Jack didn't even put on his jacket. He's wearing a short sleeve, aqua golf shirt. His hands are stuffed in his khaki pants pockets and his biceps are bulging.

"No, you're just going to keep telling me what to do. Why are you being so mean?" My teeth begin to chatter and body shudders from the cold.

"I'm sorry. I don't know... I'm confused. I'm worried about you. I'm an idiot. Come back inside, please."

"I don't need to be coddled."

"Understood," he puts his hands up in surrender. "Now, please come back inside. It's freezing out here."

I walk towards the deli, not waiting for him, but he gets there first to open the door for me.

"Thank you," I mutter.

The booth is still empty and our food remains untouched. I slide into my spot and Jack slides in after me, surprising me. He puts his arm around me and slowly rubs my shoulders and back. His other hand rubs my thigh.

"Are you warm?"

"Getting there," I say quietly. I can feel heat radiating from his body, so it warms me up, but his touch excites me, so it makes me tremble. I'm also trying to stay mad at him, but with every caress on my thigh, the anger disappears.

"You're still shivering." He holds me tighter.

"Really, I'm fine. Finish your dinner." Jack removes his arm from around me and starts to slide out, but I put my hand on his to stop him. He looks at me questioning. "Can you stay on this side? You're like an oven," I say.

He smiles, "Of course." He sits back down and pulls his sandwich over to him, picking up half and taking a large bite.

I pick mine up and do the same.

We eat our sandwiches in silence. I don't know what to say to him. I know I have feelings for him, but I don't like seeing that side of him. He acted like this the night he made dinner for me and many other times when he was trying to get me to change my mind about Steve. He has to know that he can't force me to think or act a certain way.

I wrap up the other half of my sandwich, while he takes the last bite of his. We finish our bottles of water and he slides out of the booth to put all of the garbage and recycling away, but he doesn't sit back down.

"Are you ready to go?"

"Sure."

"I can drive you to your car. I'm just parked outside. I was lucky tonight."

"You can actually drive me home, if that's ok. I'll probably run or go to yoga tomorrow. I'll pick it up then." We're talking cautiously to each other, politely even. My heart hurts.

"Sounds good." He wraps his coat around me just before we step outside and I start to protest, but he points through the window. I'm parked right there. You need it more than I do."

The drive to my house is deafeningly quiet. I don't know what to say and Jack doesn't say anything at all. He doesn't even look at me.

When he pulls into my driveway and puts the car in park, I squeeze out a "Thank you" just before I start crying and run to my door. I fumble with my purse to find my key and when I put it into the lock, I can feel Jack standing behind me.

I keep my head down and say, "I'm fine, Jack. Thanks for everything." I open the door, walk in, and quickly key in the alarm, but he follows me inside.

"What do you want?" I walk into the kitchen and keep my back to him, throwing my arms up in aggravation. Tears stream down my face.

The door closes and I hear him take a few steps, feeling him standing behind me. He puts his hands on my shoulders and turns me around, but I look down, not wanting him to see me cry. He tips my chin up with his fingers and I whip my head away. Instead, he wraps both of his arms around me and holds me tightly against his chest. I continue to cry and I know he can feel me shudder against him, but I don't care. It feels good to let it out and to be embraced like this.

After a while, my tears finally subside and I slowly pull away from him, without saying a word and walk to the bathroom to clean up. The face that stares back at me in the mirror has puffy eyes, a red nose and no idea why the crying occurred. I shake my head and analyze my feelings. Mr. Baker brought up some intense emotions, but I thought I dealt with them. I'm not mad or sad, but I feel frustrated. All day, I was so happy and then Jack's mood changed everything for me. My mood reflects his? Or am I affected by his mood? Why am I letting this happen?

I hear Jack rummaging around in the cupboards and turning the kitchen sink on and off. I clean up my face the best as I can. I'm going to have to face him before he leaves. I take a deep breath and open the door.

"I'm sorry I was emotional. It must be the whole Mr. Baker ordeal. I needed a release, I guess."

"I'm sure that took a toll on you and it's not easy to forget, but you don't have to apologize." He opens the fridge and takes out the milk. "I'm making you some tea."

"Oh. Thank you." He's using my aunt's teapot again.

"Do you want to talk?"

My heart jumps. "About what?"

"Anything."

"Do you?"

He looks at me like he did this morning. "Can we sit down?"

"Sure."

Jack brings the pot of tea and my mug to the kitchen table. I grab the milk and sugar and we sit side by side.

"This morning you said you felt different. Why is that?"

I take off my coat and hang it up on the back of the chair. "I don't know if I want to explain it to you."

"Colleen, I can see a change. Even your house is different. It's back to normal, I mean. Something got into you. What happened?" He pours tea into my mug.

"I don't want to get into it." I drop some milk and sugar into the tea, stirring it.

"Why?"

I take a deep breath and sigh, "Because that would mean that you were right."

He smiles. "I like the sound of that."

"Not funny," I smirk and drop my forehead onto my arms. "You were right about Steve."

"I'm not happy or proud to be right about that. I wish you never had met him and I wish that you didn't have to find out the type of man he really is." He rubs my back and shoulders. "I wish that I could take your pain away."

"That's the thing. I don't have pain or heartache anymore." I look at Jack. "It dissolved when I went to see him."

"How? What did he do?"

"From the moment I walked into his grungy apartment, I knew I was wrong about him. He showed me a different side of him and I didn't like it. It was like seeing him for the first time." I wrap my hands around my mug, feeling the heat.

"Did you try to seduce him?"

I snap my around to look at him. Should I tell him the truth? "Yes." I take a sip of the warm, soothing liquid.

His eyes look pained. "Did it work?"

"I realized how wrong I was before anything happened." Slightly true.

"You didn't sleep with him?"

"No way," I cringe. "Yuck!"

"Really?"

"Well, I hit him in the groin and banged his head with the door on my way out."

"You did?" The incredible smile on his face is infectious.

"Yup," I laugh and beam proudly.

"That's my girl." He rubs my hand, but immediately pulls away, standing up. "Anyway, I should go."

He's so random. What's with the mixed signals? "Oh. Ok." I don't want him to go, but I stand up to walk him out.

"Call me if you need anything." He opens the door.

"Does your locksmith guy do alarm installations? I need to add some motion detectors to my basement window and upstairs?"

"You don't have motions detectors on all of your windows?" He closes the door harshly.

"No, but it's ok. Mr. Baker's in custody."

"He's not in custody, Colleen. He's been released."

10.

I lose my breath. "What? How could he…" My head is spinning.

"The jails are overcrowded and apparently his own mother became surety for him."

"What does that mean?"

"She agreed to be responsible for him with conditions. He's living with her and he's not allowed to have weapons or any contact with you or his family. His grandmother also paid the twenty-five thousand dollar bail."

"He's out already? I don't understand." I reach thoughtlessly for the kitchen counter to steady myself, but it's not there and I stumble. Jack grabs my waist and stands me up. "How do you know all of this? They told me yesterday…"

"I went into the detention centre this morning." He leads me into the living room and sits me on the couch, remaining on his feet with his hands on his hips. "Listen, I'm going to stay here tonight and call Curtis in the morning."

"No, no, no." I'm numb. I'm not safe. Will I ever be safe again?

"I'm staying."

Snap out of it, Colleen! "Obviously, I'm not going to be able to talk you out of it, so I'll get you your blankets." I don't move. I look at the ground and trying to wrap my head around everything. I don't understand how he can be free after everything he did.

"Stay there. I'll get the blankets." Jack leaves the room to find them.

I do feel slightly better knowing that Jack will be here tonight and I'm sure after the motion detectors are installed, I'll feel one hundred percent safe. For now, I need to remain strong. Jack's here and he's staying overnight. He can't see me fall apart again. "Do you want some tea?"

He drops blankets on the couch and follows me to the kitchen. "No, thank you."

I open the fridge. "I don't have any beer. Do you want some orange juice?"

"I'm fine." He resets the kettle and it starts bubbling right away.

"I already have a full pot. I can do that if I need more."

"Just sit down. I got it." He waves me away.

"Jack, you're doing it again."

He looks at me questioningly.

"You're bossing me around." I cross my arms in front of my chest.

"This is called taking care of you. Can't you just let me do something for you?"

The tone of his voice is soft, so I don't argue. "Ok. Thank you."

He cares about me, but it seems like he doesn't want to get close to me. He pulls his hands away quickly when we touch accidentally, but will warm me up when I'm cold. Is it only that he wants to protect me, like a brother would? I thought he had feelings for me. Maybe he has moved on.

"I'm going to change. I'll be right back."

I'm so confused about the way he's treating me. Perhaps it's for the best. I shouldn't rush into anything anyway. What am I expecting? A full-blown romance? Marriage? Being friends first is a good idea. Christine said to take it slow and that's exactly what I'm going to do.

I keep my bedroom door open and step into my walk-in closet. What should I wear? I step out of my clothes and place them in the laundry basket, standing in my light pink bra and panties looking at my clothes. I run my hands over my stomach and up to my ribcage and look out towards the outside hallway, quickly shaking my head. What am I thinking? I just told myself to go slow!

I grab a pair of black spandex and a long-sleeve, hot pink workout shirt and put them on. My sheepskin booties complete the outfit. I look in the full-length mirror and pat down my hair. Not bad. I start to head downstairs, but change my mind, thinking I should brush my teeth and I stub my big toe on the door frame. I yelp and hop over to the bed.

"Are you ok?" Jack calls up.

"Yes, I just stubbed my toe!" I'm so stupid.

I brush my teeth and calmly walk downstairs. Jack has already made more tea and brought the teapot on a tray to the coffee table. His eyes scan my body as I come into the room.

"Thank you." I sit on the couch, putting my legs beneath me and I grab one of the blankets to cover up.

"You're welcome. You know, I think I prefer you in workout clothes rather than office clothes." He sits down beside me.

"Oh yeah? Is it because spandex is tight?"

"That could be one reason, but I think of you as a sporty, athletic girl, not as a…"

"What? Not as an intelligent, nerdy psychologist?"

"You said it, not me," he laughs.

"Whatever." I try to swat his leg, but he moves out of the way. "I'll get you back for that."

I reach for the tea, he does too. "I got it. Just sit back and relax," he says.

"I could get used to this." I smirk and pull the blanket up to my chin.

"Oh no, am I creating a monster?" He passes me my mug, winking at me.

"Maybe!" I giggle.

He looks at me for a few seconds and I can see he either wants to say something or he's thinking, but his eyes flicker and he says, "What's on television tonight?"

I hand him the remote and he channel surfs, talking about each program. I barely pay attention as he zips through, but nod, agreeing to a movie with Will Smith. It's the one with the robots that seems to repeat on T.V. every weekend. I sip my tea and watch distractedly. I wonder what Jack's thinking about.

"Colleen, did you hear what I said?"

"What? No, I didn't. Sorry."

"I asked if you were going anywhere tomorrow."

"No plans. I might go for a run. Do you want to join me?"

"I'm not sure that I can. I have a couple of clients in the morning. I was asking so I could text Curtis and tell him when to come over." He waves his phone at me. "Can he come over first thing?"

"Sure." I'm disappointed. That was my first attempt at asking him out and he declined.

Jack looks down at his phone and pushes the hair out of his eyes, but it just falls right back into them. He keeps texting and I stare at his jawline, covered in blonde scruff and then down to his full lips. My eyes fall lower and I keenly observe the outline of his chest and how the shirt clings to his abdominals. His belly lifts and lowers with each breath, but barely. I bet he's got great abs. He has one leg crossed over his knee and I notice that he's taken his shoes off. He has some pretty big feet! I smile to myself.

"What are you grinning about?" He puts his phone in his pants pocket.

I blush and take a sip of tea. "Nothing."

"Are you looking at my boats?

"Boats?"

"My feet. I know they're huge, but you know what they say about big feet?"

I stare at him, shocked. He's not going to go *there*, is he? I put my tea on the coffee table.

"Big feet, big shoes."

"You're a geek," I laugh.

"I'm a geek?" He jokes, turning toward me, smiling. "You're the geek!"

Without warning, he grabs my ankles and I try to kick him away, but he holds on and pulls me toward him, blanket and all. My whole body sprawls out my head falls onto the couch. He moves fast, pins my legs by sitting on them and under the blanket, he squeezes just above my knees, tickling me. I squeal and try to squirm away, but he travels higher up my legs. He's smiling and having fun torturing me, but I'm not sure if it tickles anymore. I'm enjoying his playfulness.

When Jack's hands get to my waist, his legs are straddling mine, but with a blanket barrier in between us. My shirt rode up when he pulled me to him, so he's touching the bare skin of my stomach. It burns where his fingers are. I pretend to struggle and laugh to encourage him, but he slowly stops, staring at me, unsmiling.

"You're trouble, do you know that?" He backs off and pats me lightly on the thigh, ending up at the far side of the couch.

What just happened? I scramble to sit up and face the television again. Will Smith has figured out that the robots want to enslave and control humanity and he fights to save the world. I stare blankly at the screen. I can't even figure out how one man's mind works.

"I'm ready for bed." I jump up. "You know where everything is. Make yourself at home. Thanks for staying." I don't even look back as I head upstairs.

"Good night," I hear him call out.

I pull back the heavy duvet and crawl in, but tear off my clothes, remembering how warm the comforter makes me. It's only ten o'clock and I'm wide awake. I look around and seeing the phone reminds me to check my messages:

"Hi, Colleen. It's Jack. I got your messages, but I've been away in Calgary for a workshop. I hope you're ok and will contact you tomorrow as soon as I fly in. Take care."

He did leave a message. I listen to it again. I like how he says my name. I repeat it again. All right, I've lost my mind. I hang up the phone, knowing full well that I didn't delete the message.

Jack cares or he wouldn't be here, right?

11.

Sleep consisted of thoughts turning into dreams that I kept waking up from. I hoped Jack might come to my room and get into bed with me. He didn't, but in my dream he lied down beside me and held me tight. I replayed the tickle fight in my mind and it turned into a make out session in my dream. I even imagined going downstairs in my bra and panties, or even changing into some sexy lingerie to get a glass of water, 'forgetting' that Jack was there, but I didn't think I could pull it off. In my dream, I accomplished the act and he was happy to see me. No dream really ended either, just like my thoughts.

Now, it's six a.m. and I'm up, but I don't want to disturb him, so I draw a bath. I add some mango-scented bubbles and get in, closing my eyes. The heat relaxes me and I slowly move my arms around, letting them float to the surface.

In what only feels like a few minutes later, a noise disturbs me and I open my eyes.

"I'm sorry!" Jack states loudly, already turned around in the doorway, but not moving.

I look down and there are barely any bubbles left in the tepid water. I'm sure he got an eyeful. "Do you need something?" I unplug the tub, get up and grab a towel, staying in his line of sight. Strangely, I'm not embarrassed at all.

His back remains to me. "I'm so sorry. I knocked on your bedroom door and you didn't answer and when I came in, I didn't see you and your bathroom door was open. I didn't know you'd be in the bath." He's rambling. "Curtis is here."

"What time is it?" I wrap the towel around me.

"Seven-thirty."

I fell asleep! "I'll be right down."

Jack starts to leave, but he quickly looks back at me. "Sorry again!" I think he's smiling!

I giggle and dress into some running clothes. Maybe I can talk him into a run.

At the bottom of the stairs, I see Jack, but no Curtis. "Where is he?"

"Downstairs. He's going to install the motion detectors and whatever else you need. I have to get going."

"What? No waffles?"

He smiles, "Not this time, trouble."

"I'm trouble? You're the one checking me out in the bathtub."

"Don't you use bubbles? I mean, I could see everything." He says the word 'everything' slowly and deliberately, while looking me up and down.

"I wasn't the one who was embarrassed," I declare, not fazed by his flirting

"Either was I." His eyes are very suggestive. He shakes off his gaze, "Anyway, tell Curtis what you need and I'll talk to you later."

"Have a good day, peeping Jack."

"Keep it up, trouble."

I laugh, close the door behind him and skip down the stairs to see Curtis. "Hey, are you down here, Curtis?"

"Yup, over here." I see him by the window, screwing in some mechanism. "I'm just installing the first of your motion detectors. Jack said they are to go on every window in the house?"

"Jack's being a tad over-protective, but I don't want to cross him, so yes, one on every window please."

"No problem. I'll be here most of the morning. Will you be here?"

"Yes, I have some stuff do around the house. Thanks for everything."

"No problem. Jack's wish is my command."

I smile and wonder what kind of connection they have and why Curtis owes him. "Call me if you need me."

The only room I haven't cleaned yet is my office, so I walk directly there. It's not bad, just a good dusting is needed. I get down to work and when I'm finished I sit in my yellow, leather chair. My newest psychology journal catches my eye and I scan the articles, seeing if anything peaks my interest.

When a Marriage Is Over – Moving Onwards and Upwards

That ought to do it. I begin reading.

'Many people feel as though they are ready to move on immediately after a marriage is over, without fully working through the healing and recovery process. Divorce can be severely debilitating. It can disrupt your life on many levels, from work to your social life to your physical health. The journey to healing after a marriage is over is a long one, and it is not easy. However, by dealing with your divorce, you can ultimately find yourself in a much better place; eventually, you will make it through the rough times and be able to move on.'

When Steve left me, I thought that was the end and I worked through my feelings by creating the Sex Project. The project and my obsession surrounding it disrupted my career, friendships and I totally had blinders on when it came to realizing my true relationship with Steve. The project helped me heal, though. The final outcome brought me back to reality. I'm definitely in that better place now.

I scan the article and skip the part about building your self-esteem and overcoming negative self-thoughts, but putting a 'social price' on myself intrigues me.

'If you are ready to enter the dating world, it's important to set appropriate personal standards. In particular, will you play hard to get or be an easy catch? These standards are one's 'social price'. The more you have to offer in a relationship, the

more you can expect in return, thus increasing your appropriate social price. Factors that help determine your social price include your ability to bring desirable traits such as inner strength, kindness, intelligence, and affection to a relationship. Singles seeking relationships assess unseen qualities in others based on social price as it is reflected in actions, body language, and verbal communication. Those exhibiting self-confident assertions of dating standards are perceived as holding relatively more promise as marriage partners. Conversely, those who appear insecure and desperate call a love interest excessively or engage in sexual activity too soon, send signals that they hold inferior unseen traits.'

I need to cool it with Jack. If it happens, it happens. I'm not going to push or look desperate!

Finally the article outlines five key tips when seeking out a new partner:

'1. Develop A (New) Support Group'

Christine is good for me, even though she's not divorced. She always has great advice.

'2. Assess Your Self-Worth'

I've never lacked direction and have always been a positive person. I'm good-looking and intelligent, with plenty to offer. I can see a bright future ahead of me. I think I'm good there.

'3. Plan Activities'

I already started that 'to do' list the other day. I'm not going to be sitting around, watching television or lying in bed.

'4. Curb Unhealthy Cravings'

I'm not an over-indulger. I don't have to worry about that..

'5. Prepare for Pitfalls'

This one actually might be tough. Christmas is just around the corner and I have no one to celebrate it with this year. I'm not sure if I'd feel right tagging along with Christine. When I get to that point, I'll figure something out.

'You know yourself best, so trust your inner wisdom. If you are ready to find new love, take heart: More than 40% of weddings in Canada are remarriages. But don't feel obligated to rush into another marriage, either—the 2001 General Social Survey reports that 60% of second marriages end in divorce. Now that you're single it's perfectly acceptable to remain so if that's what you prefer. What you do with your life now is up to you.'

Well, that isn't comforting at all.

12.

Curtis is explaining how to set the alarm to 'Away' or 'Stay' and how it's directly linked to the police, but I'm not listening. I've been in the house long enough and had my running shoes laced up two hours ago. I want to run. He says something about pressing some buttons to notify the police in case of a break-in, without letting the intruder know, but I look at my Garmin watch. I'm itching to run.

He notices my indifference, "Here's the manual, just in case you weren't listening."

"Perfect. Thank you so much. How much do I owe you?" I grab my purse.

"It's taken care of."

"Come on, that was a lot of work. Jack couldn't have paid for it all."

"Take it up with him. Have a good day."

He leaves and I don't even wait for him to back out of my driveway. I run past him waving and stick my earbuds in.

As soon as I fill my lungs with the fresh, crisp air, I realize that I have missed running, but's it's like I never stopped. My breathing rate automatically aligns with the beating of my heart--it's like clockwork--I inhale when my left foot hits the ground and exhale on the right step. It's a physiological wonder for me, just like how the stress in my neck and shoulders spontaneously disappears as I increase my pace. My body is made to run.

My metaphorical power button has been turned on and suddenly, I'm fully charged and alive! I feel strong, and powerful! I look around quickly. Can anyone see what's happening to me? I hope I'm inspiring the people driving in their cars. They should be thinking, *'Maybe I can run and my life could be better'*. It's so true! Running gives me such confidence. I never want to give it up again.

The gravity of my optimism even sheds positivity on the gray, bleak November day. It's cold and I'm glad I wore a light sweatshirt, but the weather hasn't deterred the Torontonians either. I have to maneuver around the Saturday shoppers, tourists and everyday commuters to get to the waterfront. It's a fun obstacle course and I make a game of hopping over the subway grates and trying to run across the street at least once every block.

I get to Lakeshore Boulevard and head down Cherry Street, crossing the bridge, to run on the Martin Goodman Trail in Cherry Park. Right away, I see a jogger that looks familiar. It looks like Jack! Flip flop. I quicken my pace to catch up to him. It's strange that he's wearing a black baseball cap. I've never seen him wear a hat before.

Getting closer, I notice that the runner's gait is 'off'. Jack's arms don't swing like that when he runs. It's not Jack. My disappointment slows me down. *Shake it off!* I'm not running for him, I'm running for me!

Despite Cherry Park's name, there isn't a traditional 'park' here. There's limited lawn space at the northern end with some outdoor grills and picnic tables, but no fountains or gardens, orderly paths or park benches. I turn down a path that takes me to Tommy Thompson Park, which leads to various trails in the man-made Peninsula.

I see some children sticking long branches into mud and getting dirty. I smile. My practice is doing well, but I'd really like to get involved with the community. I've always wanted to be a Big Sister, but that's only *one* child. I wonder how I could help more at a time. I'll have to research groups around Toronto who do that sort of thing later.

As I turn down a different path, a jogger who's fifty feet in front of me raises my heart rate exponentially. It definitely is Jack. What do I do?

I pick up my pace, just as Pink starts singing *So What*. I'm going to pass him quickly and casually, like I don't recognize him. I take a deep breath and step to his right, resisting the urge to slap his bottom.

'Na na na na na na na I wanna start a fight, Na na na na na na I wanna start a fight.'

"Colleen!"

I hear Jack's faint call, but I keep running and singing,

'I am a rock star, I got my rock moves and I don't want you tonight.'

The song's a lie for what I feel about Jack. I do want him, but I can have the attitude. Come on and catch me, Jack.

After a few minutes, I slow down and turn my head slightly, using my peripheral vision. He's there. Flip flop. He just can't catch up.

Jack falls into step beside me and reaches out to touch my arm.

I pretend to be surprised and pull out my earbuds. "Jack! Hey!" I keep running.

"You just passed me."

"I did?"

"Yup, you just zipped right past me and I called you, but you didn't hear me."

I laugh, "You caught me now."

"Barely." He slows even further.

I match his speed, "Do you want to keep running?"

"Sure, but only a mile or so."

We both put in our earbuds and continue on the path into the furthest part of the trail, then loop around, coming back to where we started. I lead and head toward Lake Shore Boulevard. I can't help smiling to myself. I could see us running together regularly in the future. Steve never wanted to come with me and now I know why. I roll my eyes. He was probably banging someone…or maybe he just became a lazy fat bastard. I laugh out loud.

Jack pokes me with his elbow. "What's so funny?"

I take an earbud out. "Just something that happened a couple of days ago."

"Please share." He stops running and places his hands on his upper thighs. "I can't run anymore." He looks up at me. "Don't you ever get tired?"

I'm jogging on the spot, not needing any recovery. "I guess, just not today."

"One day I'll be able to keep up with you."

"I'm going to hold you to that." I hold my hand out to him.

He takes it, stands up and gives it one hard shake. "Deal." His eyes are playful, but I know he means it.

We walk down Lake Shore and I realize that it's about an hour walk to my house, but I don't want it to end there. How can I keep him here with me?

"Where do you live, Jack?"

"On Hazelton, off Berryman."

"Oh, by the Whole Foods store?"

"That's right."

"That's a swanky neighbourhood." He doesn't say anything. "You're a little further than I am. Do you want me to drive you home?" I ask, crossing my fingers.

"I was hoping that you'd ask me in, so I can rest before I go. Maybe I could take an hour nap on your couch."

Or in my bed! I get excited and don't know what to say. He's coming over!

He bumps his hip into mine. "I'm kidding. I'm fine. I'll walk you back and get home from there."

"Oh."

"Hey, is that ok?"

"Yeah, no problem." I hide my disappointment. "Did you run all the way to Tommy Thompson Park?"

"Yes, I've been building up my endurance and I always have high hopes, but I can never make it back home."

"What's your goal?"

"The Mississauga Marathon at the end of April."

"Right, I remember you telling me that you were going to do a marathon. Do you have a training schedule?"

"I have something I found online."

"I have the best book for training."

We talk all the way to my house about how and when to train, and I give him tips and other information that has helped me in the past.

At my walkway I say, "Come in and I'll give you the book I was talking about."

Jack hesitates, "I don't want to take your book."

"I don't use it anymore. It's all up here," I point to my temples, smiling. "Come on." I pull on his shirt sleeve.

"Ok."

Flip flop. I don't want him to leave yet.

We get inside and he just stands at the entryway and he looks awkward.

"You can come in." Why is he acting so weird? He always gets right in my house, even when I don't want him there, and makes himself comfortable. I give him one last look and run to my office to grab the book. I walk slowly back, skimming the pages.

"I dog-eared the useful pages, but this one," I flip the book open to a certain page. "This is the eighteen-week training schedule to run a marathon." I stand right beside him with my shoulder against his chest, trying to ignore the energy between us, and read from the book: *"Do not increase either your weekly mileage and/or long run mileage by more than 10 percent a week. Doing so greatly increases the chances of incurring an injury."*

Out of the corner of my eye, I see Jack staring at me. My voice fades and I slowly look up at him. He doesn't look away. The electricity returns and my body buzzes with familiar sensations.

I move closer to him and part my lips. I want to kiss him. Flip flop.

Jack slowly bends his head down toward mine and I close my eyes, waiting for it.

After a second, I feel him step away.

"I have to go."

What just happened? "What's wrong?"

"Nothing."

I take a step toward him. "But why… Why don't you want…?" I don't know what to ask him.

"I have a date tonight."

Now I really don't know what to say. "A date?" I stare at him, dumbfounded.

"Yeah, I should be going." He backs toward the door.

"Sure. Oh. Here, take the book." I want to throw it at his head.

"Thanks." Our fingers touch in the exchange and I feel the volts of electricity again.

"See you later." He's almost out the door when he turns one last time, "Make sure you turn your alarm on. I know the cops said they'd be outside your house again tonight, but you need to have it on at all times."

"Goodbye." I slam the door on him.

Bewildered, I stare at the door. He has a date? He's been pursuing me for weeks, if not years, waiting for my marriage to fall apart, which he predicted would happen and now, he just walks away? He has to see that I'm willing…that I was interested…And he has to feel the same way still. No?

"Fine!" I don't need him anyway.

I lock the door, reset the alarm and walk in a confused circle in front of the door. Did he really just leave to go on a date? Looking out the window one more time, I snap back the curtains and kick the bottom of the door.

"Jerk!"

13.

It's 10:15 p.m. and I'm pacing in my kitchen. I should've known better to think that Christine would be on time. I called her after another long bath and an attempt at reading a magazine, begging her to take me out. I couldn't stand being alone anymore. She already had plans, but was excited to take me and told me to be ready for ten o'clock.

I pace back to the bathroom and check my reflection for the hundredth time. I straightened my hair for a change and I keep running my fingers through it, untangling the roots. It looks pretty good. I picked out a slinky, black dress that I haven't worn in years and black, suede boots. I'm undecided about the look. It's very sexy and I'm not sure if I'll get the right kind of attention, but if Jack doesn't want me, I'll have to keep playing the field! Do people still say that? Whatever. I'll keep dating, but without the casual sex. That's just too complicated.

A faint honking outside brings me to my senses. I hurry to pick up my purse and head out the door.

"Where are we going?" I ask as I get into her car.

"Love your hair!" She grins at me. "And it's a surprise."

I roll my eyes, obviously expecting something outrageous. She's got on glittery heels, but I can't see what she's wearing under her coat. I'm sure it's stunning.

"What made you want to come out tonight?" She pulls out a lipstick at a red light and applies it heavily.

"Jack," I state bluntly.

"What happened? What did he do?"

"He's going on a date tonight."

She narrows her eyes, "No way! I don't believe it. He's so into you. I bet he's playing games."

"Well, he left me today after what I thought was a moment," I air-quote with my fingers. "He's been really wishy washy with me. At times, I feel he's really into me and other times he's almost prudish and untouchable. It's like he doesn't know what he wants or maybe he's just not interested anymore."

"Strange." Christine turns down Richmond Street. "He could be just trying to make you jealous. Men do that when their desperate."

"I don't know. I've shown him that I'm interested. He doesn't have to be desperate." I stomp my foot. "I don't want to play games anymore! If that's the type of guy he really is then I don't want to be with him."

"Forget about him tonight. Let's go have some fun." She pulls into a parking lot and pays the attendant. "Sorry about the hike, but this place is awesome. I have a table booked for ten people. My work friends are coming."

We walk a couple of blocks and then I see a line of about fifty people in front of a black building with the word, 'Chill' in white block letters across the front.

"I've heard about this place."

"You're going to love it."

We're greeted at the door and I look around while Christine sorts out her reservation. There's a heavy freezer door beside us and behind the reception desk, I see a large lounge area with hanging antler chandeliers. It has a chic wood cabin feel.

"Blue or red?" asks the hostess. She's standing behind the counter at a sort of reverse coat check. Behind her, dozens of fur-trimmed parkas are hanging up in rows.

"Blue." I give her my wool coat to check and she hands me a blue coat, along with a pair of thin grey gloves. When I put it on, it's more of a tent-style cape than a coat. I'm both disappointed and relieved that no one can see my tight dress. Christine covers her own red, one-shoulder dress with a red cape.

Once we're suited up, a scantily clad hostess guides us through the heavy freezer door and through an ice hallway. The walls are made out of glassy ice blocks and the word 'Chill' is carved into it. It looks like a crystalized glass castle.

"Did you want me to take your picture?" she chirps, smiling.

Christine and I look at each other and politely decline. We're not in our twenties anymore.

The lounge casts an eerie, bluish glow and I feel the frigid temperature immediately. The hostess leads us to our ice table, complete with ice chairs. It's only one of two seating alcoves. It's a small area, with ice chandeliers, ice curtains, an ice bar, an ice DJ booth bar and many ice sculptures. It has a unique ambiance.

"The freezer is kept at a chilly minus five degrees Celsius, which keeps all the furniture completely frozen. Your reservation will end in forty-five minutes, but if you can't last that long, you can always head into the warm lounge."

"Thanks."

It's not a very big room. Only a handful of people are milling around the ice sculptures, snapping selfies and drinking from their ice cups. The sculpture display includes a mini CN Tower, a giant Stanley Cup, a dangling chandelier and a smiling, buck-toothed snowman. All sculptures are intricately detailed.

"Isn't this place great?" She touches the wall with her gloved hand. "I can't believe that everything's made of ice."

"It certainly is cool," I enunciate the word cool, stretching it out.

"Ha ha. You're so funny. I'm glad we're the first ones here. It'll give us more time to catch up."

A waiter comes up to our table. "Hi, ladies. What can I get you to drink?" He's short, cute and full of energy.

Christine points to a cocktail sign, "Two Chill Cosmos, please."

"Be right back with those." He does a hop turn and scurries away.

"So, how's life after Steve."

"I feel great about everything. I started running again and I'm going to focus on my practice, but I'm also going to make time for you. I'm excited about starting fresh."

"I'm so happy for you, especially the part about making time for me."

"I can't believe that I neglected you for so long. Why I listened to Steve for all those years is beyond me. I'm smarter than that."

"You were in love. What could you do? Steve didn't like me and hated that I valued our friendship more. I didn't fall prey to his advances and it squashed his ego. I guess when I called him a dick and warned him to treat you better he didn't like the threat hanging over his head."

"I'm sorry that I was blind and stupid. It'll never happen again." I put my arm around her and give her a half hug.

At that moment, a group of Christine's friends is lead to our table by the same hostess. Christine stands up and embraces and introduces each one of them to me. I'll never remember all of their names.

Christine busies herself with them and I get up to look at the ice sculptures. I even venture to sit on the massive, majestic ice throne. I'm surprised it doesn't freeze my bottom. I move around and see if I stick to it. Nope. I sit and take it all in. The television is encased in ice too. Amazing!

The same, little waiter walks toward me, carrying my Cosmo and I start to get up out of the throne.

"No, sit! Drink it while you're sitting there. You look beautiful."

"Thanks." I sit back down and marvel at the glass my drink is in. It's actually made of ice. I sip it, feeling like I'm in a wonderland, until other patrons come up to the throne with cameras and ruin my fantasy.

There's really nowhere else to wander, so I sit back down with Christine and her friends just as the waitress brings over a round of shots on a ski. Four people must down the shots at the same time. It's handed to me and three others to my right. Once we're set, we count to three and lift the ski and the attached shot glasses to our mouths. I immediately gag on the Jagermeister. Not my favourite, but it warms me up. I listen in on the work gossip and down the rest of my drink, trying to get rid of the black licorice taste.

"Colleen, what should Carmen do?" Christine pokes me.

"Carmen?"

"Yes," she points to the pretty brunette sitting across from us. "Tell her the story Carmen."

"I can't tell her!" Carmen squawks.

Christine passes me another Cosmo. "She doesn't know you and she's a psychologist. She can help."

"Fine. Ok. Here goes. I'm falling in love with my boss."

"Keep going," I urge.

"I've worked for him for six years. We talk about our personal lives, eat lunch together, go out with the office for drinks regularly and find ourselves hunkered down in a corner usually. He's everything I want in a man, except he's married."

Carmen continues to talk, but I get angry. She loves a married man. I look sternly at Christine and she just shrugs. Adultery hits too close to home and it angers me. I chug my drink.

"We hooked up for the first time last weekend and I'm having a hard time concentrating at work and find when I'm away from work I'm annoyed—

I finally interrupt her when I can't take any more of the stupidity, "He's married. Move on."

"But he says he's unhappy, which I know doesn't make it ok, but I just am crazy about him!"

"Carmen, put yourself in his wife's shoes. How would you feel if another woman did the same to you? If you really respect yourself, then you should understand that the only thing you'll end up doing is breaking up a family. You'd be a home wrecker. Do you want that label?"

"Well no…"

"Why on earth would a beautiful and intelligent woman like you, want to settle for a man who can't be committed in a real relationship? Wouldn't you be better off looking for a single man who'd be fully dedicated to having a real relationship with you?"

"I understand, but I love him. It'd be hard to break it off now," she looks at me with puppy dog eyes.

Grow up! "You can't control who you fall in love with, but only to a point. You need to break it off now before you get in any deeper." I stand up, needing to get away from this imbecile. "I'm going into the warm lounge."

Christine follows me, "Wait up!"

"Fuck! Why would you tell me to give her advice about that? I want to strangle her."

"I knew you'd give her the best advice since you've been through it yourself and because you don't put up with stupidity."

I laugh, calming down a bit. "You're damn right about that." I put my hands up to my chin, "But I love him," I mock.

Christine giggles and puts her arm around me, "Let's go get warmed up!"

Going through another door at the back of the ice lounge, we hand over our capes and gloves to different hostess. I tug at my skin-tight dress, trying to urge it back down toward my knees. It's much warmer out here and I adjust to the temperature quickly. I hear a piano and someone singing, *Uptown Girl* loudly.

"You look fantastic," Christine says.

"You do too." The red dress has a cut-out at her rib cage and the one shoulder is made of lace, which is also on the edge of her skirt. "Let's get another drink."

A man suddenly comes up behind Christine and surprises her, picking her up off the floor and swinging her around. Christine shrieks, "You made it!"

He kisses her on the cheek and they keep talking intimately. I don't want to interrupt, so I walk over to the bar and try to find a spot to stand. It's busy. People crowd around tables made from barrels and the faux red leather couches are completely full, too. I can't even get close to the bar.

"Are you trying to get a drink?" A guy with the most horrible mustache and goatee asks.

"I'm trying, but not getting anywhere."

"You're hot. I'm sure if you just smile at the bartender, he'd do anything for you."

I smile faintly and nod, but turn to look in the other direction. I'm not interested, buddy.

At the front reception, I see a man helping a beautiful blonde into her red cape. When he turns to get his own parka from the hostess, I see that it's Jack. Flip flop. I don't think that *flip flop* was excitement. It was more like dread or shock. He's here? With his date? What am I going to do?

Without thinking, I turn to the guy that was hitting on me before, "Can I buy you a drink?"

His face turns from bitter to surprise, "Sure." I just made his night… Or his entire life.

I look back at Jack, but he's stepping into the cold lounge freezer door. Shit! I should've waited until he came out to talk to this loser. His mustache is really thick. He looks like the guy from the movie, 'The Hangover'. Not the hot one. Shit! Where's Christine?

"What made you change your mind? You didn't seem like you wanted to talk before." He puts his hand on the small of my back.

"I was preoccupied with something, but I figured I should shake it off." Much like your hand. I take a step backwards and turn. His hand has nowhere to go but back in his pocket.

"That's what Taylor Swift would say."

I smile, having no idea what he means.

"You know, shake it off, shake it off," he sings horribly.

"I don't know the song. Sorry." Where are you, Christine?

"Hey, did you get me a drink?" Christine comes to stand beside me. 'Hangover' guy blatantly checks her out.

"Thank God, you're here. I'm still waiting. I can't even get close to the bar. This place is crazy."

Before I can say anything, Christine pushes through some guys, stands up on the brass foot rail under the bar and puts two fingers in her mouth, whistling shrilly.

The bartender turns and smiles, "Chris! What can I get you?"

"Two Coronas, please."

"Make it three," I tug on her arm.

"Three Coronas." She steps down. "Who's is the third for?"

"It's for…" I point to the 'Hangover' guy. "What's your name?" I ask him.

"Matt," he smiles and shakes my hand.

"I'm Colleen. This is Christine."

The drinks arrive and I pay for them, passing them to Matt and Christine. I lean over and whisper to her, "Jack's here with his date. They just went into the cold lounge."

"Shit." She thinks for a minute, "It's ok, here's the plan. It's time to play your own games. Focus on Matt, get all in his stuff and act like he's the only man for you." She pushes me toward him and I bump into him.

"Falling for me already?" He snorts.

I laugh awkwardly and turn to sneer at Christine, but she's hanging over the bar with her bottom swaying in the air, chatting with the bartender. They're making a lot of thirsty people angry, but they're also entertained with the booty show. Only Christine could pull that off. What happened to the guy who lifted her up? They seemed very familiar with each other. I can't keep track anymore.

My thoughts are interrupted by 'Hangover' guy Matt, "So, have you been here before?"

I cringe and drink half of my beer. How am I supposed to act like Matt's the only man for me? There are about twenty men in this bar, maybe more, that have to better than this guy. He's on full flirt and score mode. He's touched my hand, my arm and is now standing super close to me, talking into my ear. I even felt his lips on my ear at one point. His curly haired beard nauseates me. It looks like little pubic hairs.

You have to do this! I have to waste time talking to Matt and keep him at bay, so I can use him to make Jack jealous. It seems so juvenile, but I watch for Jack to emerge from the cold lounge. I don't have any other ideas.

I scan the crowd for Christine. She's moved on from the bartender to a new guy with longer, slicked back hair. An Italian stallion. She's touching his hand and they're laughing. She puts his hand on her bare shoulder and he smiles at her, leaning in to whisper something in her ear.

How come I get stuck with 'Hangover' guy Matt? Now, he's rambling on about his last business trip to Las Vegas and how he rented a Harley to ride and visit the Grand Canyon while he was there. He has a passion for motorcycles, which I can't fathom. He doesn't look like the biker type. More like a scooter or an e-bike kind of a guy. I don't need this. I finish my beer, getting ready to ditch Matt and walk around the bar, but he just went up to order another beer for me. Should I just ditch him? I'm sure he could find some other poor, unfortunate girl to hit on.

Jack suddenly walks into the warm lounge and he doesn't look happy. Hot, but unhappy. The blonde is trailing behind him, trying to run in her eight-inch heels and he just keeps walking. Their capes are off and I see that she's wearing a sleeveless, midriff-baring top and a barely-there mini skirt. She's rubbing her arms, trying to warm up. They didn't last very long in the cold. Perhaps if she was wearing more clothes…

The blonde calls for him. I hear her high-pitched shriek, "Jack! Wait!" and he stops in the middle of the bar and waits. He looks around and his eyes come to rest on me. He looks surprised, but not pleased.

My heart flutters and my stomach drops. I'm not sure if it's a flip flop. I stare back, not knowing how to read him or how to appear. Should I be happy to see him or act angry?

Matt comes back at that moment with our beer and I quickly grab his arm, leaning in to talk into his ear, "What do you do for a living, Matt?" I'm going to act indifferently.

"I'm an electrician."

"Really? That's awesome," I fawn and rub his arm. "You must be a busy man."

"I sure am. I own the company." His chest seems to puff out and continues to talk about his responsibilities. "I design, install, maintain and troubleshoot electrical wiring systems. These systems can be located in homes, commercial or industrial buildings, and even machines and large pieces of equipment."

I'm not even listening. I take a drink of my beer and casually scan the crowd and look to see where Jack has settled, but smiling as if I'm interested in Matt. I don't want Jack to know that I'm looking for him.

Christine leans in abruptly and whispers, "Jack's here and he's seen you. Actually, he can't take his eyes off of you."

Flip flop. What am I doing? I didn't want to play games! I should go to Jack and tell him that I have feelings for him. I'm sure he'd appreciate that. We can get everything out in the open and deal with it.

"Should I just go talk to him, Christine?"

"Definitely. He doesn't look interested in his date."

I hold onto her hand and turn to Matt, "Hey, I need to go see a friend of mine. It was nice meeting you."

Matt looks disappointed. "Sure. Nice meeting you."

Turning back to Christine, I squeeze her hand, "Wish me lu…" I stop mid-sentence when I catch a glimpse of Jack getting mauled by the blonde. They're sitting on a couch and her legs are draped over his lap, while she kisses his neck. My stomach plummets, but I can't look away. She bites his ear and fondles his chest playfully. I barely notice Jack staring at me.

When our eyes lock, I quickly turn away, questioning his character. Once a player, always a player? My heart's beating wildly and I feel completely disoriented. God, I can't read men! I feel so stupid. I mentally kick myself. Enough belly aching! I keep my back to Jack and down the rest of my beer. Fuck!

"Ci-Ci, don't worry about it. He's not touching her. She's the one all over him. Look! He's still staring at you."

"He's not stopping her, is he?" Turning around, I give Jack the longest, darkest stare. He needs to know how much he hurt me. I can't believe I was so wrong about him.

Looking around, I spy Matt at the bar, so I push my way through the crowd and rub his back lightly, "Hi, Matt!"

He turns around and grins from ear to ear. "You're back."

"Yup, I'm all yours." I look up at him through my lashes and touch his waist.

He looks stunned. "You are?"

"Yes!" This time I stand on the brass foot rail, put my fingers in my mouth and whistle at the bartender. Everyone looks at me. "I want tequila shots for everyone!"

The bar breaks into a frenzy of hoots and hollers. The men beside me hold up their hands for me to hive five. I wave two one hundred dollar bills and hand them to the bartender. He gets out twenty shot glasses and starts pouring Don Julio.

"I want six of those shots, please," I tell the bartender.

He slides them over and making sure I'm in plain sight to Jack, I toss a shot back quickly, without the lime. It burns all the way down. At least it takes away the sickening feeling away. I take another shot glass in my hand and push one toward Matt.

"Wow! You're quite a girl." He stands right behind me with his front to my bottom. Do I feel a bulge in his pants already?

I toss my hair back and glide my hand up his arm. "You have no idea." With that, I down the tequila. It makes me warm and my legs feel like jelly.

Matt puts his arm around me and nuzzles my neck, but then, backs away slightly and slides his hands down my shoulders and arms. They come to rest on my bottom, giving it a slight squeeze. "Do you want my shot?"

"Sure." I take it and put it to my lips, turning my head slightly to look towards Jack. He's staring at me and he looks angry. I down the tequila shot, not taking my eyes off of him and slam the glass on the table.

Matt swoops in and starts kissing my neck. After what seems like a full minute, I realize what he's doing and I don't like it. His beard is scratchy and his pubic hair beard repulses me.

"I need to visit the ladies room." I push him away and stumble backwards into a couple of guys. I smile apologetically and get my bearings, walking toward the bathroom. Inside, I find an empty stall and lock the door behind me. I pull up my skirt and sit down.

What am I doing? I need to go home. I don't need to be getting drunk and making out with strangers. Fucking Jack! I put my head in my hands. Fuck him and his blonde girlfriend. Who cares? I don't need him. I can have fun too. Matt likes me and he'll take me home. I'll show Jack that someone wants me.

Outside the ladies room, I walk down the hall and then make an abrupt U-turn when I remember that I should be walking in the other direction. With my hair in my eyes and the alcohol slowing my senses, I bump straight into Jack's chest and bounce off of it.

"What do you want?" I glare at him.

"I'm taking you home," he demands.

"Stop bossing me around. You're so bossy," I tap his chest with one finger.

"You're drunk. You're stumbling everywhere and I don't trust the guy you're hanging around. You're doing too many shots with him. He just wants to get you pissed drunk, so he can get in your pants."

"What do you care?" I hit his chest with my fist. "You've got that blonde whore. She's all over you. Go take her home." I stagger and push past him, looking for Matt.

He's right where I left him, pubic beard and all. "Let's go, Matty Matt Matt."

"Where?"

"Home. I'm taking you home." I reach out to take his hand.

"Ok!" He grasps my hand, smiling broadly.

I walk up to Christine and state, "I'm taking Matty home."

"Are you sure you want to do that?"

"Yesssss," I slur.

"Colleen, you're drunk." She puts her body between me and Matt, breaking our contact and addresses him, "You're not going home with her."

"Yes I am."

"No, you're not. She's a little too inebriated for a good time. I think you should exchange numbers and go out another time."

"She said she wants to take me home." He tries to walk around Christine, but Christine pushes him back.

"Be a gentleman and think about this," she's asking him politely, but for a tiny girl, she's pretty scary.

He looks around at the people gathering to watch the scene and spits out, "Fuck you. Leave us alone."

"Christine, I'm fine. It's ok."

"No, it's not. You're not going home with him." She steps between us and puts a hand on Matt's chest.

"Listen, bitch, get the fuck out of our way." Matt knocks down Christine's hand and grabs my wrist, dragging me away.

I trip and feel myself fall forward. I can't stop. I brace for impact, but suddenly feel an arm around me. I float in mid-air for a few seconds, wondering why I didn't fall.

"Are you ok?" Jack rescued me.

Always the hero. "I'm fine." I brush off his arm and straighten my dress. Matt comes to my side, putting a possessive arm around me. I pat his chest, "I'm going home with Matt the plumber."

"I'm an electrician. Who's this guy?" Matt asks.

"No one. Let's go, Matty." Jack's livid. I see a vein popping out of his neck.

We step outside and the cold air slaps me in the face. My eyes start to water and everything seems blurry. I take a few deep breaths and try to sober up. The tequila isn't sitting well.

"I'll get us a cab. Stay here." Matt releases his grip on me and heads to the street, flailing his arms as cabs race by.

What am I doing? I don't want to go home with him. He called Christine a bitch and wasn't nice to her. Jack's furious with me and I completely snubbed him. I didn't want to make Jack mad, but he was with another woman! And I totally lost it! Why am I so crazy! I've been foolish and reckless. I almost went home with the ugly 'Hangover' guy. I need to get away.

As a group of people walk by, I step toward them and grab onto a young girl's arm. She looks at me, alarmed and starts to push me away, but I say, "Shhhh, I'm trying to hide from a guy. He's such a loser." She laughs and tells the group to help surround me, to conceal me from the so-called loser. We all continue walking and I don't even look back.

After walking a few blocks, I thank the group and stop to hail a cab, but they stay with me to make sure I'm safe. After a few drive by, the group helps me out by jumping and whistling loudly. Finally, one pulls over and waits for me to get in, while the young girl pulls me in for a hug goodbye. I cry all the way home.

14.

The cab pulls up behind the police car in front of my house and after paying the driver, I just wave to Officer Leeds who nods, and go directly into my house. I don't feel like making small talk and they might smell the alcohol on my breath or see the tears in my eyes. I'm pleased to see them there. I temporarily forgot about Mr. Baker tonight. No matter what I do during the day, the fear always returns. I'm always going to be afraid. He's out there…somewhere and it frightens me. If the cops weren't there, walking up to my dark house would be nerve-wracking. Never mind actually going in.

I reset the alarm and look in the fridge, shifting the bottles and containers around. I'm hungry, but don't find anything appealing and bending over makes me feel dizzy. I'm exhausted and I just want to erase the last couple of hours. Time for bed. I shut off the lights and head for the stairs.

A banging on the front door makes me jump and I stumble forward, in a panic. I steady myself on the bannister and look at the door with my heart pounding in my chest. Is it the officers?

"Colleen, it's me. It's Jack." He bangs a couple more times. "Open up."

I'm relieved, delighted and nervous all at the same time. I don't think it's going to be a friendly visit. I wasn't very nice to him at the bar.

I turn off the alarm and open the door, but Jack pushes past it and me, "Is he here?"

"Who?"

"You know who," he scowls at me. "That loser you were with. Is he here?"

"No." I feel my temper flare. "Loser? At least I wasn't making out with him at the bar."

Jack has one foot on the bottom step of the stairs and his hand on the rail. "Colleen, who the hell was kissing your neck then," he snickers.

Did Matt kiss my neck? I don't remember any of that.

"Is he up stairs waiting for you?" He takes two steps upstairs.

"No, he's not here!"

He comes back down and walks toward me, taking my hand. "You scared me. He was such a douchebag. You have to be careful about—

I pull my hand away, "Why do you care who I'm with? I'm tired of this! Is it that you just want to be my hero and that's it? I don't need a fucking hero. I can take care of myself."

"A hero? I just don't want to see you get hurt."

"I'm a big girl, Jack. I don't need a babysitter or your pity." I take a few steps backward.

"Colleen, it's not pity. You were so lost when Steve left you and then with everything that happened with Mr. Baker, I thought you needed a friend." He steps toward me. "You know, someone to lean on. And seeing you tonight, I know you're still not yourself. You're making bad choices and you need my help."

I go to the other side of the kitchen table, keeping distance between us. "I'm making bad choices? Who was that tart you brought to the bar? She was really a grade A, prime choice selection. Really classy. How do you live with yourself?"

"What are you talking about now?"

"She was all over you at the bar like a dog on a bone. It was disgusting. Where's she now? Is she waiting for you at your house?"

"How much did you drink?" He laughs. "Dog on a bone?"

"Not enough to ignore her tongue in your ear."

"Are you jealous?" He's still smiling.

I laugh frigidly, "No, not at all. Why are you even here with me? You should be banging her by now."

"You're jealous." He puts his hands on the chair in front of him, looking at me childishly.

He's making me mad. "No, Jack. I'm not. If you want to date a woman like her, who am I to say anything? But come on, she's a blonde whore!"

He throws his hands up in the air, "You *are* jealous! Why now? You've been pushing me away for weeks and *you* made it very clear that *you* weren't interested. Fuck! Are you just on my case because you had too many tequila shots and couldn't get laid?"

"Is that what you think I want? I could've had sex with that douche bag, but life isn't about getting laid. It's about meeting someone and connecting with them." I get quieter, inhaling deeply, getting ready to swallow my pride and take a chance, "Listen, I'm mad because today... We were having fun today and then you left me because you had a date. I don't understand why you'd rather go out with her instead of me."

"So now, just because it's over between you and Steve, I'm supposed to jump for joy and take you in my arms, forgetting about all of your constant rejection?" He tilts his head to the side, "Did you forget about that? I haven't and I'm not going to be your second choice."

I shake my head, but I don't know what to say. He has every right to think that way. That's exactly how it played out for him, but I see it very differently. "I'm sorry, Jack. I can see how you'd think that," I say sensitively.

He adjusts his stance, but doesn't say a word.

"While you were completely right about Steve all along, couldn't you see that I had to figure it out for myself? Finding out was my right and actually my grieving process. I failed at my marriage and I had to come to terms with it in the way that I did," I talk slowly, finding the correct words. "It took some time, but now Steve is out my mind and out of my life and I'm so happy to move on."

Jack thinks for a few seconds. "You're right and I'm sorry. I'm glad you figured it out and I do understand the need to do it on your own terms. I jumped the gun and I didn't give you time. I was being selfish."

"It's ok. You tried to help me through a rough time."

"Colleen, I just tried to save you the heartache. You've always deserved to be happy."

"Thank you." Even with all the yelling, he still has kind words for me. I take a step around the table, closer to him. "I'm glad you came over, even if it was just to scold me and beat the living hell out of some guy."

"You're not kidding," he laughs. "I was about to go postal."

"I bet. I had the same thoughts about your date."

"Really? I can't see you taking anyone down."

"Probably not, but I was pretty angry."

We both have our hands on the backs of the chairs in front of us and I don't know what to say. I can only keep staring into his blue eyes. He's not saying anything either. *Go for it, Colleen. Tell him.*

"Are you—

"I need—

"Go ahead, you first," he says.

"I need to tell you something." I look down at my hands, not knowing how to begin, but determined to let him know how I'm feeling.

"Ok," he says quietly.

"You've been on my mind since the first time we ran together. I mean, you've always been a great friend and we've gotten along for years, but when we ran, I started thinking about you differently. For one, I don't lend my favourite Garmin watch to just anyone, you know."

He smiles, but says nothing.

"We've been through so much and you're always there for me, but that's not why I've been thinking about you." I remember him kissing me right in this kitchen and I blush, looking down again. "You're definitely not second choice," I say quietly.

"Why are you thinking about me?"

I look up to his unsmiling face and it makes me nervous, "Oh… I remember the times we've been together, you know, here at my house, running, the times we ran into each other… I find myself looking for you at the café every morning and I went to the deli the other night only because I thought you'd be there, which you were."

"Buy *why* are you thinking about me?"

"I don't know."

"You have to know why," he urges.

"Because you give me flip flops!" I exclaim exasperatedly, not knowing how to explain myself.

"What?"

"I get butterflies when I think about you. The way you look at me and touch me… I like how I feel when I'm around you." I can't even look at him now, but I notice him stepping closer to me. Our elbows touch.

"Flip flops?" He places his hands on my waist.

"Yup, I just got one now when you touched me."

"So, they're a good thing?"

"Oh yes, definitely."

He pulls me close to him by placing his hands on my lower back. The smell of him is intoxicating.

"Did that give you flip flops?"

"Yes," I murmur.

"Look at me."

I raise my head and stare into his eyes. God, he's gorgeous.

"You're definitely trouble."

"No, I'm—

Jack gently lowers his head and places his lips on mine. The flip flops are unbearable. My whole body trembles and my legs feel like they're going to give out.

His lips are so soft and I open my mouth slightly to flick my tongue out to touch his upper lip. He groans and opens his mouth, sliding his tongue out to meet mine. Our tongues make contact and pull back at the same time, rhythmically. It's a slow, sensual dance.

I slide my hands up and down his arms. The bulge of his muscles is a turn-on. I can feel the definition of his biceps and shoulders and I finger the dimple of his triceps, while pushing my tongue deeper into his mouth.

Jack responds by grasping my hips and pulling them into his. I get up on my tiptoes and feel the hardness against my lower stomach. It's me who groans this time.

Suddenly, he puts his hands under my bottom and lifts me up, wrapping my legs around him. My dress rises to my upper thighs. One of his hands remains on my behind and the other climbs up my back to the nape of my neck. I hear his ragged breath as he kisses me hungrily. I squeeze his torso tightly with my thighs and bite his bottom lip.

He groans again, but slowly pulls away from my lips and places me on the kitchen counter. He backs away slightly, putting his hands on the counter and dropping his forehead to my mouth. I kiss it lightly.

"What's wrong?"

"Nothing," he pants and looks up at me. Our faces are inches apart.

"Then why did you stop?" I caress his arms and peck his lips.

"I can't do this now?"

"Why?" I try to pull him closer, but he's like a rock. He means what he says.

"It's late," he shakes his head. "It's not right."

"Yes, it is," I grab his face and lift it up.

"No, it's not how I want to do this with you." He steps back and puts his hands behind his head. "No, not this way."

I jump off the counter and pull my dress into place, stepping towards him. "I want this." I place my hands on his chest and get up on my toes again to kiss him. "I want you."

He throws his arms around me and kisses me roughly. Our tongues stroke each other, in and out and swirling around. Our heads tilt in different directions, trying to devour each other.

I grab at his waistband and pull his jeans away from his hips. "Come to my bedroom." I keep kissing him, so he doesn't change his mind.

"No. No. No." He steps away and tries to break all contact, but I pull him back by his belt loops.

"Why? Don't you want me?"

He loosens my grip gently and walks toward the door. "Yes I want you, but I can't do this now. I'm sorry, Colleen."

I'm so confused. I shake my head slowly, trying to figure out what went wrong.

He walks back to me and kisses my forehead. "I'll call you tomorrow, ok?"

I nod, still not understanding. He wants me, but is leaving?

"The cops will be here all night, but don't forget to set your alarm."

Then he's gone.

I hurry to the window and watch him talk to the officers in their patrol car. He looks back toward my house, but then he gets into his car and drives away.

15.

It's Sunday. Day of rest, my ass. I'm unrested and miserable. Along with a hangover, I didn't sleep for more than two hours. Fucking Jack.

My mind was racing last night and it's worse now. I'm trying to make sense of Jack and his 'it's not right' speech. What wasn't right? Everything was more than right.

I kick my legs, shaking the heavy duvet off of me. 7 a.m. is the perfect time for a run. I throw on some spandex, put my hair up and do some quick stretches. My body is achy from yesterday's run, but an easy run will do my body good and clear my monkey mind.

Outside, the police car is gone already, but I feel pretty safe at this hour. I head down my street toward the waterfront, but change my mind and turn completely around. Jack said that he runs to Tommy Thompson Park to train and I really don't want to bump into him right now, so head out toward Craigleigh Gardens near Rosedale. It's a quiet park in the middle of Rosedale and the perfect place to be a hermit for a day. It's hidden beneath a canopy of trees and is basically never busy, so it's a good spot for some quiet, alone time.

On weekends, Aunt Anna would sometimes take me to Craigleigh Gardens, but it was only one of the many places where we'd hike in and out of the Toronto area. We'd drive to Rouge Park and walk the Mast Trail, which for any child is an extremely challenging trail. It leads up and over a ridge with some steep climbs and descents either way on the trail. Each time, I'd try to keep up with Aunt Anna and keep the complaints to myself, but I didn't really like that trail. I'd suck it up so she'd take me to the Toronto Zoo afterward. That was my favourite part.

Sometimes I'd beg her to take me to the Royal Botanical Gardens in Burlington. I didn't care for the nature sanctuaries or the walking trails along the Niagara Escarpment. I had just wanted to see the brides in their beautiful gowns getting their pictures taken among the gardens. Aunt Anna had thought it was too extravagant and unrealistic to have the photos done in a park. 'Marriages are not fantasies', she'd say. She was such a feminist. I, on the other hand, had loved to see newlywed couples in romantic poses. They had looked so happy.

Getting to Craigleigh Gardens is a quick jaunt down Sherbourne Street and Elm Avenue and then to the discreet entrance of the park at Castle Frank Road. There aren't any castles on that street, but I used to think that the old and beautiful mansions were very regal. Castle Frank Road is named after the first son of John Graves Simcoe, lieutenant-governor of the new colony of Upper Canada and Elizabeth Simcoe, accomplished painter. I love the historical aspect of this area.

Inside the park, I run the trail that leads to an opening in the middle of its northern side which has access to the Milkman Lane. Aunt Anna told me that the short gravel lane has existed for more than one hundred and thirty years and was originally intended for horseback riding and commercial transport, including, presumably, deliveries of milk. Currently, Milkman's Lane is prone to severe erosion resulting from various water sources, steep grades and lack of erosion control features. It leads down into a majestic ravine and winds its way through the trees on a steep hillside and eventually into the Don Valley. I think the uneven trails intimidate people, but I love the rustic quality of them.

However, the people at the off-leash dog park are in abundance and are irritating me today. I just want to run freely and not have to sidestep into the grass to avoid a hyper dog on a leash wanting to chase me or stop dead because a dog runs in front of me. I curse under my breath when a Shih Tzu tries to nip at my heels as I run by.

Why would Jack just leave like that? *No! Stop!* That same question has been repeating in my head all night. He must still be angry about turning him down, so he got me back by making out with me and giving me hope. What a jerk! He doesn't want to be with me. That's all there is to it. I think… That sounds so malicious. He's not like that. He did say he wants to be with me and that he wanted to go upstairs with me… I can't figure him out at all!

Breathe. Focus on breathing. I run up the final hill and out the other end of the park by Mount Pleasant Road, heading home. Running didn't help my mood at all, but it was a tough run. I should be tired out.

Just as I'm about to cross the street, a silver Jetta stops abruptly in front of me. "Hey!" I stop myself from angrily slamming my hands onto the hood of his car. "You're supposed to yield to me!"

I lower down to look at the driver and my stomach drops. It's Mr. Baker. He's leaning towards me with his hand on the passenger seat, making sure that I see him. I back away quickly, almost tripping on the curb and he leers at me with his black, beady eyes. I could turn and run, but I'm frozen at the small intersection with only a Rogers media monument behind me. There isn't a building that I can escape into, just a walkway above me, but I still can't move. Why aren't there any pedestrians walking by?

Mr. Baker keeps his car at the juncture for what seems like an eternity, until the vehicle behind him honks his horn. Even then, he doesn't drive forward right away. He just keeps staring and I want to scream at him to stop or to go away. Sweat drips into my eyes and down my back.

Finally, he smiles lewdly at me and puts his car in motion. As the rear end passes me, I go into survival mode and memorize his license plate: *BEVE 291… BEVE 291… BEVE 291.* I repeat it over and over and frantically sprint across the street, not knowing where to go. My office is just down a few blocks, but he knows that. I can't go there. *BEVE 291.*

I start running home down Jarvis Street, but stop at the Allan Gardens Conservatory to hide and catch my breath. The greenhouses are open seven days a week and there are always tourists around. I step into one of the Tropical Houses and mix in with the few visitors who are looking at the orchids and begonia. *BEVE 291.*

Mr. Baker was supposed to be staying with his mother. Is he allowed out of the house? Shouldn't she be with him when he's out on the street? Is this considered harassment? *BEVE 291.*

It's crowded in the greenhouse. A short woman pushes past me and I bump into a table covered in purple, Cattleya orchids and my heart races. It suddenly feels really hot in the greenhouse and I start sweating more than I already was. I also feel strangely claustrophobic. I push through the people, "Excuse me," and fling open the greenhouse door, feeling a bit of relief from the cool November air.

BEVE 291. I sprint the last half mile home and write down the license plate as soon as I get into the house. I drop the phone once, scrambling to pick it up again and dial Officer Nicholls' number. He doesn't answer, so I hang up and try again, while I reset my alarm. When his voicemail comes on again, I huff infuriatingly and leave a message, while looking out the window for a silver Jetta.

    I hold my hands out, watching them shake. *Come on! Relax!* Mr. Baker won't come here during the day. The alarm is on and it's a brand new, state-of-the-art system. Jack saw to that. He can't get in without me knowing and the cops circle by here hourly. I'm safe in my house. Completely safe. I take my cell phone upstairs with me and try to calm myself further by taking a bath.

16.

BEVE 291. I wake up flustered and chilled to the bone. The bathwater is cold and my fingers are pruny. How long have I been in here? I step out, dry off and head right to my bed completely naked. That'll warm me up.

It's 1:30 p.m. already? I'm amazed that I had a two-hour nap with the stress that I was feeling. Stress usually keeps me up at night. How could I just fall asleep? Must've been the bath. I'll have to remember to take a bath when I'm feeling tense. My phone should've at least woken me up. Officer Nicholls had to have called. I don't think he'd ignore the lunatic message like the one I left. Where's my phone? Dammit! I jump out of bed, go back to the bathroom and snag my phone off the counter, running back to get under my heavy duvet.

Three missed calls and a text? I slept through all of that? The first message says,

"Colleen, it's Officer Nicholls. I received your message. Please call me back."

I'll listen to the other messages first, before I return his call.

"It's Officer Nicholls again. I'm going to send a car over to your house. Please call me back."

Nope, it'd probably be better to call him back now. I hit redial.

"Officer Nicholls."

"Hi, it's Colleen Cousineau."

"Colleen, I was worried. Did the cruiser come by?"

"I don't think so." I need to get some clothes on. "I've been upstairs."

"Tell me what happened."

"Mr. Baker drove by me in a silver Jetta, license plate BEVE 291."

"Ok," I think he's writing it down. "What did he do?"

"Well… I was running and when I went to cross the street, he pulled out in front of me, so I couldn't go anywhere. He blocked me at the intersection and stared at me."

"Is that all?"

I feel silly now. "Yes, that's all he did, but isn't that harassment?"

"Not really."

"Oh. His mother wasn't with him! Actually, no one was with him. Isn't that a violation of some sort?" I'm grasping for anything that makes me look sane.

"His conditions require him to report to the police and obey a curfew. He also can't possess weapons, drink alcohol or communicate directly or indirectly with you, his e-wife or his child, but he can do day-to-day things, like drive around."

How is he allowed to be out on the streets by himself? He's a criminal! "In a way, he was trying to communicate with me indirectly." He definitely wanted to intimidate me.

"Listen, I'll stop by his mother's house and remind him of his conditions, making sure he knows not to harass you."

"I'm sorry for flipping out and wasting your time." I'm embarrassed.

"You have every right to flip out. He's a criminal. I'm sure you were scared when you saw him up close and you did the right thing. Call me whenever you want. You're never wasting my time."

"Thanks for being patient."

"No problem. Take care."

How humiliating! I slap my forehead and kick my feet wildly under the covers. I have to stop being so over-dramatic. All Mr. Baker did was drive by me and try to scare me. He got the response he wanted. Just like when he was outside my house the other night. He's pushing my limits, but I can't let him get to me. *Stop being such a baby!*

After a few more slaps to the forehead, I listen to my third message:

"Ci-Ci, you bitch! You'd better be ok. I sent Jack after you to make sure you didn't actually go home with that dick! Call me back!"

I cringe with guilt, but I can put that off for a minute while I look at the text. I lose my breath when I see it's from Jack:

"I'm sorry I left so quickly last night. I'll explain later. Have a good day."

That's it? That's all he wrote? When's 'later'? Christine may have the scoop. I call her quickly.

"What?" She roars into the phone.

I flinch, "It's Colleen."

"You'd better be calling to apologize."

"I am. I'm so sorry, Christine. Jack pissed me off and I had to get out of the bar, so I just used Matt as an excuse."

"Matt's a huge dick."

"I know. That's why I ditched him outside the bar. He didn't come home with me."

"Good. I told you to use him to play games, not to play with him. He was pretty gross. What was with his beard? It looked like a face full of pubes."

I start laughing, "I thought the same thing! Why didn't you say something last night?"

"Like I said, I didn't think you were going to take him home! And anyway, I tried to stop you, but you were hell bent on going home with him. Remember?"

"I know…I know," I feel guilty. "It was the mix of alcohol and seeing Jack with his date."

"Did you talk to Jack? Did he go to your house?"

"Yes," I say warily.

"What happened?"

"Nothing!" I huff. "We started kissing, I mean, really kissing and he just stopped and said he couldn't do *this* with me. Then he left!"

"What?"

"Yeah! It was really intense, to the point where I asked him to go upstairs with me and he said it's not the right time and left."

"The right time? I've never heard that one before. I don't know what to tell you."

"I just got a text from him and all it says is that he's sorry for leaving and he'll explain later. Did he say anything to you about me at the bar?"

"Not really. He was pretty angry about you going home with that guy, but I didn't have to tell him to check on you, he was already going to do that. It was apparent that he was worried about you."

"Does he care about me or doesn't he?" I'm so frustrated.

"He does care about you. I think he needs to figure things out. If you like him, you'll have to be patient."

17.

    This drama is depressing. It's supposed to be a romantic movie, but with Bill Murray and Scarlett Johansson as the key characters, I just don't see it. The action and dialogue is so slow that I tap my foot incessantly while constantly looking at my phone. When is it going to be 'later' Jack? This movie was nominated for Academy Awards? Maybe it gets better. I convince myself to only check my phone during commercials. I even put it on the table across the room, so I won't cheat and look at it, focusing on the movie.

    By the end of the film, I feel I have to do something productive…or something life-changing. The movie was so disheartening that I can't just sit on the couch and wait for Jack's call anymore. That's not what life is about. At least that's what the movie taught me. I leave my phone in the living room and go to my office. My best thinking and hard work had always taken place there.

    The only thing I can think of doing for myself right now is to deep-clean and re-arrange my office. *How humanitarian of me*! But it is Sunday and too late in the afternoon to really do anything else. It's not charitable or metamorphic, but I do shred some files, dust, vacuum and move my desk to the wall beside my window.

    I sit in my yellow, leather chair and survey the new look. I don't like it. Dammit! It doesn't flow. I'm looking at a stupid wall, with my back to the door! I'm satisfied with the deep-cleaning, but I angrily move the furniture back to the way it was.

    Just before bed, I finally look at my phone and don't see a message from Jack. That's when I lose my last ounce of patience. I turn it off, throw it into my purse and go to my room. "Fuck him." It takes a while, but I finally fall asleep.

    Now, walking to my office on Monday morning, I find myself still swearing out loud, "He said he'd explain *later*. Well, it's fucking later." I park and walk straight into my office, not even looking down the street at the café. If I run into Jack, I'll lose it.

    Work. Work. Work. Focus on work. Wasn't I thinking about volunteering and donating my time to help children? I'll research that right now, before my first patient. I'm determined to keep my mind off of him. I hang my coat up in the closet and sit down at my desk, immersing myself in Google searches.

    The front door opens and I call out, "Good Morning, Margie!"

    "It's not Margie."

    Flip flop. "Hi, Jack." Dammit! I'm not supposed to be excited to see him. I'm angry with him. He comes into my office and I weaken even more. God, he looks amazing. He has a brown leather jacket on with a pale blue, button-down shirt underneath that brings out the blue in his eyes. How can I be mad?

"Good morning. I brought you a cinnamon latte. When I didn't see you at the café this morning, I thought I'd bring it to you in person."

"That was very sweet of you. Thank you." I take it from him and when our fingers touch lightly, I almost drop the latte as the pulse of electricity is so strong. I try to calm myself and raise the latte to my lips, but the aroma of cinnamon instantly reminds me of Jackhammer John's cinnamon cologne. I almost gag and quickly place the cup on my desk.

"You don't like cinnamon?"

"I do. It's just too hot."

"Where were you last night?"

"I was home. Why?" I ask curiously.

"Shoot. I called your cell, but your voicemail picked up right away. I didn't bother calling your house because the last time I did that, I got the idea that you don't check your messages."

"My phone died," I lie. I'm starting to feel guilty for losing my patience and being mad at him. He doesn't seem like he's being vengeful, but he still left me without an explanation. I have every right to be angry…or a touch annoyed. Those beautiful eyes…

"Listen, I'm sorry about the other night. You don't understand how much I wanted to stay and be with you."

"Ok," I don't look at him. I'm trying to remain upset.

"I have a very good explanation for leaving. One of the reasons is that you were drunk."

"No, I wasn't," I remark, frowning at him.

"You downed three shots in five minutes, completely collided with me and almost fell inside the bar. Luckily I was there to catch you."

I just shrug and look away. I wasn't drunk. The walk halfway home sobered me up.

"Anyway, it wasn't the right situation for me to stay."

That was only one reason and it doesn't really explain anything. Maybe he's leading up to it. I keep my hands occupied, brushing away imaginary particles off my desk, but Jack comes to sit on the edge of my desk, directly in front of me. I have to roll my chair away for him to fit.

"I have a question for you that may be none of my business, but I need to know. Did you have sex with Steve when you went to his apartment?"

"No, I already told you that. What does that matter?"

"Did you do anything with him?"

I pause and look up at him. "No." Nothing meaningful anyway. "Is this why you didn't stay? You thought I had sex with Steve?"

"Sort of. I just needed to know." I roll my eyes and stand up, walking away from him, but he grabs my hand. "I need to know if you're over him."

"I am! I'm not sure what I have to do or say for you to believe me, but I'm over Steve." This time I look him right in the eyes, willing him to believe me. I even squeeze his hand and bring it to my chest, to solidify my statement.

He stares at me for a full minute before he asks, "Would you go out to dinner with me on Thursday?"

His invitation surprises me. I didn't see it coming. "Dinner?"

Jack pulls me toward him. "Yes, I want to take you on a date."

Flip flop. Oh, those blue eyes. "Ok." I don't care why he thought the situation wasn't right before. I'm done fighting. I look down and stare at our clasped fingers, hoping he doesn't feel me shaking.

His other hand lifts my chin back up. "I want to do this right. I want to start fresh and get to know you."

My chin pulses with electricity. Actually, my whole body is charged up. "That sounds like a great idea," I whisper.

"Is that what you want?" He takes me in his arms.

I nod and he lowers his head, kissing me gently. I savor the softness of his lips, but he pulls away instantly. I keep my eyes closed, loving how his arms feel around me.

After a few seconds, I slowly open my eyes to see him smiling at me. I blink a few times, fluttering my eyelashes and shake my hair back, smiling subtly.

"You're trouble."

"Why?" I lick my lips and part them slightly, wanting him to kiss me.

He takes my face in his hands and skims my bottom lip with his thumb. "You're beautiful." He kisses me again, but it's urgent. His tongue nudges mine immediately and when I counter, prodding his tongue with my own, he groans.

One of his hands cups the nape of my neck and the other slides down my back. I feel the heat of his palm through my dress. I place my hands inside his jacket on his chest, grasping his shirt and pulling him close.

His hands stroke my back and shoulders and then go down to my waist. He grasps the sides of my body and his hands rise up to my rib cage. I feel his thumbs pressing on my ribcage, just under my breasts. He cups them slightly and I moan into his mouth, but he quickly slides his hands back down to my waist.

I reach my arms higher, running my fingers through his hair and giving it a gentle yank, urging him to keep going, but Jack suddenly moves his hands to my upper back and lightly caresses my arms. His kisses become gentler and then he pulls back two inches from my face. "I'm going to take you right here on your desk if we don't stop."

Flip flop. I'm very ok with that. "Can't we go on our date tonight?" I kiss him softly.

He grumbles, "No, I can't. I'll be back late Wednesday night."

"Back?"

"Shit! Sorry, I forgot that I didn't tell you. I'm going to Niagara Falls to see my parents. My dad's having gall bladder surgery and I want to be there for him and my mom."

"Oh," I'm disappointed, but see him in another positive light. He keeps getting better and better. "That's thoughtful of you. I hope everything goes well."

"Thanks." He plays with my hair, pushing it back over my shoulders, but takes one curl and wraps it around his finger. "Can I call you when I'm gone?"

"Yes, please." I smile and nod excessively.

He laughs, "Stop looking at me like that."

"Like what?"

"All sexy and…" he kisses me, "And tempting."

"You find me tempting?"

"I always have. I just wasn't able to act on it before."

"You can now." I get up on my toes and kiss him passionately. I want him to know that he can have me any time.

"Good morning, you two," Margie's voice startles us and we pull away from each other.

"Hi, Margie," I say, completely embarrassed.

"Hi, Margie," Jacks echoes.

Margie laughs and steps into the reception area.

"You got caught," he whispers in a sing-song voice. "You're gonna get in trouble."

I laugh and swat him, but he catches my hand and pulls me close again, kissing me. Flip flop.

"I should get going. I'll call you when I get to the Falls," he whispers, staring into my eyes.

"Drive safe."

"You bet." He releases me and steps away, winking his goodbye.

I exhale loudly. That was so intense! I can't even remember why I was so angry at him last night or this morning. His eyes…his touch… I'm so weak around him, but I love it! He wants to be with me! That's all I wanted. He could've taken me right here on my desk and I wouldn't have stopped him. I smile and hug myself. How am I supposed to get any work done now?

18.

Play day Monday is a blur. I entertain and devote the time to my patients all day, knowing that they're getting something out of it--a bond, attention, friendship--but I'm not fully present. I can't stop thinking of Jack.

When Janie comes in as my last patient of the day, I make the promise to give my one hundred percent to the session.

"Hi, Janie. How are you doing today?"

"I got a dog!" She exclaims proudly, clapping her hands.

"You did? Tell me about him." During our last appointment, I suggested to her parents that Janie would thrive emotionally and socially if she were to get and take care of a dog. Dogs offer unconditional love and Janie needs that bond to increase her sense of self. I'm glad they took my advice.

Janie rattles on about the type of dog it is and how she takes care of it, but my mind starts to wander. I stare at my desk, imagining the sex that could have taken place on it this morning.

"Dr. C, did you hear me?"

"What? Yes. Your dog sounds wonderful. What's his name?" God, how inappropriate of me. *Pay attention!*

I already told you and it's a girl, not a boy," she huffs.

"I'm sorry. I was thinking about… about the dog that I had when I was young," I lie, and regret it instantly. I'm trying to build her self-esteem and focus my attention on her, not on me.

"You had a dog?" She asks softly, looking at her feet as she kicks the table.

"Yes, but I want to hear about yours."

"No, it's ok," she says softly.

Dammit! I've lost her. "Come on, what's your favourite thing about her?"

She picks up a stuffed rabbit from the table beside her and doesn't look at me. She plucks its ears, trying to make them stand up.

"Does your dog give you kisses?"

Nothing.

"Does your dog sleep in your bed?"

"She's not allowed."

Phew. "Does your dog do any tricks?"

"Not yet. I'm trying to teach her to shake a paw."

"That's great! Do you give him treats to reward him?"

"It's a her!"

Shit! "Sorry. Do you give her treats?"

"Yes, I give her dog food."

"That's a good idea." I keep asking her questions and praising her about how she takes care of her dog. Those repeated successes will help her develop self-esteem. Her past accomplishments will show her what it takes to face new challenges and her success will make her feel good about herself.

The session ends and I feel horrible for almost blowing it, but as she skips out and tells her parents that she's going to work harder at teaching her dog to do tricks, I feel better.

"Janie, would you like to bring your dog with you during our next visit? I'd love to meet her. It has to be ok with your parents though."

She looks at her parents and they nod. "You'll love her, Dr. C!" Janie jumps up and down excitedly.

"Great! I'll see you soon."

I'm happy that I didn't totally blow that session. This whole thing with Jack is throwing me off. I was always so focused when I started dating Steve. I had a plan and I followed it. Why am I so unfocused now? What's the difference?

Steve had controlled me. He had told me what to eat, when to eat, how to improve my volleyball skills and was involved daily in my life…and nightly too. I suppose I had worshipped Steve and listened to everything he said because I had him on a pedestal. He was the first and only man that I was with and I wanted to please him. I became the woman he wanted me to be, but he ended up resenting what I had become.

Is Jack on my pedestal now? I cringe. It wouldn't be a horrible thing to adore Jack, but I won't let him have power over me. I don't want that toxicity ever again. I'm surprised that I can't stop thinking about him and wanting to be with him. It's almost juvenile. I giggle to myself. Look at me! I'm giggling. I'm excited to start some kind of relationship with him. It's not just the sex. I want a normal relationship with him and I think he wants to be in one with me. I slam my hands on the desk. Not being able to move forward is frustrating. We just need time together to talk and to figure things out, but he's in Niagara Falls! I push myself away from the desk, grab my belongings and head to the reception area.

"Colleen, thank you for the beautiful flowers. It was such a nice surprise," Margie says.

"They arrived?" I see them on her desk and I put my nose up to them, smelling deeply. "They're so pretty! You're very welcome. You deserve them for all you do and all you put up with." I adjust the red carnations and yellow daisies.

"You're very sweet." She gives me a quick hug and disappears into my office and comes back with some files that were on my desk. "Any plans tonight?"

"No, just home to sleep."

"You're not seeing Jack?" She raises her eyebrows.

I smile and shake my head, blushing. "No, he's in Niagara Falls until Thursday."

"That's good."

"Why do you say that?"

Margie hesitates, "Can I be honest with you?"

"Of course."

"You just had closure with Steve. You don't need to jump into a new relationship right away."

"I thought you told me to call him the other night and to go out with him as a friend," I use air quotes with my fingers when I say 'friend'.

"I've been thinking about it and I might've been wrong. You've been obsessed for weeks, if not months, trying to get Steve back and suddenly, you're making out with Jack in our office."

"It's not been sudden. We've done it before when—

"I don't need to know," she laughs. "I can see that you're happy and I'm so glad that you're over Steve, but you need time for you."

I speak slowly, trying to understand her point of view, "That makes sense and I'm grateful for your input, but I really like him."

"If you really like him, then those feeling will remain while you hang out with your single friends, like Christine. You can go for drinks, meet new people and try new things."

"True." I'm not sure that I want to have a social life like Christine's. It seems too chaotic and wild.

"I read somewhere that the most common rule for dating after divorce is to be alone one year for each of the four or five years you were married. This is supposed to give you time to get back to the real you."

A year? "That seems like a long time."

"You're such a strong, intelligent woman, Colleen. Do you really need to get into another relationship right away?" Before I answer she states firmly, "No, you don't need it! Be alone! Find out who you are again."

I nod, agreeing with her. I've known this all along, but I've been very caught up with my feelings for Jack in the last couple of days.

"You have so much to offer to your practice and to anything you put your mind to. You can find happiness on your own. Just think about it."

"Thanks, you're absolutely right."

"You're not mad?"

"Not at all. I needed that kick in the pants. Thank you."

"You really are different now, Colleen."

"Yes, I am."

19.

"Hi, Colleen. It's Jack."

Flip flop. "Hi, Jack." I'm lying in bed, reading a fashion magazine that I picked up at the convenience store on the way home. A bag of peanut M & M's are open beside me, along with a glass of wine. My plan was to veg out all night and not think about anything. It was working until now. "How was the drive?"

"Not bad at all."

"How are you?"

I close the bag of M & M's and sit up against the pillows. "I'm good. I'm just reading a magazine in bed."

"Sounds cozy and quiet. It's a little rowdy here. I'm at my parents' house and we just ate my mom's famous lasagna, but my dad's grumpy because he's not allowed to eat anything before his surgery tomorrow. I made the mistake of saying it was delicious and he hasn't stopped swearing. My mom and I have been hiding and laughing in the kitchen all night. It's been fun."

"It sounds like fun. Are you close with your parents?"

"We get along fine, but I don't see them much."

"Why not? Niagara Falls isn't that far."

"I'm usually too busy with work and to be honest, they begin to annoy me after a day or two. My dad always wants me to work on the car with him and my mom coddles me." He changes his voice to a high-pitch whine, "*Are you hungry, Jack? Can I get you something to eat, Jack? You look cold, Jack. Do you want some soup, Jack?*"

"That's sweet. She loves you."

"I know, but it gets on my nerves."

"Oh." That's sad.

"What's wrong?"

"Well..." I don't know if I should comment.

"Colleen? What?"

"If my parents were alive, I think I'd make the time to visit, no matter how much they annoyed me." I clench my teeth together, cringing. I know that some families aren't close for one reason or another. I don't know Jack well enough to lecture him on family matters. Did I step too far? It's quiet on the other end. "I'm sorry. It's none of my business."

"No. Stop. You're completely right. Shit! I knew your parents passed away when you were young. I'm sorry for being so insensitive."

I remain quiet now. I didn't mean to make him feel guilty.

"You must think I'm a horrible person."

"Not at all. You have your reasons. I shouldn't have said anything."

"Colleen, I'm glad you did. I was being selfish. Thanks for giving me a new perspective on my parents."

"Go give them a big hug for me."

"I will and maybe you'd like to come to Niagara Falls with me next time. Lucy and George might be more bearable with you by my side."

Is he asking me to meet his parents? I like that he wants to take me, but…to meet his parents? Isn't that supposed to happen much later in a relationship? Are we in a relationship? I don't know how to respond, so I stay silent again.

He swears quietly and clears his throat. "I realize that I just asked you to meet my parents," he says slowly.

Yup, that was a faux pas. I just smirk and wait to see how he recovers.

"Um… Let's leave that topic for another time and change the subject. Ok? How was your day?" His voice almost cracks.

He's so cute. I laugh, "It was great. And it's fine, we can talk about going to Niagara Falls anytime. It'd be fun."

"Really? Are you just saying that because I just made the worst relationship blunder ever?"

"That was funny, but I mean it. I'd go the Falls anytime with you."

"I'd like that, but we can talk more about that later. Now, you mentioned that work was great. Why was it so great?"

"I shouldn't say it was great. I was a little distracted, but my day ended well. I had an epiphany, you could say."

"Was I the cause of your distraction?"

Yes, but I'm not going to tell him that.

"Your silence speaks volumes," he laughs.

I giggle along with him. "You only distracted me a little."

"I don't believe you. I know you were thinking about me."

"Of course I was! You kind of left me high and dry."

"Literally?"

"Jack!" We laugh some more. His laugh is so contagious. "Weren't you thinking about me?"

"I haven't stopped," he pauses. "I want you in my arms right now."

Flip flop. "That sounds good," I murmur.

"You're a great kisser. The best I've ever had."

"You're even better. Your lips are so soft."

We're both quiet. I wonder if he's picturing this morning's incident too.

"Before this turns into phone sex, what epiphany did you have?"

Phone sex! That should've been a goal for my Sex Project. "Oh! It was just that I'm a strong woman, capable of anything."

"You've always been that."

"Thank you, but I realize now that I can be alone and not have to count on anyone, but myself. I can do what I want and reach my own goals. It's exciting! I'm free to find my own happiness without anyone's help."

Jack doesn't say anything.

"Does that make sense?"

"Sure."

I brush off his lack of enthusiasm. He might not understand it. "Is you dad's surgery tomorrow morning?"

"Yes, first thing."

"That's good. Did you save him any leftover lasagna?" I joke.

"Yeah, we did." He doesn't laugh with me.

Something's changed. "Are you ok?"

"Sure," he pauses. "Listen, I should go. My dad's in bed, but I'm sure my mom's stressed about the surgery, so I should help calm her nerves."

"Make her some tea," I suggest.

"Good idea. Thanks."

"I'll talk to you later?"

"Sounds good. Take care, Colleen."

"You too."

What happened? He was in such a playful mood at the beginning of our conversation and then he fell flat. Maybe he's more worried about his dad's surgery than he's letting on. But he was talking about kissing me and phone sex… Did I say something wrong?

I'm disappointed with how our conversation ended, but if I learned something today, it's that I make my own happiness. It's probably not as bad as I think. I turn off the light and fall asleep easily.

20.

Focusing on patients is easier today and I pull out all the stops, helping them to the best of my abilities. I made a promise to myself to concentrate on my practice and not worry about Jack. If Jack wants to be with me, it'll happen. Work comes first right now.

The highlight of my day is visiting with eight-year-old Brandon, who was unfortunately knocked down by a hit-and-run driver, as was his grandmother when they were crossing the street to attend church. His grandma broke her leg and he suffered a concussion with mild neurological affects which have since disappeared. Brandon was directed to me when he was still unable to cross a street and talk to his mother about the accident. He's still very high-strung, irritable and emotionally sensitive.

Brandon's only been in twice to see me, but both sessions consisted of playing and replaying scenarios where a family minding its own business is interrupted by intruders whom he felt compelled to challenge. Today, he has the figurines playing at an imaginary park and two large monsters become involved, pushing over the figures, but his own figurine beats up the monsters. His energy is intense and aggressive.

"Are you trying to save your friends?" I pick up a monster that was knocked down and stand it upright.

"Yes, the monsters are being mean." He makes noises like explosions when he jumps on the monster that I just stood up with his own figurine.

"I see that. Those monsters are definitely being mean. Do you think that the car that hit you and your grandma was mean?"

He looks at me and quickly looks away.

"The car that hit you *was* mean. It hurt you and your grandma. It's ok to think that." With that, his figurine attacks the monsters again and one goes flying off the table. We watch it fall to the floor. Turning back to him, I smile and ask, "Do you think about the accident a lot?"

"Yes."

"Do you think about how you could've helped your grandma?"

"Yes, I could've pushed her out of the way. I'm big. Dad tells me to stay tough," he starts to cry a little.

"You are a big boy and I can see that you're pretty strong too, but I'm sure the accident happened pretty fast. It might have been difficult to push your grandma away in time. What do you think? Did it happen too fast?"

"Kind of," he sniffs.

"Accidents happen quickly and they happen all the time. I don't think there was any way you could've saved her. And I know your parents wouldn't have expected you to do that. Do you think your dad could have saved you if he was there?"

"No, the car was too fast."

"Right! It was too fast and there wasn't enough time to think, but it's really nice that you wanted to save your grandma, though. I bet she's proud of you no matter what."

"She likes when I push her around in her wheelchair."

"Wow! You can do that? Wheelchairs are hard to move."

A big smile spreads across his face. "It's easy."

We continue to talk and think of ways he can help his grandma now, and to help keep his family safe outside. Brandon's obviously been thinking about his family's safety and rattles off many rules, most legitimate, but some being unrealistic. He's being overly protective of his family.

I find a book on the shelf called, *Safe at Play: Outdoor Safety*, and let Matthew read it, while I step outside to talk to his parents.

"Mr. and Mrs. Chapman, Brandon is feeling vulnerable and guilty about the accident, but he also thinks you want him to be tough about it. He's putting on a show for you. He thinks that he should have saved his grandmother and he feels bad for not doing anything to help her." I can see that his parents are broken up about this. His mom covers her mouth and shakes her head.

"Brandon saw me cry when he was in the hospital. He doesn't need to stay tough," Mr. Chapman says remorsefully. "Does he think I'm mad at him?"

"No, not at all." I put my hand on his arm briefly. "His reactions are completely normal. They're typical for the trauma he's just gone through. You need to remind him that it's all right to be sad and upset. He'll get over his fear of crossing the street, I promise."

"Thanks, Dr. Cousineau."

"I still want to see him. You can make another appointment with Margie." I smile at them, walk back in my office to wrap up the session and say goodbye to the Chapmans, knowing that I need to do something for myself.

Dr. Wylie's number is still on a sticky note, stuck to my computer screen. I dial it immediately.

"Good afternoon, Dr. Wylie's office."

"Could I please make an appointment to see the doctor? This is Colleen Cousineau." Thinking about Matthew's troubles, make me think that I may need assistance with some underlying issues that I might still have. I need a clear head before I pursue anything with Jack.

Once the appointment is made, I grab my gym bag and head out the door. I packed my clothes for volleyball this morning, not knowing if I was going to go, but after such a good day, how could I not?

I rush to the university and the overwhelming smell of the stale and rank gym is soothing to me. I'm itching to get out on the court and amplify my mood, so I change quickly and head out to limber up.

After I finish a lap around the gym and stretch my quads, I bend over to loosen my hamstrings, hugging my calves and burying my face in my shins.

"Nice view, Superstar."

I stay down and shake my head, laughing. "Grow up, Ryan."

"That's it, keep talking to me from that position. It reminds me of certain things."

"Ok. Ok. Enough!" I stand up and punch his shoulder. "Are we on the same team today?"

"Wouldn't have it any other way."

I high-five him, "Let's get it on!"

"Superstar! You can't talk like that."

"Volleyball, Ryan. Think volleyball."

"Gotcha!"

The next two hours fly by and we annihilate the six teams we play. We should actually be our own two-man team. We were on fire and dominated the plays as usual, passing it to each other, completely snubbing our teammates. They must hate us. We were even so ignorant as to not introduce ourselves to them. I had the best time.

"Do you want to get a beer with me? We could go to Hoops?" Ryan asks.

"Sure."

"Really? You want to go?" He's very surprised.

I laugh and swat him, "Yes, I'd love to get a beer." This time it's different. I don't want to take him home, Steve's not hanging over my head and I think I'm in a relationship… Even if I'm not, I'm allowed to have fun. Not that I want to start anything with Ryan. I just want to relax and enjoy myself.

"Awesome. I'll see you in a second." He disappears into the change room.

I change into black leggings and a fleecy, pink sweatshirt, trying to fluff my hair after getting rid of the elastic. It'll do.

When I step out of the change room and turn, Ryan intentionally bumps into me and picks me up, putting me over his shoulder.

"I'm driving," he claims.

"Put me down!" What's with this guy and picking me up? It's irritating.

He slaps my bottom and jogs out to his car. I force a laugh and ride it out. He'll put me down eventually, which he does at his car.

"I'm glad we're going out." He eyes me flirtatiously.

I climb into his car, not knowing what to say. I like his honesty and friendliness. I especially like our unreal connection on the court. It was never that fierce with Steve. We rock! But I'm afraid he might be getting the wrong idea.

"How's life in the world of psychology?" He starts driving.

"It's great. I love my job. How's the lawyer thing working for you?"

"It's working," he smirks.

There's nothing wrong with Ryan. From what I can see, he's caring and attentive and I'm sure he'd treat his girlfriend or even wife extremely well. He's also an amazing lover. I blush and look at him from the corner of my eye. All those qualities are everything a woman would want in a man, but I can't get past something. I don't know what it is. I can't put my finger on it.

"We're going to my condo."

21.

"Ryan," I warn. "That's not a good idea."

"I was just testing you," he teases. "There's a small lounge near my place."

"Much better, but I thought we were going to Hoops?" I calm down a little, but a lounge sounds cozy and romantic.

"This place is much more fun." After a few minutes, he parks, opens my door for me and when I get out he takes my hand, leading me down the sidewalk.

Is anyone looking? I frantically look around. He's holding my hand! Ryan's charming and very forward, but I don't appreciate his efforts. I just want to be friends. Maybe this was a bad idea.

Ryan stops in front of a dimly lit building. "After you," he holds the door open for me.

I walk up the staircase in front of me, which is rather sketchy-looking and keep looking back to make sure Ryan is following. At the top of the stairs, we walk into a vast lounge, surrounded by leather booths and numerous tables, all brightly lit by red Japanese lanterns and white string lights.

"Good evening and welcome to *Game Play*. Will you be playing games tonight?" A young girl asks us, but not taking her eyes off Ryan.

Games? Was that an innuendo? I scope the room, looking around for sex toys.

"Yes, please," Ryan says.

"Follow me."

She takes us to a booth and as we get comfortable, she points toward the television, "If you're looking for classic board games, they're in the unit by the T.V." She then points back toward the entrance, "The strategic games are over there."

"Thank you," Ryan says and leans forward on the table to look at me.

"You server will be with you shortly." She places menus on the table and stares at Ryan an extra second. He ignores her.

"I've never been here. At first, I was wondering what kind of games we were going to be playing! I was worried," I grin.

"Dirty girl! Would you have been ok with any other games?" He smiles lewdly and winks.

"No! This is perfectly fine," I say quickly. I shouldn't joke with him like that.

"This place is pretty cool and very laid back. I've only been once. The food isn't the best, but the drinks are good. Do you want wine or a martini?"

"No, I think I'll just have a draught beer."

"That's why I like you. You're a beer kind of a girl. Now, what about food?"

"I'm not hungry, but get what you want."

"I'll get the nachos and you can pick at them, little bird."

I cock my head, remembering that he called me that before... It was the night at his apartment after we got out of the hot tub. I stutter, "What... what game do you want to play?"

"Why don't you pick out something while I order?"

I agree and get up to start browsing the bookshelves. I see childhood games, like *Scrabble* and *Monopoly*, in between games I've never even heard of, like *Seven Wonders* and *Settlers of Catan*. I pick up a beat-up version of *Cards Against Humanity*, having heard positive reviews about the game, but after I read the directions, I realize it's not meant for two players.

Then I see *Guillotine*, a *'card game with a French Revolution theme'*. I laugh out loud. Why not?

Ryan is already sipping his draught when I get back to the table and I place the game in front of him, sitting down to take a sip of my own.

"Guillotine?"

"Yup."

He reads from the box, "*The revolutionary card game where you win by getting a head?* Really? This is what you picked?"

"Yup, it sounds like fun." I open the box and set up the cards in a line, placing the small, cardboard stand-up guillotine at the end of the table. "Isn't this cute?"

"You're sick and twisted."

Laughing, I say, "The goal of the game is to collect heads of French Nobles."

"We're executioners? You're seriously morbid."

I explain the rules to him and we begin to play. There's some strategy involved and I begin to manipulate the order of the line of beheadings to benefit me.

Ryan goes first. "Let them eat cake!" He exclaims and he beheads Marie Antoinette.

"But she was at the end of the line!"

"This card says I can chop her head off at any time."

"Dammit! She was worth five points." I don't want to lose to him.

The game is fun and with us both being extremely cutthroat, it gets heated. We mess with each other's strategies, trying to outwit one another.

Ryan makes some silly wisecracks like, "Heads are gonna roll!" and "Off with his head!" He thinks he's hilarious, but it's excessive. I peek beside me to see if anyone's watching when he drips salsa on the cardboard guillotine and says, "It's a bloody good time!" I think he's trying to impress me, but it's completely embarrassing.

When the line of beheadings is finished, we add up our points and Ryan boasts, "I win! I win! I win!" He's acting like a child.

"We're playing again," I say bitterly as I shuffle the cards and set up the game quickly.

"So, it's not just volleyball that brings out the spitfire in you. You're just a big, ol' bloodthirsty, competitive freak."

"Shut up and pick up your cards." I slide them in his direction.

He slaps his hand on them to prevent them from falling into his lap. "Whoa! You're really taking the loss hard. There's no need to get testy. I'll play again, but let me order two more pints first."

I'm not listening. I cross my legs underneath me and figure out my strategy. I realize that the game is purely based on luck, but I need to beat him. I can't stand his arrogance.

Our beer arrives and he holds his up, "Cheers to a friendly competition."

I smile falsely and clink his glass, "You do remember who you're playing with, right?"

"I'm trying to remind you that it's just a game and just because I'm going to beat you again, it shouldn't cause you any grief."

With that, I collect the Clown's head and give it to Ryan, giving him a starting total of negative two.

"Is that how you're going to play?"

We continue to egg each other on and drink our beer, and joke about who's going to win. While Ryan is trying to figure out his next move, I watch him. I'm not actually mad at him. It's a harmless competition that's brimming with arrogance, but I'm used to that kind of egotism in sports, so it doesn't bother me. God, he's so good good-looking. He's also funny, sweet and sexy… What is it that I can't seem to get over about him? Maybe it's the fact that I used him for my Sex Project. Or maybe he's too much like Steve.

"Booyah! Three points for the Baron's head," he gloats.

"Sorry, chump! I'll take this Palace Guard's head and add it to the other two I've collected and get what? How many points do I get?" I feign ignorance.

"Nine."

"What was that? Nine points?" I do a happy dance on the bench seat.

"Well done."

"Thank you and I believe I win."

"Now we're tied. Can you live with that, Superstar?" His eyes tease me.

"Actually, I'm very fine with that."

"I don't believe you. Don't you want to come out on top?"

"No, really. We both won. It's good."

"Don't you want to have the chance to dominate me?"

Another sexual intimation. "Ryan, a tie is a good finish."

"You didn't *come* this far to walk away without the *climactic* victory."

"Ok, enough!" His sense of humour exasperates me. Why does everything have to be so sexual in nature?

"But I had a good one about winning being so hard and beating me is going to be even harder."

"Ryan, this was great. I've had so much fun, but I should get home."

"You're killing me, Superstar." He stands up hesitantly. "Think about coming to my condo while I pay the bill."

Ryan's amazing in many ways, but I just don't see us together. Christine would kill me right now. She told me that he's that unattainable man… He's in the news as the best and youngest lawyer in Toronto… He's the elusive bachelor. And he wants me. I should give him her number, but he'd probably be offended.

"Have you decided?" He holds out his hand.

I take it, "Home please."

He doesn't say anything and leads me into the hallway, to the top of the stairs and stops, "I know you said that you weren't ready for a relationship, but I think you keep coming back into my life for a reason." He steps closer to me, taking my other hand. His face is inches away from mine. "I had fun with you tonight. The best I've had since the last time we were together. I don't want you to go home. Come home with me." He tilts his head down and kisses me.

It's a nice kiss and I don't stop him, but Jack's face pops into my head. Jack's scruff would be tickling my chin right now. A light bulb turns on and it's the brightest bulb I've ever seen. That's it! That's why I'm not interested in Ryan. The passion's just not there. Not even a flip flop. Of course! It's Jack!

I pull back slowly, "Ryan, you're such a great guy." He releases my hands. "I just can't do this with you now."

"I understand. I can't make you change your mind." He looks so hurt. "I'll take you to your car."

Music from the radio is the only noise in the car on the ride back to the university. The song that's playing is *All at Once* by the Fray.

> "*Maybe you want her, maybe you need her*
> *Maybe you've started to compare to someone not there*
> *Maybe you want it, maybe you need it*
> *Maybe it's all you're running from*
> *Perfection will not come.*"

I feel guilty for going out with him. But that's not fair. Did I lead him on? "Ryan, I sense that you're angry or disappointed. Should I have not gone out with you tonight? I mean, we played so great on the court, I thought a beer wouldn't hurt."

He sighs, "No, you're right. I shouldn't be mad." He pats my thigh and returns his hand to the steering wheel awkwardly. "Colleen, I go out. I go on dates. Not all the time, but I meet women. A lot of women."

Where's he going with this? "Ryan, you don't have to—"

"Colleen, listen. I meet a lot of women and no one, I mean, no one compares to you."

Is he serious? "Ryan…"

"Please, I don't want you to say anything. I'm just telling you why I'm so upset. I get it, though. You're not ready to date. Your ex-husband ruined that for me." He laughs. "I'm kidding. I can live with that and hope that you'll change your mind one day."

I nod and smile at him. I'll let him have his hopes. I don't want to crush him completely.

In the parking lot, he helps me out of his car and walks me to mine. "No scratches, dents or tire damage. Your stalker must still be in jail."

"Actually… he's not. He was released on bail and is staying at his grandmother's house."

"Fuck!" He shakes his head angrily. "This is what I have to deal with every day: Canada's limp noodle justice system. Was house arrest ordered?"

"No, he's allowed out on the street."

"Such bullshit…. Sorry. Ok, this just means that I'm following you to your house and making sure you get inside safely."

"You don't have to do that. I think the cops are parked outside my house watching it."

"I don't care. Get in your car, Superstar."

"Yes, sir!" Another bossy male, but when it comes to Mr. Baker and my safety, I accept it.

The police are in front of my house like I said and when Ryan pulls up behind the police car, I feel ashamed. I told Officer Nicholls that I didn't want to date anyone and now he'll be seeing Ryan go into my house with me. Jack's presence is understood. As far as the police know, Jack was involved in my abduction and that's why we have a relationship, but Ryan… Shit! I'll have to get him out quickly, so they don't think there's anything going on between us.

We walk up the driveway and I wave to the officers nervously. I see a hand wave back, but I can't tell if it's Officer Leeds or Officer Nicholls. I look down quickly, fumbling for my keys and try to balance all my belongings.

"Here, I'll open it." He takes the keys from me and unlocks my door, letting me go in first.

I shut off the alarm and turn to look at Ryan, but he's on his way upstairs. "What are you doing?"

"Inspecting your surroundings."

He'd be an amazing boyfriend…to someone else.

"The house looks good, Superstar." He calls out from upstairs. "It's clean."

I wait until he gets downstairs before I answer, "Thanks for noticing that I cleaned up."

"Oh, I notice everything," he grins at me.

"No bras for you to pick up off the floor this time."

"You're right. There weren't any bras, but..." He pulls out a lacy, black thong from his pocket. "I took a different souvenir."

"Ryan!" I try to grab the panties, but he holds them above his head. "You're awful. Give them to me!" He slowly brings his arm down and I snatch the thong out of his hand.

"Can't I keep them?" He seems serious.

"No way." I look at him strangely, but then he winks. "Ha ha. Funny guy."

"I guess I'll leave if there's nothing you need from me. I'd be happy to oblige doing anything demanding or physical in nature."

"I'm good, Ryan." I smile and swat him with the panties. "Thanks for a great night and for making sure I'm safe."

"No problem, Superstar. Call me if you need anything." He starts walking toward the door.

"I will. Good night."

"Good night." He gives me one last look before shutting the door.

That was way too quick for the cops to think that I had sex with Ryan. I sigh with relief.

I take my cell phone upstairs and check for messages and texts and even emails from Jack. Nothing. Should I just call him? Is it too late? I'll just text him:

"Thinking about you."

22.

The next morning, I get up early to make it to my appointment with Dr. Wylie before I'm scheduled to start work. I'm nervous to see him, but I'm pretty grounded with everything now. If I had seen Dr. Wylie last week, he may have committed me or at the least been concerned with my behaviour. I've been deliberating whether or not I should tell him about my Sex Project. I'm still on the fence about that.

Dr. Wylie's office has moved since I last saw him and the new location is beautiful. It's on Queen Street by Nathan Phillips Square. The square is a site for concerts, art displays, a weekly farmers' market, the winter festival of lights, and other public events. During the winter months, the reflecting pool is converted into an ice rink for ice skating. I used to go skating with my dad here a long time ago.

The office is easy to find and when I open the door I'm surprised by the lack of class or formality within the space. It's sparsely decorated, with only a handful of chairs, and a sad end table with beat-up, old magazines. The outdated wallpaper on the main wall is peeling and the other walls are in need of a fresh coat of paint. An ancient ghetto blaster on the floor is playing 'The Tide is High' by Blondie. I've stepped into the eighties?

There's another door which I assume is the entrance to his office and I sit across from it feeling unnerved. His old office was state-of-the-art, with a three-hundred-gallon saltwater fish tank and televisions on every wall. He also had a secretary, but she's not here now? I did talk to one to book the appointment… It must be a service.

Suddenly the door opens and Dr. Wylie pokes his head out. He's aged as expected, but he looks worn out, almost sad.

"Colleen!" His eyes light up. "It's so nice to see you. Come on in."

"Hi, Dr. Wylie. How are you?" I watch him hobble to his big brown, leather chair. I loved that chair. He let me sit in it when I was feeling sad about my parents.

"Can't complain. Sit down and relax."

I choose the couch over the high-backed chair as it doesn't look comfortable and the couch is directly across from him. "I like your new office," I lie.

"Oh, I had to downsize when I got divorced." He looks around. "It's not as fancy as it used to be, but it does the job."

"I'm sorry about that." That explains everything, I guess.

"Thank you, but it was a couple of years ago. Now, tell me what you've been up to," he smiles encouragingly.

The couch molds to my body as I delve into my experiences since college: Meeting Steve, getting married, opening a practice and our separation.

"How did you feel when he told you he thought you were a robot?"

"Awful. I thought I was living my life the best way I knew how. I thought I was a strong, independent woman, but also a good wife. I thought I had everything balanced." I fiddle with my purse strap remembering how I felt. "I figured out that I always was those things, but it was him who was unhappy and no matter what I did I could never make him happy. I knew it wasn't my fault that our marriage dissolved."

"You're in a good place. You seem very confident and happy."

"Yes I am. I'm figuring out what I want and focusing on my practice. There's so many things that I want to do. I've learned so much in the last few months."

"I'm proud of you. You thrived despite all of your difficulties. Is there anything you're not telling me?"

I start to laugh and Dr. Wylie smiles. He always asked that question during our sessions. "Well... my patient and I were abducted by her father. Her parents were divorced and he was denied custody, so he held us both at knifepoint and drove us to Windsor. The police think he was going to try to sneak us over to Michigan or just her. He was probably going to *dispose* of me," I almost whisper the last sentence.

"Dear Lord! That's something." He leans forward looking into my eyes. "But you're ok? You're here now, so his plan was obviously unsuccessful. What happened?"

I nod and smile, "A man that I know followed us and saved us. He fought my abductor and freed us. I don't know where I'd be if it wasn't for him."

"What a brave man. Is he a friend?"

"He was one of my ex-husband's friends, but we started running into each other after the separation."

"Do you like him?"

I blush, "Why do you ask?"

"Your eyes lit up as soon as you started talking about him."

"Oh. Yes, I like him. We aren't in a relationship yet, but we've had...some moments."

"Are you sure you should be getting into a relationship so quickly?"

It's probably not a good idea to tell him about the Sex Project. "I think I've had plenty of time to think and I had closure with Steve. I feel secure with this man."

"Is that the only reason? You feel secure?" Is it because he saved you?"

"No," I defend myself. Why did I use the word secure to describe him? "No, he's very sweet and kind and we have fun together." I feel like I'm making up reasons.

"Colleen, maybe you should take some more time, but if you're going to pursue him, just take it slow. Or you could date other men and find out what else is available out there?"

"Ha!" I burst out and then clear my throat quickly. "Sorry, I don't want to date anyone else."

"There's nothing wrong with dating."

"I know, but I've met a few men in the last couple of weeks and this one is different. I really like him. I'll be cautious and take it slow, I promise."

"You don't have to promise me. Just make sure you're dating him for the right reasons."

"I understand."

"Our time is up. Do you want to make another appointment now or do you just want to call later." He stands up and starts ushering me to the door.

"I'll call you." Or your service.

"Great. It really was wonderful seeing you. I'm so proud of what you've accomplished."

"Thanks, Dr. Wylie." I want to hug him, but he doesn't give me any indication that he wants the affection, so I head for the door.

"Take care."

Preoccupied with my thoughts, I get into my car and start to drive to work. That's two people who've told me that I need to take it slow. I can understand the need for caution if I was still hung up on Steve or I was destroyed by the impending divorce, but I'm over it. It's not like I'm looking to jump into a relationship with the first guy that excites me. This is Jack. I've known him for years, he's been in the background quite a bit and I've developed a crush on him. Further, I already did the dating, I've met some wonderful men and some idiots and I've had casual sex. I'm stronger than I've ever been before. I don't need to take it slow. I want to date Jack.

My phone beeps as I put my car in park outside my office. I rummage through my bag and click my phone open. Flip flop. It's a message from Jack:

"Dad's surgery went well. He's home and we're eating leftover lasagna. He's happy. I hope you're enjoying your new-found freedom."

New-found freedom? I wrack my brain. Is this a private joke? Am I forgetting something? Does he mean my freedom without Steve? I text him back:

"I'm glad to hear about your dad. I guess he's not swearing anymore. New-found freedom?"

I wait a few seconds and put my hand on the handle to exit the car, but my phone beeps again. I sit back in my seat.

"The other night you said that you're free to live your own life and that you don't need anyone to make you happy."

Uh oh. I get it now. Is that why he got quiet on the phone the other night? After I explained my stupid epiphany!

"No, you've misinterpreted my words. I definitely didn't mean it that way."

I pause with my finger over send. What else can I say? I need you? That's way too soon. I should take it slow, right? Wait, do I? I'm so confused. I hit send.

I tap the steering wheel and stare at my phone, willing it to beep again. Come on, Jack…

"We'll talk on Thursday. Have a good day."

Shit! He's right. We can't have a discussion like this via text. This is too important. I type one more text:

"Can't wait to see you."

Margie knocks on my window, scaring me. "Good morning," she shouts through the glass.

"Hi, Margie," I say as I get out of my car and shut the door.

I gloomily walk with her to the door as she chirps about her evening out with her husband. They went to dinner and to see the new Tom Cruise movie. I'm frustrated that I have to wait until tomorrow to see Jack. I need to reassure him about my feelings. He can't think that I don't need him. He shouldn't have any doubts about my feelings.

"Are you all right?" She holds the door open for me.

"Yes, I'm fine."

She lightly pinches my arm as I pass by her. "I don't believe you. You look sad."

"I don't know what I am," I sigh. "Both you and my own therapist told me to take things slow with Jack and it's frustrating! I'm going back and for the in my head: Should I get involved with him or should I wait? I think about him all the time!"

Margie laughs, "Are you crushing on him?"

"You caught us making out! What do you think?" I laugh and put my hands on my flushed cheeks. "That wasn't the first time either. He's such a good kisser!"

"Do you just want to… you know… do it?" It's her turn to blush.

"Margie!" I feign surprise and shyness. "Of course I do! He's amazing. I want more than that though. I want the whole she-bang! I want to date, I want a relationship and I just want to be with him!"

"Then tell him or just let it happen naturally. I think he likes you or he wouldn't be kissing you," she giggles.

"But you told me yesterday that I should wait and—

"Don't listen to me. I'm just an old married woman." She pats my hand. "I was just laying out some of your options. Do what makes you happy."

"I'm trying to do the right thing," I lower my eyes at her. "That's why I listened to you."

"You're a silly girl. Ever since I've known you, you've done the right thing. Follow your heart this time, wherever it leads. You're allowed to make mistakes and if this isn't a mistake and it turns out to be fantastic, enjoy it."

"Thanks, Margie." I hug her briefly. "That makes me feel so much better."

"Good. It's great to see you open up to me again. You weren't yourself for quite a while."

"I know. Steve did a number on me."

"Speaking of emotional and physical damage…your last appointment today is with Connie Baker."

My stomach sinks. "Really?"

She looks at me sadly, "I know, but what can you do?"

"Nothing." I shake my head woefully. "She needs me. This is why I became a psychologist. I'll be fine."

23.

Knowing that Connie is in the reception area, I take a few deep, long breaths to calm my nerves. She's just a little girl and I shouldn't be scared, but it's that sinister father of hers that frightens me to the core. Connie needs me. She's probably upset by the fact that her dad's in jail and needs me to reassure her that everything's going to be fine. I can do that for her, even though I don't know if it's true.

"Send her in," I say through the intercom.

Connie skips in and when she sees me, she runs toward me and gives me a hug. "Hi, Dr. C."

I pat her back lightly, "Hi, Connie. Thanks for the hug. Do you want to sit down?"

"Can you sit beside me?" She takes my hand and pulls me to the couch, waiting for me to sit down first and then she snuggles in close to me.

I try to assume a posture of rigidity and remoteness with my patients, but there are times that I have to interact with warmth, empathy and spontaneity. Since the abduction, I've let Connie hug me, so I can't stop now. If I re-affirm our boundaries, I think it would deeply affect her. We have a special bond. "How are you, Connie?"

"Good." She extends her legs, trying to touch the coffee table with her toes, but can't reach it, so she lets her legs drop heavily against the couch.

"What's new?"

"Nothing." She's now kicking the couch with her heels.

"Do you want to colour or play a game?"

"Can we play *Pick Up Sticks*?" The kicking stops.

"Sure. Go find it on the bookcase."

She races over and gets up on her tiptoes to pull it out. She knew right where it was. "I want to set it up."

"Go ahead."

Connie holds all of the coloured sticks in her hand vertically over the table and releases, letting the sticks scatter. "I want to go first." She focuses on a green stick and picks it up easily. "Your turn."

"How's school?" I pick up a yellow stick.

"Good." Her next stick is yellow too.

"How's your mom?"

"She's outside. It's your turn. Go."

I take my time getting a stick. "Are you being good for her?"

"Yes."

"Have you seen your dad?" Connie doesn't answer. "Connie, have you seen your dad?"

"No," she says quietly.

"What's wrong?"

"We had to move again because of dad. He hurt mommy."

"Is she ok?"

"Her face is purple and yellow."

"Oh, honey. That must've been scary for you."

Connie starts crying soundlessly. "Mommy was sad. Someone told her to move out because all of the noise and we did, in the middle of the night."

I put my arm around her. Why didn't I know this? "Do you like your new house?"

"We live with grandma and she smokes. It stinks and her backyard is too small to play soccer in."

It must be the grandmother on her mother's side. "Do you still go to the same school?"

"Yes."

"Well, that's a good thing. How's your best friend? Do you still go to her house?"

We continue talking and I let Connie beat me at *Pick Up Sticks*. I'm concerned about Connie. Children who are exposed to battering become fearful and anxious with everything. They're always on guard, watching and waiting for the next bad incident to happen. Connie doesn't seem to be too affected, but this is only one visit. I need to talk to her mom.

When we step out of my office, I see Mrs. Baker and her bruises immediately. She rushes to embrace me and I awkwardly pat her back.

"Are you ok, Mrs. Baker?" I ask quietly.

"Yes," she whispers, looking over at Connie.

"Connie, would you like a piece of candy?" Margie takes her to her desk.

"You don't look ok."

"Martin did this to me just before he was sent to jail. He forced his way into the house and I couldn't stop him. I can't believe he was released. His mother has no idea what he's done. He's such a good liar. I guess we'll just have to pray that he goes back quickly."

"Did Connie see what happened between you?"

"No, she was in her bedroom, but she heard everything and she saw my face right after the beating."

"Please call anytime to update me on anything that arises. I hope that something like this never happens again, but please tell me about any incident, no matter how big or small. It'll help me plan for our appointments."

"Oh, yes. Sorry about that. I didn't even think to call you."

"It's ok." I pat her arm briefly. "How is she doing at home and school?"

"Not great. She doesn't want to leave me alone. She hates going to school, she won't go to her friend's houses very often and she makes me lock the door, double-checking it throughout the night."

"It's very normal, but you're doing a great job with her. Keep showing her love and support and you'll both get through this. Don't worry. Make another appointment before you leave for next week. I can see her more often if you'd like."

"That would be great. She always asks about you."

"She's a sweet girl."

"Thank you."

Margie makes the appointment for the Bakers and they all say goodbye, leaving together. I grab my purse and coat to head home, looking forward to a relaxing bath.

When I turn off the lights and take a step out the door, I can feel my cell phone vibrate through my purse against my leg. I rush to find it, stepping back into the office. It's an unknown number. "Hello?"

"Aren't you all cozy with *my* family?"

"Mr. Baker?" My stomach plummets and I weaken, falling against the door. It slams shut causing me to jump. Has he been watching me? I lock the door and try to duck out of view from the windows.

"You can call me Martin since we're so acquainted now. Did you have a nice visit with my daughter Connie?"

I don't know what to say. I back up towards Marge's desk, thinking I should call the police with her phone.

"Where's your boyfriend tonight?" Are you going to see him again soon?"

My boyfriend? Does he mean Jack?

"You don't have to say anything. I always know where you are at all times. Have a good night."

The line goes dead.

I can't go outside. What if he's still there watching me? I look at my phone. The last time I called the police I felt stupid. It's just a phone call. What if he's waiting for me outside? I need to call someone.

Suddenly, there's banging on the front door and I fearfully slump down to hide behind Margie's desk, dropping my phone. Is it Mr. Baker? I can't catch my breath. My heart is hammering through my chest.

"Colleen? Are you still in there?"

That's not Mr. Baker. It's Jack. I stumble to stand up. "Jack?"

"Open up!"

My shaky hands fumble with the lock and when I open the door, I usher him inside, slamming the door and throw myself into his arms.

"Hey! What's wrong?"

"Mr. Baker just called me on my cell. He's watching me. I think he's outside."

Jack releases me quickly. "Stay here, lock the door and call the police."

"You're leaving?"

He kisses my forehead quickly. "I'll be right back, I promise." He steps outside and I lock it, dialing Officer Nicholls number.

"Officer Nicholls."

"Hi, it's Colleen Cousineau. I'm at my office and Martin Baker just called me on my cell. He was watching me. I had an appointment with his daughter and he wasn't happy. Jack is now outside looking for him."

"I'll send the unit over. That's not my area, but you've dealt with the officers before."

"Right. Sorry." I feel stupid again. I should've known to call the other officers.

"No problem. They'll be right over."

"Thank you."

After I hang up, I look out the window to look for Jack or Mr. Baker. What's Jack doing home a day early? I'm so happy and… Wow! What timing. My heart's still thumping like crazy, worried about Jack.

Jack finally comes into view and walks up to my office door. I unlock and open it for him. "Well?"

"I couldn't see him anywhere."

"Oh." I'm relieved. It's for the best. Mr. Baker is a dangerous man.

"Are you ok?"

"Yes, just frazzled. He still gets to me."

Jack takes me in his arms and I wrap mine around his waist. He smells fresh and clean, like he just showered. I bury my face in his chest.

"I'm so glad you're here."

He pulls away slightly, "Are you?"

I look into his eyes, "Of course. Why would you ask that?"

"Is it just because I keep you safe?"

"No… Not *just* for that reason." That's what Dr. Wylie asked.

"Then why?" He steps back a little more.

"Jack, what's wrong?" I reach for his jacket, but he pulls away.

"I need to know how you feel about me."

A knock at the door interrupts us and Jack stares at me for a few seconds before he opens it, letting the officers in. I grab Jack's hand, squeezing it tightly, as I explain the evening's events.

24.

"Thanks, officers."

"Stay safe." Officers Ackerman and Lajoie leave my office after a quick discussion. This incident was just added to the rest, without any consequence. Mr. Baker can deny that he called me and he didn't call me from his mother's house, so the call couldn't be traced. It's my word against his. There's nothing they can do. We have to wait and maybe he'll get caught.

Jack slams the office door. "The police are useless. Martin Baker can do anything he wants to you and get away with it? It's so fucking stupid."

"It's fine, Jack. They'll catch him eventually."

"Whatever," he states and turns to me, "I'm sorry." He takes a breath. "Are you ready to leave?"

"Yes, what are you going to do?" I don't want him to leave me.

"I'm driving you home and staying the night."

Flip flop. "Ok." I can't help but smile. I'm not going to argue with him at all.

He guides me outside, waiting for me to lock up and at the sidewalk he stops at an oversized, black truck, unlocking the door. A running board extends when the door is open as a step to get into the vehicle. It screams hi-tech manliness.

"Is this yours?"

"Just picked it up from the dealership," he grins. "What do you think?"

"It's huge."

He laughs, "No, I'm not compensating."

"You're funny. I like it." I take a big step up into the truck and he closes the door. It smells new. When he gets inside I ask, "By the way, why are you home early? You were supposed to be home tomorrow."

"Well, I was supposed to get home tonight and just see you tomorrow, but I couldn't wait. Surprise," he says unhappily. "Mr. Baker ruined my surprise."

"Not at all." I lean over and give him a peck on the cheek. "I'm very happy to see you."

He plays with a curl, pulling it straight. "I hope so." I think he's going to kiss me, but he just releases the curl and starts the ignition. "Let's get you home."

The truck begins with a loud, rumbly roar and as it runs, it vibrates through the seat and under my feet. It is a man's truck. It's rugged and safe, kind of like Jack. There's that word again: Safe.

I sit back in my seat and look straight ahead, irritated at my own thoughts. I like him for other reasons and I shouldn't have to validate my feelings. I take a quick glance at him. If I'm questioning why I like him, I can understand why he's being so aloof and guarded. Am I giving him mixed signals? I thought I was pretty clear when we made out in my kitchen and in my office. We need to talk, but not here.

"Do your parents live near the actual Falls?" I try to make small talk.

"No, they're closer to Brookfield."

"I've never heard of it."

"It's close to Welland."

"Oh, I bet you've seen the Falls a hundred times."

"Nope, just once, when I was twelve."

"Really? That's strange."

"Not really. How many times have you been up in the CN Tower?"

I think for a minute and laugh, "Only once! I guess if you've seen it once, why see it again. We don't have to see the Falls when I meet your parents," I joke, elbowing him.

"I'm so sorry about that." He runs his fingers through his hair. "It came out all wrong. I didn't mean to pressure you."

"Don't be silly. I'd love to meet your parents."

"It'll have to wait until George is feeling better. He's a grumpy son of a bitch. Although, if I finally brought a girl home, he'd probably change his tune, especially to see a girl as pretty like you."

Jack's mood is shifting and my heart sings. "Is that so? I'd like to meet Mr. George Fraser. He sounds like a smart man," I say playfully.

"You'd like him. He'd make you his famous Cosmopolitan and tell you stories about working at a bar in the seventies. He's got some great stories about meeting Don Cherry and Darryl Sittler."

"No way!" Sittler wore the Maple Leaf on his chest for twelve seasons. My dad always talked about The Darryl Sittler and he became my hero.

"You two would get along great."

"I'd say so and I'd love to go to the Falls sometime too. Isn't there a whole strip of tourist attractions, like a wax museum and a Guinness Book of Worlds Records?"

"Both. Wait, does that mean you've never been to Niagara Falls?"

"Never. My aunt didn't like crowds too much."

"That's a travesty!" He laughs, "We'll definitely have to go then. I'd go there again just to take you. I hear it's beautiful in the winter."

I look out my window and notice that we're going the wrong way. "Hey! Where are we going?"

"I decided that we're going to my house instead. I've been away a couple of days and I need to get some stuff done. I already told the officers that they didn't need to watch you tonight."

Flip flop. "Oh."

"Is that ok? I don't want to leave you alone, but I can't put off a few things at home either."

"No, that's fine." It's better than fine.

"Good. It wasn't a request anyway," he smirks with cheekiness.

I laugh and swat him. "Knowing you, I wouldn't expect an invitation."

He pats my hand, but pulls away quickly. "We're going to get along fine."

Please stay in your good mood! "Does this mean we're having our date night tonight?"

"How about a pre-date date? I have to unpack, do some laundry and finish some paperwork."

"I'll make you dinner."

"You don't have to do that. We can order something."

"You deserve more than just pizza. You've made me both breakfast and dinner before. I owe you a good meal."

"Suit yourself. I'm just not sure what I have in the house."

"I'm sure I can make do with what you have." Jack pulls into a detached garage, minutes away from my office and I ask, "Do you live here?"

"Yes, why does that shock you?"

"I mean you told me that you live on Hazelton, but I didn't know you were so close to my work."

"It's close to my work too."

I keep forgetting that he works one block away from me on Isabella. I have to start paying attention.

He opens the truck door for me, helps me out and we walk down the sidewalk. "This is my house," he points.

"Jack, your house is stunning." It's not actually a house, but a townhome. It reminds me of Carrie Bradshaw's brownstone on *Sex and the City*. We walk up the steps and I begin to realize that I don't know Jack at all. The area where he lives is a mix of extremely high-end buildings and restored historic Victorian homes which results in an extremely high-valued housing market. Considering the neighbourhood also happens to be located in perhaps the most ideal central-midtown corridor, close to the city's best shopping, dining, entertainment and transit, the homes rent and sell among the highest price ranges in the country. A house in this area is worth close to four million dollars. It's very intimidating.

He unlocks the door and holds it open for me, flipping on the overhead chandelier which illuminates the almost completely white colour scheme. A few feet from the foyer, a frosted glass wall separates an ascending stairwell from the living space, which is vast and immaculate. The white leather living room couches and chairs are ultra-contemporary and are paired with orange and gray accent pillows and throws. Even the large painting above the fireplace mantle is in those three colours. Beyond the couches is a dining room with black leather, swivel chairs and a frosted glass table.

"Before you say anything, my parents bought this house as an investment and had it renovated by a designer. They lived in it for a year and I bought it off of them for a small fee, but it's really not my style. I really haven't had time or the energy to change it."

"It's gorgeous."

He takes my coat and hangs it in the closet. "Do you want a tour?"

"Yes, please."

He takes me by the hand and leads me to an entrance between the living and dining rooms. We step into the gourmet kitchen that's complete with a range built for a chef, stainless steel cabinets, wood countertops, and gray glossy floors. The stools behind the island are bright orange leather.

"Very nice. I could cook you the most perfect meal in here."

"Good, but again, I haven't been grocery shopping in a while. The take-out menus are in this drawer. Just in case," he taps under the island. "A bathroom is right here and the spare bedroom is through that door," he points. "There's a patio garden outside those doors, but it's too dark to see. It's nice enough, but it doesn't have a lot of room for entertaining."

I nod in awe at the modern interior. Jack is basically a stranger to me and I'm disheartened by this. How much more don't I know about him?

"You have to see my favourite room." He leads me back towards the living room and we head upstairs.

"Your bedroom must be up here. It's your favourite room? Shocking," I joke.

"No, you big ball of trouble." He tugs my hand.

We do enter the bedroom and it's the only room on the second floor. It's decorated in shades of blue and white, but with lighter wood accents. His walk-in closet puts me to shame. My jaw drops and I stop to gawk at it. Natural light from a skylight floods the closet, it has floor-to-ceiling shelves, and he even has an ottoman in the middle of it. I could live in there.

"I know. My closet is a woman's dream come true. Come this way." He releases my hand to open double doors at the back of his room, leading to another room surrounded entirely by windows, but completely unlike the rest of the décor.

The fireplace is contemporary white marble, but everything else is homey. His bookshelves are lined with all sorts of books, trophies and photographs and the deep couch looks worn, faded and very comfortable.

"Is this your dorm room?"

"You could say that, but I call it my man cave. I do most of my work here," he pats an antique-looking roll-top desk.

"I love it."

We stand looking around awkwardly and then he says, "I have to go get my bag out of the car. Make yourself at home."

When he's out of sight, I pick up a framed picture from his desk and see Jack with his arms around an older man and woman. It must be his parents. His dad has the same scruffy beard, although a bit gray and he has his eyes too. Jack looks so happy and so hot!

I hear the front door open again and I carefully put the picture frame down. I walk through his bedroom, eyeing the bed on my way out. It's a king size, I think. It looks very spacious. Flip flop.

In the kitchen, Jack surprises me when he comes out of a hidden door beside the fridge. "That's the laundry room in there."

"Oh, you startled me."

"I'm going back upstairs, but I shouldn't be too long."

"No problem." I start looking in the fridge for available food and I feel him slap my bottom. I turn around and smile at him.

"I couldn't resist." He winks and disappears.

That's a good sign. I'm encouraged by his friskiness and start humming while hunting for food. There are a few things in the fridge that stand out, but I continue to look in the cupboards for other options. I decide on a meal and whip around the kitchen, baking the chicken, making pasta and drinking some wine that I found in the fridge. I wanted to go upstairs with a glass for Jack, but I didn't want to bother him. He can have some with dinner…if there's any left.

During a brief pause in preparation, I kick off my heels and wander into his immaculate living room. I wonder if it ever gets used. I head over to a wall-to-ceiling bookshelf in the small inlet beside the foyer that I didn't see before. I scan the book titles: *'History of Modern Art', 'Twentieth Century Design' and 'Nineteenth Century French Art'* are amongst the titles. They can't be Jack's books. There aren't any personal objects or picture frames, just expensive candles and pretty vases. This must all be just for show.

Standing back, I look up at the beautiful, crystal light fixture and as I my eyes scan down, something catches my eye on the very top shelf of the entire unit. It's a large, well-used book lying on its side. I look around and grab a chair, dragging it over to the bookcase. Standing on the chair, I slide the book toward me and see that it's an album. I'm intrigued.

I take the album back to the kitchen, put it on the counter and open it to the first page. The pictures are of Jack, probably during his first year of university. There's a group shot of a bunch of guys in someone's living room and another one of him sitting on a couch with a bunch a guys, drinking beer. They look like they're half in the bag. Jack has such a baby face. No scruff at all and super short hair. It's a buzz cut! He's so cute.

There are a bunch of action shots of him playing hockey for the University of Toronto. I didn't even know him back then. It's a shame. If I wasn't so focused on volleyball and Steve, things could've been completely different.

Turning the page, my stomach drops when I see a picture of him with a pretty girl sitting on his lap. She has long, blonde hair and it looks like she's wearing a tennis outfit. I can definitely tell that they were a couple. Jack's got a look of adoration in his eyes. Ugh! *It's university, Colleen! Get a grip.* I flip to the next page harshly.

"Where did you get that?"

I jump slightly when he comes into the kitchen. "It was on the top of the bookshelf in the living room."

Jack grunts, "I wonder why that's down here. I haven't looked at that in years." He stands next to me, his chest touching my one shoulder. "That was when I was young and stupid," he points to picture of him sitting on a motorcycle.

"That's hot."

"It is?"

"Absolutely."

He places his hand on my back. "What about this picture?"

Flip flop. My heart starts to beat quickly. I look at the photo. He's sitting on a sidewalk curb, holding a paper bag-covered bottle of booze. He looks like a bum. "You're hot there too."

"Bullshit."

"You were hot then and you're super-hot now." I look back at him, throwing my hair over my shoulder.

He gently pulls back the last couple of strands. "Is that so?"

I turn slowly toward him and reach up, pulling on his hair with one hand. "I do prefer this over the buzz cut though."

"I liked the buzz cut. It's so much easier than this mop." He pulls me toward him. "I thought about getting it cut like that again."

"No," I cry, but before I can protest further, he kisses me.

His lips are soft and gentle and the intensity of his kiss makes my legs quiver. I take his face in my hands and run my fingertips over his scruff and then gently pull on his earlobes. I hear him moan quietly and it gives me confidence. Standing on the balls of my feet, I push my hips into his and wrap my arms around his neck, probing my tongue deeper into his mouth and caressing his tongue. I can't get enough. The butterflies are so intense that I'm sure he can feel me quivering with excitement.

Jack's hands slide up and down my back and drop lower to my bottom, where he squeezes softly, pulling me toward his hips. I feel his hardness through my thin dress, which seems to be rising.

I suddenly feel his hands on my bare skin at the top of my thighs, fondling my cheeks. I want him badly. I press my breasts into his chest and lift my foot off the ground, resting my inner thigh against the outside of his hip.

The oven timer sounds and it's not a normal beeping sound, it's a musical tune. It throws me off and I try to ignore it, but Jack slowly pulls away, releasing my bunched up skirt. It drops, swishing around my thighs.

"Saved by the bell." He walks to the oven and starts singing to the timer. "Your dinner is ready. Your dinner is ready. Please come and get your dinner. Your dinner is ready."

"You made up a song to your timer?"

"It was so annoying that I just made it up one day," he shrugs. "Do you want me to take the food out?"

"We can have dinner later." I follow him and pull on the back pocket of his jeans. "We were just finishing the appetizer."

"As appealing as that sounds, I'm starving and this smells amazing," He takes my hands. "But I'll make sure I save room for dessert."

"Dessert is the best part." I grab the oven mitts and pull the chicken out of the oven. "We're having basil pesto chicken pasta with artichokes and sundried tomatoes."

"I had all of that in my kitchen?"

"You sure did." I serve it on two plates and we sit at the island to eat. "Do you have any more wine?"

"There's some in the fridge. I'll get it."

"Oh, that's gone," I laugh.

"I'll get some from the other room." He goes into the hidden door laundry room and returns with a bottle. "Do you still prefer white?"

"Good memory."

He pours two glasses and sits down, passing me my glass. "Here's to you and this mouthwatering dinner." We clink glasses and start to eat. "This is absolutely delicious." He puts another forkful into his mouth and closes his eyes.

"Thanks."

"Didn't it bother you to cook for all of those dinner parties that Steve wanted?" Jack asks between bites.

Why is he talking about Steve? "Not at all. I liked doing it."

"You sure put up with a lot."

I don't say anything. I don't like the conversation and search my mind for how to change the subject.

"He wanted everyone to like him and used you to increase his value. You were the trophy wife who provided it all for him. He never could've gotten where he did without you. Do you know that he—

I cut him off, "Can we talk about something else?"

"Is it still a sore subject?"

"No, I just don't want to talk about my ex."

"Why?"

"I've moved on. I think we have more in common than just Steve, right?"

"Well, yeah…" He puts his fork down. "I'm just concerned about how you're dealing with everything. I'm going to be incredibly honest here. I don't want to play games anymore. It's not a surprise that I have feelings for you and I want to pursue a relationship with you, but I'm afraid that you're not ready."

He does want me. "I'm great, Jack. Truly and honestly." The flutter in my chest makes me breathless. "I want the same with you. I'm ready for you to pursue me," I grin.

"How do you know that I'm not just a rebound fling for you?"

The Sex Project was a bunch of rebounds. "I've had a lot of time to think and I told you that when I met Steve that night, I knew I was already over him."

"But you were so adamant about winning him back. What changed?"

"It was like I had blinders on during our entire relationship. He was my very first boyfriend—"

"What? I thought you met in university?"

"We did. I never dated until I met him."

"You've only been with him?"

How do I answer? If I say no, he'll know that I've been with other men since Steve and I split up. Do I tell him about the Sex Project? "Well, no. But that doesn't matter. The point is that I thought he was a God and that he could do no wrong, but from the moment I walked into his disgusting apartment, I knew that I was completely wrong about him and I had made a huge mistake."

"That must hurt."

"Not really. I know that I didn't do anything wrong. I didn't cause him to be a jackass, he just was one and still is."

"You're not sad or feeling…I don't know, alone?"

"I'm angry in the sense that I wasted years of my life being with him and I feel stupid that I never saw him the way everyone else did, but I'm not depressed or lonely." I put my hand on his. "I'm excited for the future."

"I'm excited that you're excited," he laughs and places his hand over mine. "That sounded completely cheesy."

"It was sweet. I want you to be happy for me, but now I have a question for you."

"Shoot."

"What about you?" I ask.

"What about me?"

"You've never had a serious relationship in your life and that concerns me. You're so troubled with how I'm dealing with issues and making sure that you're not a rebound, but you're afraid of commitment."

"I deserve that, but you're wrong."

"How can I be wrong? You always had a different date at my house. It was never the same girl twice."

"You noticed?"

"Of course I did."

"Do you think you might've had feelings for me way back then?"

I did look forward to my dinner parties and it wasn't because I wanted to impress Steve. Sure, I wanted Steve to be successful, but I didn't like to entertain his co-workers. Jack made everything tolerable and much more fun. I enjoyed talking to him in the kitchen and I even made sure I looked my best. I always bought a new outfit and he never failed to compliment me on it.

"What are you thinking about?"

"There was one year that I had a party around Christmas and you didn't attend. I thought you were coming, but when you didn't show up, I was so bummed out that I barely left the kitchen. I also burnt the chicken and forgot to put baking powder in the popovers." I put my napkin on the table. "You know, I remember that I had bought a pretty red dress for that night and I was disappointed that you wouldn't see it. You always noticed what I was wearing."

"I remember missing that party. I had to go home to see my parents because they were leaving to go on a Christmas cruise and I was disappointed too." He smiles and touches my thigh. "I always noticed your dresses. The more leg the better."

"You're a leg kind of a man?"

"I'm a Colleen kind of a man."

I shake my head, giggling. "You know, you were definitely on my mind back then. I think I started having two parties a month, just so we could catch up. I had to brag about the Leafs to someone."

"I thought you were crazy to host so many, but I was always happy to go. No girl knew sports quite like you and to watch you bend over and work in your kitchen was my favourite part."

"You're awful," I hit him with my elbow. "Those poor, poor girls that you brought with you! They must've been so bored. You barely talked to them."

"Listen, I only brought them for show and honestly, I did it to keep your husband occupied."

"What?"

"Come on, I know you saw it. He was all over them and that always gave me the chance to be alone with you."

"Wow, you were scheming."

"It wasn't very nice of me. I'm sorry."

"It's not as if you made him stray. He was always like that and it doesn't matter now. So, you would bring a different girl each time, like a buffet for Steve?" I laugh.

"Yup and I never had a second date with any of them."

Kind of like my Sex Project. "That brings us back to my original question about being afraid to commit."

He tilts his head, thinking and starts to nod, "Right. No, I'm not afraid of commitment. I actually had a long term relationship in university."

The girl in the photo? "What happened?"

"We started dating in our last year of high school and two years into university. She was everything to me and I thought I was going to marry her. I proposed and gave her a ring, but she cheated on me into our fourth year together. She broke my heart."

"Oh, I'm so sorry."

"We had big plans for the future. We wanted to live in a smaller city and I wanted kids right away, like five of them."

"Five kids? You're crazy!"

"I love kids! Don't you want any little Colleens running around? I want little Jacks."

"Sure, I want kids, but I don't know about five of them. Little Jacks would be so cute." Their blonde hair would flop in their faces.

"Of course they would and so would little Colleens with curly hair. They'd be adorable," he leans over and pulls some of my curls, watching them spring back in place.

"One day, I suppose. So after you had your heart broken you swore off women?"

"I wouldn't say I swore them off," he snickers. "I didn't ever want to feel that hurt again, so I just dated casually and then it just became habit. I could never see myself settling down with any of the women I dated and I didn't care to give any of them the chance. Yes, I was a player, but I did it to protect myself."

"Women don't see it that way."

"I was a pig. I know I was horrible, but then I met you at the café on that one morning and I knew I wanted to be a better man. I couldn't do that to women anymore."

"Wait. Which time at the café?"

"It was the morning that I blindsided you with information about Steve. I told you that he had cheated on you and had been seeing his secretary for months."

"I remember that."

"You were wearing a pale blue dress and looked beautiful."

I drop my head down shyly. How did he remember my dress? "Why did you want to become a better man that day?"

"For you. I wanted to be a better man for you." He takes both of my hands in his. "Colleen, I've had a crush on you since you talked hockey with me in your kitchen, while you made your homemade Caesar dressing, poured wine for your guests, drank beer with me and taught me to make those silly napkin pockets. You made me make them every time!"

I laugh, remembering those pockets. "I'm Suzy Homemaker. You like that in a woman?"

"You're way more than that. You're beautiful, smart and funny." He touches my face softly. "Anyway, when I saw you in so much pain that day, I knew that I wanted to help you or be there for you if you'd let me. Maybe I was preying on a newly separated woman and maybe I had my own best interests in my mind. I just knew that I had to be in your life one way or another."

"I pushed you away so much. I'm surprised that you kept trying."

"You were definitely tough on me, that's for sure. But I told you, I knew I wanted you."

"You do?"

He moves his chair closer to mine. "I do." He kisses my cheek and then my lips. He pulls away abruptly. "I do want to be with you, but I also want to take things slow."

"Why slow?" I want to groan.

"I want to get to know you and date you."

"What happened to talking me on my desk at work?"

"Oh, that'll still happen," he smiles slyly. "But I still want to try to take it slow."

"The key word being *try*."

"Yes," he laughs. "I will *try* my best not to take you on every surface of this house too."

Flip flop. "Is that realistic?" I tease, flipping my hair back and looking up at him through my lashes, like I was taught. I even tickle his forearm with my fingertips.

He groans, "Not when you look so God-damned sexy." He pulls me off my chair and sideways onto his lap, kissing me roughly.

Pressing my body into his, I throw my arms around his neck and respond enthusiastically. One of his hands cradles my head and the other slides up my body to cup my breast. I gasp and throw my head back. He ravages my neck and collarbone with his mouth. His scruffy beard scrapes my chin, but it's such a turn-on. I press my chest out, yearning for him to touch my breasts, but his hand travels back down my body to my thighs.

He has will power. I bring my face down again and nudge his forehead and temple with my lips, wanting him to kiss me again and he does. The hand on my thigh massages from knee to hip and my dress begins to rise.

Instantly, he's touching my bare skin and he's inches away from my panties. I shudder with anticipation, but he stops, pulling my dress down over my thighs.

"What's wrong?" I whisper into his mouth.

"I told you that I want to take things slow." He bites my bottom lip. "No matter how difficult it is."

"But I want this. I want you."

He groans, "I want you too, but not yet." He slides me back onto my chair. "We need to be adults about this."

"This is what adults do," I pout.

Jack stands up and kisses me. "Come on, let's clean up the mess you made." He holds out his hand.

"Ok." If he wants to take it slow, I'm going to make it really difficult for him.

With every turn he makes in the kitchen, I make sure that I'm there, bumping into him. I bend over to load the dishwasher and back up enough so that my bottom hits him. When I reach up to put the rest of the pasta away, I do it as he's cleaning the counter and he bumps into my torso and breasts. When he bends down to put the freshly-washed strainer away in the cupboards, I stand next to him, pressing my hips into his shoulder as I pretend to do something in the cabinet above him.

"You're doing this on purpose."

"Doing what?" I ask innocently.

He rolls his eyes. "Upstairs, trouble. Let's relax in my man cave."

I make sure that I walk ahead of him up the stairs slowly and deliberately stop in front of him, so that he bumps into me.

"Don't do it again or I'm going to get you."

Of course, I can't help myself and bend over in front of him. He grabs my bottom, but I run the rest of the way upstairs and head to the couch. I jump onto one end of the couch and stretch out my legs, so there's barely any room for him. He comes in, looks at me and starts to sit on me. I almost protest, but he swings his leg over mine and sits at the other end of the couch, facing me, with a leg on each side of my feet. My feet almost touch his crotch and just when I'm about to toe him gently, he picks up my feet and massages them.

"Mmmm... That feels good."

"I'd really like you to stay here tonight. Not because I want to take advantage of you, but because I'd feel better knowing that you're safe."

"I'd like to stay here with you too."

"You can stay in the spare bedroom."

My jaw drops, "Are you kidding?"

"Not really. I don't trust myself."

"We'll discuss that later. Let's talk about you. I don't know you as much as you know me. Tell me about your family and if you have any brothers or sisters. I want to know everything."

25.

At two in the morning, Jack's lying on the floor in front of the couch, with his head on a pillow, looking up at me and I'm lying on my side with my arm under my head, looking down at him. We haven't stopped talking and he just finished telling me about his little brother who lives in Florida.

"We need to go to bed. I have to get you home in the morning so you can get ready for work."

"Ugh! You're right." I get up and step over him, holding my hands out to help him up.

He laughs and takes my hands. "Be careful," he warns.

I have to get into a deep squat to take all of his weight, but I get him up.

He puts his arm around me, "All right, tough girl. Let's get you to bed."

Flip flop. We step out of his man cave, but he keeps going, leading me out of his bedroom. "Seriously? You're still going to make me sleep downstairs, all alone?"

"Colleen," he grumbles. "Ok, ok, you can sleep with me in my bed, but keep your clothes on."

"I can't sleep in my dress. Can't you give me a tee shirt?"

"You're making me crazy!" He walks into his closet and comes back to throw me a plain, white tee shirt and sweatpants.

"Thank you." I start untying the belt on my dress.

"Colleen! Can't you get changed in the bathroom?"

"I'm fine right here. You've seen me naked in the bathtub. It's nothing you haven't seen before."

He groans and stomps out of the bedroom. "I'll leave then."

"It's not like you haven't seen a naked woman before," I call out to him as he races away.

I change, but just into the tee shirt. It barely covers my bottom. It's perfect. Then, I go into the large, immaculate bathroom looking for a toothbrush, finding one still in its package beside the sink. I rip open the package, find toothpaste and brush my teeth.

The bathroom is straight from a page from '*House Beautiful*' or '*House to Home*'. The lack of clutter and the pale grays in the large space make it seem like the spa where I get my massages and facials. It's very luxurious, complete with a large soaking tub and a spacious master shower that's covered in intricate tilework. I can't wait to bathe in that tub.

When I'm done brushing my teeth, I splash water on my face and smooth down my hair. I look at myself in the mirror. Nope, that won't do. I bend over and fluff up my hair, whipping my head back when I stand up. It's a wicked, sexy mess. Flip flop. Jack won't be able to resist.

Jack walks back into the bedroom at the same time I do. He looks at me and stops dead. "Why aren't you wearing the pants I gave you?"

"They're too big."

He walks past me into the bathroom, talking to himself. I can't understand what he's saying. He seems frustrated. It makes me laugh.

I pull back the soft, navy blue blanket and white sheets from the bed and sit on the end of it, waiting for him to finish brushing his teeth.

"Why aren't you in bed?" He's wearing a red Coca Cola tee shirt and red plaid pants.

"I don't know what side you sleep on."

"I sleep in the middle."

"Oh, so I guess it doesn't matter which side I sleep on." I walk to one side of the bed and we both get in at the same time, lying on our backs stiffly. How did it get so awkward?

"Can I turn off the light?"

"Sure," I say.

In the dark, I can't see him, but I know he's there and I'm excited to be here with him. I want to reach out to him, but I don't want to pressure him. It was fun to joke around and tempt him, but now I'm actually in his bed! I can hear him breathing. How am I supposed to sleep?

He starts to move and the bed shakes, shaking me and then, nothing. He moves again and stops. He groans, "This is ridiculous! Get over here!"

I move toward him quickly and something hits me hard in the nose. "Ouch!" My eyes tear up and I hold my nose, waiting for the pain to subside. Behind my eyelids, I see the light turn on. I feel a tear slide down my cheek.

"What happened? Did I get you in the nose?"

"Mmhmmm," I whimper.

"I'm so sorry. Let me see."

"It's ok, I'm fine." I release my nose and open my eyes, squinting into the light.

"Looks good." He kisses my nose, while carefully sliding his arm under my pillow. I feel his other hand touch my bare hip and then pause, yanking the tee shirt down. "This is why I wanted you to wear pants. Your thong is an immediate threat."

"Get over it already," I laugh.

"Get over it?" He pulls my hip toward him and I keep my hands and arms tucked into my chest, relishing his embrace. "Do you know how sexy you are in my tee shirt?" He makes a noise like he's in pain.

I start to stretch out my arm and reach for his hip.

"Keep your hands where they are."

I bring it back. "I can't touch you?"

"No."

"Can I kiss you?"

"No."

I lift my head off my pillow and try to reach his lips, but he turns his head.

"Not even a good night kiss?"

He makes that tormented noise again. "Fine. One good night kiss."

When he tilts his head down to kiss me, I grab onto his face and give him my deepest, lingering kiss, bringing my thigh up and over his hip. My panty-covered sex finds his erection easily and I press into it.

Still kissing me, he rolls onto his back, bringing me on top of him. My knees touch the bed on either side of his hips and I slowly rock back and forth over his length. He dips his fingers under the sides of my panties, like he's going to pull them down, but doesn't. He does press my hips down urgently onto his hips and the force of his hardness onto my sex is agonizingly sensual.

Jack releases my hips and his hands roam under my shirt. They glide up the sides of my body, feeling every rib and when he gets to my breasts, he moans. I took off my bra. He cups both breasts and pushes them together, while his thumbs lightly graze my nipples. It takes my breath away and I moan loudly into his mouth, arching my back, giving him more access to explore.

He does it softly again and I push my sex up and down his erection. I want his mouth on my breasts. I sit straight up and look at him demurely. His hands fall to my hips and he stares at me, questioning me.

I stare back at him and grab the hem of the tee shirt, easing it up over my head. I throw it the floor.

"God, you're beautiful."

I bend back over him and purposely rub my breasts on his chest, kissing him gently. I move a bit lower and kiss his neck and his chest. I try to go lower, but he flips me off of him onto my back and planks on his elbows over me.

"We're going slow," he breathes into my ear.

I tug at his shirt. "Take this off, please."

"No."

"Please," I stretch the word out, begging and pull his shirt up.

He laughs, "You're horrible. No, I'm not taking it off." He pulls it back down, balancing on one elbow. "And you should put yours back on."

"Are you really going to deny me?"

"Tonight, yes. But I do like hearing you beg."

"Is that so?" I wrap my legs around him and hold onto his upper back, lifting myself off the bed.

"You can't take me down. I can hold this position all night."

"Oh yeah? What if I do this?" I hold him tightly with one arm around his neck and lightly dig my knuckles into his ribs with my other hand.

"That's not fair," he cringes and wiggles around. Suddenly he drops all of his weight onto me, laughing. "See what you get?"

"It's what I wanted." I start pushing my hips up, grinding against him and kiss him slowly, sucking on his bottom lip.

"Baby! Please stop!"

"Do you really want me to stop?"

"I don't know anymore. It's too late. I want you badly, but I'd like to wait a little longer." He planks over me again, brushing some hair away from my face. "Is that ok?"

"Yes, I can wait." He called me baby.

He rolls onto his side. "Now put your shirt on. You're driving me crazy."

I smirk and sit up in bed, looking for it. Before I put it on, I make sure he gets one more eyeful.

"Argh!" He groans and puts a pillow over his face. "I don't know how I'm going to sleep next to you. I always thought you had a fantastic body, but it's even better naked. Get over here."

I fall onto him and splay one leg over his thighs, kissing him again. The electricity builds up instantly.

Jack moans harshly, "Turn over. I'm going to spoon you. You're not to be trusted with those vicious kisses of yours."

When he pushes into my backside, I feel that his excitement hasn't died down. I push back against it. "Are you sure this is a safer position?"

"It would be if you stopped moving."

"Oh! Ok. Good night, Jack."

"Good night, trouble."

I haven't felt this comfortable going to sleep in a long time. I relax into his body and take a deep breath, slowly exhaling.

After what feels like only minutes, I feel a sensuous pressure between my legs increase. It's a gentle throbbing and it pulsates throughout my entire body. I stretch my legs and then relax, basking in the pleasure that's growing inside me.

"Jack, what changed your mind?"

"I couldn't wait. I need to be inside you."

"Make love to me, Jack."

"Colleen."

Yes, Jack?"

"Colleen."

"Make love to me."

"Colleen, wake up."

"What?" My eyes flutter open. Was I dreaming? I turn to see Jack staring at me, resting his chin on his hands.

"Wow! You talk in your sleep."

"I do not!" I'm so embarrassed, hiding my head under the blankets.

"Oh yes you do!" He pulls the blankets down.

"What did I say?"

"Wouldn't you like to know?" He kisses me on the forehead.

"Tell me!"

"Nope. Time to get up and get you home."

"Can't we stay in bed all day?" The dream made me horny.

"Nada."

"I can take my shirt off again," I tease.

"No, no, no." He starts to get out of bed, but I grab his shirt, pulling him backwards. He falls back down.

"Come back to bed."

"No, I'm being the adult here. Get up!" He pulls away from my grasp. "I'm going to make coffee."

"Ok, I'll get up. By the way, do you always wear clothes to bed?"

"Never. I don't wear anything to bed."

He leaves the bedroom and I hug myself, content and ecstatic for what happened last night and for the future. I roll over and bury my face in Jack's pillow, breathing deeply. It smells like him.

I leisurely roll out of bed and walk over to my dress that I laid out on a chair. I pick off some lint from the sleeve and take Jack's shirt off. I adjust my panties and just as I'm about to pick up my bra, I hear Jack come up the stairs. I turn my back to the door, waiting for him come into the room. I can't help teasing him.

"Hey. Colleen! Do you like cream and sugar…?" He walks slowly toward me.

"Yes please."

"Oh my… Can you be any sexier?" He comes up behind me and places his hands on my hips, pulling me close. He's already hard.

I lift my arms up and reach back, grabbing the back of his head, pulling at his hair. He kisses my shoulder and neck and I arch my back as his hands move over my ribs to my breasts. He covers them with his hands and squeezes my nipples. I moan and lean back into his chest. I can barely stand up.

One of his hands lowers down over my stomach, over my panties and his fingers lightly press into my sex. My hips buck into his hand and I tug on his hair. I want more.

I turn around abruptly and place my hand on his hardness, rubbing up and down over his cotton pants. I'm thrilled to feel how large he is.

"Baby, we can't do this now. We have to go to work." He places his hand on my back and pulls me close.

"I know," I kiss him gently. "This is just another build-up for that one day when you decide the time is right."

"It's going to be sooner, rather than later, if you keep this up."

"Let me get dressed. I don't want to tempt you any more than I already have."

"You stay here and I'll go dress in there," he points to his walk-in closet and leaves me.

I dress quickly and tip-toe to the closet, hoping to catch a glimpse of his naked body. I peek my head inside and he's pulling on his pants.

"Nice," I whistle.

He turns around and I ogle his well-defined torso. Every ripple of his abdominal muscles is distinct and separated, as is the outline of his chest and bulge of his arms. I knew he was muscular, but to see him bare-chested gives me butterflies.

"Are you going to ravage me?"

"Is that an invitation? Oh wait, you don't give invitations." I walk toward him.

"Go away! Don't start."

"Don't tell me what to do." I bend over slightly and kiss his chest, outlining his pecs with my tongue, and using my fingers to feel each of his six abdominal muscles. I bend lower to kiss them.

"Baby, stop." His hands caress my shoulders, but he doesn't push me away.

"Shhh… Trust me."

I get down on my knees and lick his belly button and undo the button on his khakis.

"Baby, please…"

I ignore him and unzip his fly, moving my mouth over his erection beneath his Under Armour underwear. I hear him groan.

"This isn't fair."

I quickly stand up with my hands on my hips and kiss him on the cheek, "Where's that coffee?"

He does up his pants again and grabs me by the arms. "You're definitely a lot of trouble. When we have time, I'm going to get you back."

"I'll be waiting."

We kiss passionately and I end it by biting his lip. "We have to go."

"I've been saying that for an hour."

I watch him pull a light gray button down shirt off a hanger and put it on. I sigh heavily.

"What's wrong?"

"Are you sure you want to take it slow? I mean, we have this amazing chemistry. I want to tear your clothes off and I think you want to do the same." He nods. "Then why wait?"

"I want to make sure we both want this for the right reasons."

"Right reasons?"

"You're going through a separation."

"And?"

"Do you really want to jump into another relationship or is this just a…"

"Fling? I don't do flings, Jack." Only for research.

"You don't strike me as the type either, but I want to be sure."

"We've been over this, Jack. What do I have to do to prove to you that Steve means nothing to me and that I want you?"

He shakes his head, "I don't know."

26.

Jack kisses me goodbye. "I'll pick you up at five-thirty."

"Will I be able to go home first to shower and change?"

"Yes ma'am."

"Thank you."

"Have a great day." He takes off in his big, manly man's truck. I can still hear the muffler when he turns the corner.

At my house, I only had time to freshen up and change quickly. We ended up making out one more time before we left his house and had to race to mine to make up time. Flip flop. I understand the whole 'take it slow' concept, but he has nothing to worry about. In the meantime, I'm sure I can prove it to him or break him. I smile to myself.

"Oh my goodness. Look at that smile." Margie comes up behind me at the front door of my office.

"What about it?"

"Tell me the details."

"There's nothing to tell. We're taking it slow."

"Slow? Your face says otherwise."

I grin, "We're getting to know each other, if you must know." I open the door for her.

"How in-depth are you getting?" She laughs unconvinced, walking inside.

"All right. Enough about me," I say. "Listen, I think we should start locking the door between appointments."

"Why?"

"Mr. Baker was watching us yesterday while Connie was here."

"How do you know?"

"He called after you and the Baker's left and basically told me that he was always watching. I called the cops again and Jack came to keep me company. I want us to be safe, but not scared. Screen your phone calls, don't give out information and lock the door."

"I'm always vigilant about our safety and patient confidentiality, but locking the door wouldn't hurt."

"Thanks, I don't know what else we can do."

"Do you think we need to have the police here when Connie has an appointment?"

"That wouldn't hurt either. I'll call the officers and you just let me know when her next appointment is scheduled."

"I'll look and write it down."

"Who do we have today?"

After a full morning, Margie steps outside to do some errands and I figure out what I'm going to eat for lunch. I have forty-five minutes. I could walk across the street to the market for a salad, but Jack trumps my hunger. I text him instead:

'I'm hungry, but not for food.'

Will he respond right away?

'You need to eat. Do I have to come over there and force feed you?'

That question is full of sexual connotations.

'It depends. Are you on the menu?'

'I'm coming over.'

'Good.'

About ten minutes later, Jack comes into the office with two plastic bags.

"What's all this?"

"What do you think it is? It's lunch." He walks past me into my office and puts it on the table.

I follow him and when he turns around, I attack him. I reach for his head, pulling it down and kiss him deeply.

"Where's Margie?" He murmurs.

"Out."

With that, he grabs my bottom and pulls it toward his hips and begins lifting up my skirt. "You should never stop wearing dresses." I feel his hands on my bare cheeks and he squeezes firmly.

I moan softly, "You said you liked me in spandex more."

"Nope. Dresses. Definitely dresses." He caresses my bottom and kisses me again.

I bite his bottom lip and pull away. "I don't know when Margie's coming back."

He backs off quickly and my dress falls back down to my knees. "Lunch time."

I giggle and open up a bag. "Mmmm… Fattoush? And falafels? Awww, you remembered."

"Of course. I don't know how you can eat those fucking awfuls, but I got them for you anyway."

"Thank you so much for bringing me lunch. You're very sweet."

"Anything for you," he winks.

We sit down on my couch to eat. "What time do you have to be back?" I ask.

"About thirty minutes."

"Perfect. That's when my next appointment is."

After a few minutes, I feel Jack staring at me. "What? Do I have tahini on my face?"

"No, I wanted to ask you something."

"What?"

"Remember when we were at the deli, the first time, and that guy came up to you?"

Oh shit. "What guy," I try buy time to compose myself.

"Kyle? No, it was Chris. Do you remember?"

Cooking class Chris. "Uh, yeah. What about him?"

"Did you date him?"

"Just once."

"Once?"

"Yes." Where's he going with this?

"Why only once?"

"He was newly separated and he still had feelings for his wife."

"Oh."

That 'oh' is not a good 'oh'. "Yeah, it didn't work out. There wasn't a connection at all."

"Oh."

I take a bite of fattoush and rush to change the subject, "Where did you get the food from? It's great."

"Sarai's. Now what about that guy at the waterfront?"

My stomach twists into knots. "Jack, what's wrong? Why are you asking me these questions?"

"I've been thinking. You said that you don't have flings, but you seemed to date a lot when you were separated."

"Does it matter? You've dated loads of women and I don't care."

"You're right. I'm sorry." He pats my hand. "It's none of my business."

"Jack, I want to be with you and only you. You can believe that."

"I know." He leans over and kisses my cheek. "Now you have food on your face." He dabs my lips with a napkin. "All better."

I smile at him, but my insides are in turmoil. What if he finds out about my Sex Project? Would that upset him? I can't eat anymore. I start packing up my food and put it in the fridge.

"All done?"

"I'll bring it home tonight and have it later."

"I'm done too, but I finished mine like a good boy."

"Would you like me to reward you?"

"What if Margie catches us again?"

At that moment, we hear Margie come in the front door. We look at each other and laugh.

"You'll have to reward me later," Jack smiles slyly.

"For sure."

Jack gets up and starts piling his garbage, but I place my hand on his, stopping him. "I've got it. You bought, I clean up."

"Thanks." He puts his arms around me and kisses me. "I'll see you after work."

"Can't wait."

He leaves and my day ensues slowly, finishing with the last patient of the day cancelling, giving me time to call Christine when Margie leaves.

"Where have you been, Ci-Ci? I haven't talked to you since we went to that cold bar. How are you?"

"I'm awesome. How are you?"

"Forget about me. I'm always awesome, but why are you?"

"Jack and I are dating."

"You are? That's great. Have you fucked him yet?"

"Oh, Christine!" Laughing, I say, "Not yet. We're trying to take things slow, but it's proving to be difficult. We can't keep out hands off each other."

"Why are you taking it slow?"

"Well..." I sit in Margie's chair. "Jack feels that I still need time to adjust to everything that has happened with Steve."

"Do you need time?"

"Not at all."

"Then jump him!"

"I've been trying!" I complain. "Maybe tonight? We're going out on our first real date."

"You're gonna get laid for sure."

"It's not *all* about that!"

"I know, Ci-Ci. I'm just happy that you're happy. You deserve it."

"Thanks, Christine."

"Where are you going tonight?"

"I don't—

Jack walks into the office. "Hey, beautiful! Oops, sorry."

I smile at him and put my first finger up to tell him to wait. "I don't know where we're going. Jack just walked in. I'll ask him." I take the phone away from my ear. "Christine wants to know where we're going tonight."

"Tell her it's a surprise."

I frown at him and put the phone up to my ear. "He says it's a surprise."

"That's sweet. You're getting laid!" She squeals.

"All right. Have a good night."

"You too. Good luck!"

Jack steps toward me. "Christine's a really good friend of yours, eh?"

"The best. I met her on my first day of university and she basically took me under her wing and we've been friends ever since."

"She definitely has your back."

"I know. She's always been there for me." I put my coat on and get my purse. "When am I going to meet your friends?"

"Tonight."

"Really?" I thought we were going on a real date.

"Don't worry, we'll still have alone time, I promise."

He can read my mind. "That's good. I like alone time."

"You do? Let's get started then. I'll drive you home and wait for you to get ready," he opens the front door for me and we start walking down the walkway.

"I was thinking that I can drive myself home and you can come get me when you're ready. It's silly for you to drive me when my car's already here."

"I guess…"

"What's wrong?" I stop and look at him.

"I don't want to leave you alone."

"Jack, it won't be for long. I need about an hour. It'll be much easier and I can take my time, without feeling I have to rush."

"Fine, but make sure you set your alarm when you're home."

"I will," I stand on my tiptoes and give him a quick peck on the lips.

As I start to walk again, he catches my hand and pulls me toward him. "I didn't get a chance to give you a proper hello." He stands close to me and rests his hand on my cheek, staring into my eyes. "Hello."

Flip flop. "Hi." I place my hands on his chest and kiss him gently, feeling the sparks surge throughout my body. When we part, we're both breathless.

"Hurry," he states intensely. "I can't wait to be with you again."

27.

Thirty minutes later, I hear knocking at my front door. I run downstairs in my towel and peek out the window. It's Jack, wearing jeans and a thick, knit sweater.

"You're early," I say when I open the door.

"Oh, but I'm just in time." He pulls at my towel while I turn off the alarm.

"Do you want to see what's under this towel?"

He nods eagerly, "I do. I do."

I fiddle with the edge of my towel. "Do you understand the consequences?"

"Yes, I do."

"Are you prepared to follow through, possibly taking me on the dining room table?" I take the towel in both hands, prepared to tear it off my body.

He hangs his head. "Damn, you called my bluff." He points toward the stairs, "Go on! Get dressed We've got places to go, people to see!"

Laughing, I start walking toward the stairs and stop on the second step, turning around with a dirty thought. I'm not sure if it's a good or a bad idea. "Jack?"

"Yeah?" He looks up from his phone.

I drop my towel onto the stairs, revealing my naked body. "Oops!" I smile, turn and walk up the stairs slowly.

"Colleen!" I hear him holler and run across the kitchen floor.

At the top of the stairs, I look down and see him staring up at me, with a stunned look on his face. It was definitely a good idea.

"I'll be right down."

Jack just shakes his head and scowls at me, but it turns into a smile.

I expect him to run right up the stairs, but it's quiet. I'm starting to believe that he really does want to take things slow. I head to my room and pick out clothes to wear.

After dressing in skinny jeans, black boots and layer in a long sleeve shirt, black sweater and down-filled vest, I head downstairs and find Jack playing on his phone in the kitchen.

He puts it away when he sees me. "That wasn't very fair of you?"

"What?"

"Dropping your towel."

"It was an accident."

"Sure it was. It took everything in me to control myself and not run up the stairs and ravage you."

"I would've let you."

"Yes, I know you would've. Anyway, you look great." He stands up and touches my curls. "Have I ever told you how much I love your hair?"

"No, you haven't. Thank you."

"I've never met anyone with hair like yours." He kisses me gently and takes my hand. "Let's go."

We drive downtown, sitting higher than everyone on the street in his massive truck and the traffic starts getting thicker and thicker, but Jack's truck is like a bulldozer. I think it would scare any driver in a normal-sized car, but for me it's like I'm in an armoured car.

When we turn onto Blue Jays Way, I know we're headed to the CN Tower and the Air Canada Centre. "Are we going to a Leafs game?" I ask excitedly, clapping my hands.

"Yes we are." He laughs at my giddiness. "I knew you'd like that." He takes my hand, holding it as he drives.

"I love it." Jack knows I'm a closet Maple Leafs fan. I'm just so happy to be with him, but going to a game with him makes it extra special. I lean over and kiss his cheek.

Steve had despised hockey and hated that I knew more than him about it. During one dinner party, his co-workers had been talking about the latest Leafs game and I piped in about a bad call the refs had made. Steve had laughed at me in front of everyone and tried to brush me off, but I schooled him, quoting a new game misconduct rule that was implemented for the 2014-2015 season. He had stopped talking to me for the rest of the night and for three days after. I had learned to keep quiet about my passion and shared it only with Jack in the kitchen during the dinner parties.

It's slow-moving traffic, but we finally park outside, across the street from the parking garage where Mr. Baker blocked me in. I brush that memory off hastily, I'm safe with Jack. We follow the crowd and walk toward the CN Tower. The sidewalks are bustling with people lined up to go into Ripley's Aquarium of Canada, up to the observation deck of the CN Tower or eat in the revolving restaurant, and to go across the walkway to get to Front Street, Toronto's entertainment district. The entire urban neighbourhood is lit up and packed with a wide array of restaurants, bars and night clubs. I hold onto Jack's hand tightly as we weave through the mob of people.

Jack leads me to Gate 2, which is closed and has no one in line. I look around and see a huge lineup at Gate 3. Why is this one closed? He shows the attendant his tickets and I figure he's going to tell us to go to a different entrance, but the attendant opens the door and lets us in.

"Do you have exclusive tickets, or something?"

"Something like that," he winks. "Nothing but the best for you."

We walk upstairs and I see the upscale *Air Canada Club* restaurant. I start to walk past to get to the arena, but Jack stops at the concierge desk, yanking my arm faintly.

A pretty blonde greets us, but she stares at Jack, not even acknowledging me, "Hi, do you have a reservation?"

"Yes, it's under Fraser."

She looks down at a book, "Ok, you can follow me." She walks toward the glass doors and they slide open. Her tight, short skirt doesn't leave much to the imagination. Is she shaking her butt like that on purpose? Jack places his hand on my lower back and we follow the blonde. I notice that Jack looks everywhere else, but not at her wiggling bottom. Steve's eyes would've been all over it. Jack is a gentleman. He respects me and it shouldn't be so surprising. Every woman deserves to be treated this way.

The dimly lit restaurant looks romantic, but it's completely packed and noisy with chatter. We walk past an oversized wine rack in the middle of the dining room, holding at least two thousand bottles of wine. I look to the top of it, impressed by its grandeur, but think it's out of place with the beer-drinking Leaf fans.

"This is a nice surprise," I say and Jack just smiles.

The game hasn't even started yet and all of the tables and booths are taken. Everyone has a great view of the ice. The bar is sleek, made with backlit, translucent onyx and runs the entire length of the restaurant. It's supposed to be the largest bar in the city. Every single seat is taken there too.

The blonde leads us to the last two stools left at the front, with a pristine view of the ice. I don't even care that it's not a secluded table. We can still sit beside each other, talk and enjoy the game.

"Your server will be with you shortly," the blonde ignores me.

"What do you think?" Jack focuses on me and the blonde leaves abruptly.

"This is amazing, Jack. These are great seats!"

"We do have actual seats down below in the arena, if you want the real deal. We can stay here or sit in them after dinner."

"That's great, but I thought your friends were going to be here?" Not that I want them to be.

"They're probably drinking at Jack Astor's right now and will get here when the game starts. They'll just go right to their seats."

"So we're alone." I grab his hand and he squeezes mine.

"We're surrounded by hockey fans. We're not alone."

A short brunette with pouty lips walks up to Jack's right side, "My name is Kate and I'll be your server. Can I get you something from the bar? Perhaps some wine?" She tries to squish in further, looking at Jack. She even touches his body with her hip. What's with the women who work here?

Jack turns to me, "Do you want beer?"

"Absolutely!" I fake a smile.

"My girlfriend and I will have a large draught. Anything on tap, please." He basically waves her away.

He called me his girlfriend! In front of the hot waitress! He's so sweet. Steve would've flirted with her right in front of me, explaining that he had to string her along, so she'd give us better service. I shake my head and look to the ice.

"Are you ok?"

"Perfect." The players are warming up and filling the nets with wrist shots. "That Matthias," I point to number twenty-two, "He's from Mississauga and had eighteen goals last season with the Canucks. He should be good for the Leafs." Jack doesn't say anything, so I look at him and he's just staring at me, smiling. "What?" I ask.

"Kiss me."

Flip flop. I look around, lean toward him and kiss him gently. He pulls me in for an even deeper kiss. Steve had never kissed me in public. This date keeps getting better and better. I pull back and he's still just smiling and staring.

"What?" I ask again.

"Nothing."

"Then why are you grinning at me?"

"You blow my mind?"

I laugh, "Why's that?"

"You just do." He sits back in his chair. "Want to look at the menus?"

"I'm still full from lunch. Can we wait?"

"Sure. I might order an appetizer though."

Our beer arrives and he lifts up his glass to me. "May we kiss whom we please and please whom we kiss."

I frown, but slowly bring the glass up to hit his. "I better be the only one you're kissing."

"Of course." He moves close to me again. "Do I please you when we kiss?"

"Most definitely and I'm looking forward to you pleasing me in other ways." I whisper.

"You are, are you?"

"Oh yes. Don't you want to please me?"

"I'm not sure you can handle it."

"What?" I pretend to be offended. "You couldn't handle the pleasure I can give you."

"Hey, Colleen?" The voice is coming from behind me.

I turn around and see Dr. Mark standing there. Shit! Shit! Shit! "Hi, Mark. How are you?" I remember I stole his tuke before I snuck out of his house. I wonder where I put that hat.

"Good." He's staring at Jack.

I turn back to Jack and touch his hand, "Jack, this is Mark…Mark, meet my boyfriend Jack." He called me his girlfriend earlier, so why not?

They shake hands stiffly and I'm at a complete loss for words watching them. This is not good. I just stare blankly at him, wanting him to vanish, but he keeps looming over us.

"Can I talk to you for a minute?" He asks.

I turn to Jack and kiss him on the cheek. "I'll be right back." He doesn't look too happy.

Mark is standing just a few feet away, but I walk even further, not wanting Jack to hear anything Mark has to say. "What's up, Mark?"

"I haven't seen you at yoga, so when I saw you here, I figured I'd finally have the chance to talk to you."

"About what?"

"You left me in the middle of the night."

I nod, embarrassed and angry that he's confronting me about a one-night stand. Shit! It was a two-night stand. Oh my God! Is my dream coming true? Mark had the number seven written on his chest and Christine was yelling in the background, 'no second dates'.

"Why did you leave?"

"I wasn't ready to date anyone at that time. It was just one of those…things."

"Was it me?"

"No, not at all." He's remarkably insecure.

"Are you just saying that?"

"Mark, it wasn't you. I'm sorry I left, but I'm on a date and can't talk to you now."

"I get it," there's bitterness in his voice.

"Take care."

"I don't want to bother you. I'll just *sneak* away and leave you alone," he says loudly, glaring at me.

I turn and walk toward Jack. Judging by his face, he heard what Mark just said. Hopefully, that's all he heard. I sit down, expecting the worst.

"What was that about?"

"Um… he wondered why I haven't called him."

"Called him? Did you date him?"

"Just once."

"All these guys were just once? Why didn't you call him?"

"I didn't like him."

"Did you tell him that?"

"Sort of. I told him I was dating you and that I wasn't interested."

"Oh. He seemed pissed."

"A little. Come on, the past is in the past, right?"

"I know." He plays with his coaster.

Why do we keep running into my samples? This is not helping Jack to trust me and my choices. It makes him nervous and suspicious. He pulls away each time it happens. I know he wants to be with me, but he's doesn't want to get hurt. He's opening his heart to me for the first time since university…I need to tell him…or show him how I feel.

"Jack, what are you doing next weekend?

"I'm not sure. Why?"

"I'm off on Friday and don't have any plans. Is there any way you can get Friday off too and we can spend the weekend together? Maybe we could go away."

"The entire weekend?" He seems deep in thought.

It was way too soon. "It was just a thought. Don't worry."

"No, it's a great idea. Do you really want to go somewhere with me?" He rubs my thigh.

Flip flop. "Without a doubt. We could go to Niagara Falls."

"I'm not sure we should do that yet." He shakes his head. "Not that I don't want you to meet my parents, I just don't think we have any self-control."

"What do you mean by that?" Knowing full well what he means.

"You can't keep your hands off of me and that would be weird around my parents. I can't have you all over me while we're eating together."

"Me?" I laugh and swat him. "You're worse than I am."

"It's true. I can't help myself." His hand travels up my thigh, close to my sex.

"Jack!" I quietly warn, but am turned on at the same time.

"Want to skip the game?"

Yes! I move in to kiss him lightly on the lips. "I want to do what you want to do."

He raises his hands in surrender, "Let's order some food and watch the game."

"You tease."

28.

The Toronto Maple Leafs are playing the Ottawa Senators and there's no score at the end of the first period.

"Could we have the cheque, please?" Jack asks the pouty-lipped waitress. She nods and leaves the table. She's given up on Jack. "Do you want to go down to our seats?"

"Sure." I'm a little uneasy about meeting his friends for some reason. I have a sip of beer, but when Jack figures out a tip, I down the rest of my glass, hoping it'll take the edge off.

He stands up suddenly and grabs my hand. "Let's go."

Jack finds the right section and we head down the steep steps. He keeps going and going and finally stops two rows from the glass, right behind the Leafs bench.

"No way! Here?"

"Yup! We're those two empty seats in the middle," he points.

The entire row consists of men drinking beer and they stand and smile as I walk by. I smile back, just in case they're Jack's friends.

Jack follows and I hear him greet some of the guys. When he sits beside me, he reaches over me to bump knuckles with the man to my right. "Hey, Aaron. This is Colleen."

"Hi, Colleen. Nice to meet you." Aaron is slightly balding, but has a nice smile.

"Hi." I shake his hand.

"Over here is Cam, Jeff and Dwayne." He points to three men beside him. I just wave and smile shyly.

"Want a beer?" Jack asks.

"Yes, please." I'm still nervous.

Jack waves his hand at the server for this VIP section and she's oblivious to him, staring straight ahead at the intermission show on the ice. A couple of guys are taking shots on net from centre ice for prizes. He and his friends yell for her attention, but she doesn't hear.

"I give up," Jack says

I stand up, turning to the server and put my first two fingers in my mouth, whistling piercingly loud. The server jolts out of her trance and looks in my direction. When I wave at her, she smiles and starts clambering down the aisle.

Before I sit down, I notice that every one of Jack's friends is staring at me, smiling. The guy to Jack's left, I think it's Cam, holds his hand up for a high five. I slap it, feeling pleased with myself.

Aaron leans across me and says to Jack, "She's a keeper."

I blush and Jack pats my thigh. "Yes, she is." He orders beer for everyone from the server.

The crowd suddenly erupts angrily and I stand up to see what happened. I didn't even know second period started. The Senators scored in the first forty seconds.

"Dammit!" I sit down heavily. Jack and Aaron both laugh at me.

"It's still early." Jack squeezes my knee and kisses my cheek.

I turn my head quickly and snag a kiss. "The Leafs have to win on our very first date."

"What if they don't?"

"We're cursed," I joke.

"Nice."

The arena explodes again with boos and hissing.

"What did I miss now?"

"Senators scored again," Aaron says.

"Fuck!"

"We're going to be cursed because of you," Jack says, laughing.

The server comes back with our beer and I watch the ice as Jack pays.

"No! No! Get it out of there!" I yell. It's a power play and the Senators are all over our end. The Leafs can't get it out.

"Shit!" The Senators score again.

Jack hands me my beer and I down half of it. "Come on, Toronto!" I scream.

"Baby, you're adorable," Jack whispers in my ear.

"Hey! Pay attention," I point to the ice, giggling.

Jack looks quickly at the Senators end and the Leafs left winger, Lupul gets one by the goalie.

"Score!" I jump up and down. I feel Jack beside me. He's just as excited.

"Are you happy now?" He asks as we sit down

"No, we're still down."

"I'm sure we'll even it up. Now what were you saying about next weekend?"

"We could go somewhere or just stay in all weekend. Is there anywhere you want to go?"

"I like the idea of going away with you."

"Do you think it's too soon? It's not really taking it slow."

"I think we're on the right road. It wouldn't hurt us at all."

We discuss options and are enthusiastically interrupted by two more goals by the Leafs. My faith in the Leafs is restored. At the end of the second period, the game is tied and we've decided on a trip to Coburg. One of Jack's clients told him about cottages on Lake Ontario with fireplaces and Jacuzzi tubs. It sounds very romantic. It's only about ninety minutes away and we even discussed taking the train. We're very eager to make the reservations and find things to do in the small town. I can't believe we've made these plans and haven't even been intimate yet, but I have no doubt about our passion or compatibility. I'm excited!

"Do you want more beer?" Aaron asks.

Jack looks at me and I nod. "Yes, two please."

Aaron leaves, along with the guys on the other side of Jack.

"Where do you know these guys from?"

"We've played hockey together for years. It's just a pick-up league, but we're very competitive."

"I bet. I love that you play hockey."

"We bought season tickets as a group and try to go together every game. You'll be able to see as many games as you like, if you stick with me."

"That's a pretty good incentive. You may be stuck with me."

"I don't mind." He looks around, "We're alone now. What do you want to do?" He eyes me playfully.

"Kiss me."

Jacks leans in, placing his lips on mine and kisses me deeply. My stomach goes crazy with butterflies and my heart feels like it's going to burst. I reach for his neck and feel his hand on my hip, pulling at my jeans. I'm lost in the moment and I don't care who's watching.

A few minutes later, not surprising us at all, we hear cat calls, whistling and someone yells the old catch-phrase, "Get a room!"

We pull apart and see that his friends are back. I blush and sit back in my chair.

"Grow up," Jack says, laughing with them.

Aaron walks past me and hands me a beer. When he sits down, he leans toward me, "You must be pretty special."

"Why do you say that?"

"Jack's never brought a girl to a game before. He has a cousin that he usually brings, but he brought you instead."

I smile, hugging myself. I look at Jack talking to his friends and he's so animated and…gorgeous. And he likes me. I suddenly do feel pretty special.

Jack grabs my hand and holds it the entire third period, which ends in a tie: 4-4. Three-on-three overtime follows and no one scores during the thrilling five minutes of play. This means a shootout will start and the entire arena is on its feet.

The Leafs go first and score! I go crazy with the crowd. Then, it's the Senators turn and they miss. I jump up and down and jostle Jack on purpose. He laughs and pats my bottom.

Toronto misses the next one and the Senators score. We're tied again. Jack pushes up my seat and stands behind me, with his arms around my waist, waiting for the next shots on net.

It's Lupul's turn and he skates hard across the red line, handling the puck swiftly and easily. He does a quick stutter step, a fake and then strikes the puck toward the awaiting goalie. "Ping!" The puck hits the crossbar of the net.

"That's ok. We can still win if the Senators miss."

The Senators player skates wide and brings the puck slowly around to the left of the goalie, but gets in front of him quickly, pulling back and firing the puck. It lifts off the ice and hits the top right corner inside the net. The Senators win.

"Dammit!"

Jack hugs me hard and kisses the top of my head. "That sucks. We're cursed." He takes my hand to start leading me down the aisle.

"That's not funny," I say, but not really believing in the curse.

"Are you guys coming out for drinks?" Aaron asks.

I look at Jack and he scrunches up his nose. "I don't think so. Do you want to go?" He asks me.

"No," I shake my head and squeeze his hand.

"You heard the lady. We're outta here."

"It was great meeting you." I shake a few of the guys' hands and when we get to the top of the section I watch Jack grab Stan's hand and Stan pulls him in close to tell him something. They're both looking at me and I feel slightly uncomfortable, but Jack winks at me and laughs at Stan, nodding.

Jack walks up to me, "He says you have a nice ass."

29.

"I'm going to say good night now," he says when we get on my front porch.

I glare at him, mid-yawn. "You're not going to come in for a bit or…" I rub his arm, "Overnight?"

"You've been yawning all the way home and I'm tired too. You kept me up late last night."

I pout, "Come in for a few minutes. Please," I beg.

"I'll come in to make sure you're safe, but the cops just pulled up. I know you'll be fine."

I look toward the street and see the police car. I wish they weren't here, so Jack would have a reason to stay the night. I get my mail from the mailbox and unlock the door. Inside, I turn off the alarm and Jack closes the door behind us. I throw the mail and my purse on the counter.

Jack pushes me against the counter and kisses me. I bring my arms up and place my hands on his chest. He grabs my bottom. "You do have a great ass. Stan was right."

"Is that so?" I bite his bottom lip and he winces. I release it and kiss it gently. "All I care about is you liking it."

"I love it." He grabs it tighter.

I kiss his neck and travel my lips and tongue up to his ear, whispering, "Are you sure you don't want to stay with me tonight?"

"As much as I want to say yes, we need to rest up for tomorrow night."

"What's tomorrow night?"

"A surprise."

"Another surprise?"

"Yup."

"You spoil me." I jump up and down, knocking the mail onto the floor.

Jack bends down and picks up the mail, pausing on one piece. "Oh, um… You got a postcard from your car dealer?" He questions, waving it at me. "I didn't mean to read it. It's pretty personal." He hands it to me and watches my face as I read it:

"Let me know if I can ride you in your new car. John."

Fuck! What's with these samples ruining my night and my life? Will I ever live down the stupid Sex Project?

"Why we would he write something like that?"

"I don't know," I say quietly.

"That's pretty ballsy of him, don't you think?"

"Yeah." How can I keep my Sex Project a secret if this keeps happening?

"Was he a prick when he sold you the car?"

"Kind of."

"What an asshole. I can go down there and kick his ass, if you want." A vein pops out of his neck.

"No, don't do that. It's fine. I won't ever see him again," I try to brush it off. "No harm, no foul."

"It doesn't bother you?"

"It's just flirting."

"This is not flirting. This is disgusting. I would never say that to a woman. This isn't even funny."

I snap, "It doesn't matter. He was a jerk. End of story."

He shakes his head in disbelief, "I don't get it. Did something happen with this guy?"

"Not at all. Can we stop talking about him?" I hate lying to him, but I can't tell him the truth.

"First, it was the guy at the restaurant tonight and now this. Not to mention the others we've run into. How many men have you dated since you separated from Steve?"

"Jack, come on. It's no big deal. You've dated for years. I'm sure we'll run into one of your exes at some point."

"The difference is that you told me you wanted your husband back. You had some plan, remember? Did it include dating all these men?" He takes a step away from me.

Do I tell him? "I dated, but none of it meant anything. I did want Steve back, but I learned through dating that Steve was not meant for me and I deserved better."

"How could dating teach you that?"

"When one guy opened the door for me or another listened to every word I said or made me feel pretty. That's how I knew. Steve never did any of that."

"If all of these guys made you feel this way, why are you with me? Why don't you keep dating them?"

I walk toward him and hold my hands out to him. "I want you. You have all of those qualities and more. You treat me like a princess and listen to me babble on about the Leafs and make me feel beautiful, inside and out. You make me feel like the most important person in the room, but you also make me want you to feel that way. I'd do anything for you. I hope you know that."

He takes my hands and starts to say something, but I shake my head. "Let me finish. It took me awhile to figure things out and realize that you're someone that I want in my life." I take a deep breath, "Maybe for the rest of my life, if you'll have me."

Jack stares into my eyes and seems to soften during my last few words. "Colleen," he whispers. "That means the world to me." He kisses me hard and almost desperately. I kiss him back, trying to give him the reassurance he needs.

He finally release me, "I wish this conversation took place tomorrow?"

"Why?"

"I'd make love to you."

Flip flop. "Baby, come upstairs with me." I tug on his sweater.

"No," he says roughly and kisses me again. "You need your sleep and so do I. I still want to take things slow, but you're making it very difficult. I have a lot to think about."

"There's nothing to think about it. Don't you believe me?"

"I believe you. I guess I'm the one who needs time. Just give me the night."

"Don't leave me alone," I beg.

"Don't make me feel bad."

"I'm sorry. I just don't want you to go." I rub his arms. "I'll be fine. Go get your sleep."

"Call me if you need anything. At any time."

"Ok."

"It doesn't matter what time it is."

"I understand," I say smiling.

"Meet me tomorrow morning at the café."

"Sure." I kiss him again and press my whole body against his.

"Good night."

Two seconds after he leaves, I text him:

"I miss you already."

After a minute, my phone beeps:

"Me too. Sleep well, baby."

My heart aches and I hug the phone to my chest. Before I turn off the lights, I take a peek at the police car for comfort. For a moment, I think about Mr. Baker and his threats, realizing I haven't thought about him much at all today. I've been happily side-tracked, but being alone for the first time in days makes me feel defenseless and a bit scared. I want to call Jack, but I don't want him to think I'm being a baby.

No, I'm fine. "Go to bed, Colleen!" I say aloud.

30.

Standing in line at the café, I feel a hand graze my lower back. "Good morning, beautiful." Jack kisses my cheek. "Did you sleep well?"

"Yes," I lie. Unfortunately, Mr. Baker stayed on my mind most of the night and it made me nervous, believing that the normal noises in my house were actually him. I got up a few times to check for the police car and each time it was there, but when I would go back to bed, I would hear another noise and assume the cops left. It was a never-ending cycle.

"I know I only had you in my bed one night, but I missed sleeping next to you."

"Me too."

"We'll have to remedy that tonight," he winks.

"Really?"

"Good morning, what can I get you?" The cheery barista asks.

"Cinnamon latte?" Jack turns to me.

"No," I say quickly. "Could I have a chai tea latte instead?"

"I've got this," he says and finishes ordering.

I stand to the side, wishing it was later in the day. It's going to be unbearable to have to wait all day to see him, knowing that I'm going home with him tonight and possibly having sex with him!

Jack comes up behind me, putting his arms around my waist. I hold onto his hands and squeeze tightly.

"What's the plan tonight?" I ask.

"After work, I'll meet you at your house around six-thirty."

"Ok."

"I want you to pack an overnight bag."

Flip flop. I squeeze his hands again in excitement.

"Actually, pack an over-weekend bag. I'm not sure when I'm going to let you go."

I lean back, turning my head and lifting my lips up to kiss him. He meets me halfway and kisses me gently.

"Chai tea latte and an Americano?"

"That's us." Jack grabs our beverages and I open the café door for us to go outside.

"Do we have to say goodbye? I can't wait until six-thirty to see you," I whine and take my latte from him.

"Do you want to ditch work?" He steps in close and places a hand on my waist.

"I'd love to, but that wouldn't be very professional."

"I know," he mopes, but bends down to whisper in my ear, "I'd love to get you in my nice, warm bed right now."

Flip flop. "Oh?" He must've overcome his bad thoughts about me.

"I'd take off all your clothes and kiss every inch of that perfect body."

"Every inch," I can barely speak.

"I'd start with your toes and feet and travel up your gorgeous legs and…"

"And?"

"You want me to tell you what's next?"

"Yes," I breathe.

"You'll have to wait until tonight. I'll show you."

I groan, "You're a tease."

"You're the one who dropped her towel on purpose."

"That wasn't teasing. That was an invitation. You need to learn the difference."

"Is that so?" He squeezes my waist and ribs, tickling me.

"Enough," I laugh, wriggling out of his grasp. "I'm going to spill my latte."

"Get to work, trouble. I'll call you at lunch."

Our goodbye kiss is gentle, but still tantalizing. It leaves me wanting more.

A few minutes later, I meet Margie outside the office door. "Still smiling, I see." She unlocks the door.

"Yes I am. How are you, Margie?" I hold the door open for her.

"Not as good as you."

"You're right. I'm pretty damn good. Don't know if you could beat it."

She laughs, "Stop bragging and get inside. I'm sure you have an early appointment."

Brad Atwater and his mother come up the walk at that moment. I smile at Margie and welcome them in. "Come into my office, Brad." Time to start my day.

The ten-year-old has oppositional defiant disorder, which began when he was about four. His parents thought he was just a strong-willed and emotional child, but his patterns of anger, irritability, arguing, defiance and vindictiveness lead them to seek therapy for him when he was eight.

"How are you today?" I close the door behind us.

"Good."

"Have a seat."

Before he sits down, he takes the Etch-A-Sketch off the shelf and starts playing with it on the couch across from me. I groan inwardly. He knows he's supposed to ask permission first. This is going to be trouble. "How's school?"

"Fine."

"How are your parents?"

"The same."

"What's going on at home?"

"The same," he repeats.

"Remember our deal? Answer my questions first and I'll let you play."

"Fine, I didn't want to play with it anyway." He throws the Etch-A-Sketch to the far end of the couch.

"Tell me what's been going on with your parents," I ignore his outburst. I already know that his parents have said everything with him is a hassle. Minor requests to clean up his room, do his homework, or help with housework are consistently met with protest. He can't tolerate having anyone tell him what to do and often storms to his room, slamming the door.

"They boss me around all the time. I'm ten now and can take care of myself."

"What do you do when they boss you around?"

"I get angry." He kicks his feet up and drops them down, hitting the floor loudly.

"How do you react?"

"I get angry and go to my room."

"Do you yell at them?"

"Yeah."

"Do you think yelling at them is right? Do they deserve it?"

He plays with his hands on his lap. "No. They just push me too much and make me mad."

"Do they ask you to do things when you're in the middle of watching T.V. or playing video games?"

"Sometimes."

"You get annoyed by this?"

"Yeah."

"You must be annoyed all the time. My aunt used to always tell me to clean my room, take out the garbage, wash the dishes, and do my homework. It never stopped and I hated it. Are you grumpy when you're home?"

"Yeah."

"Do you feel like you're grumpy all the time?"

"Sort of."

"Do you like being grumpy?"

"No, but I can't help it."

We've been focusing on treatment to decrease power struggles, reinforce positive behaviour and create logical consequences for behaviours. This time I remind him that his chores have to be done daily and his parents will keep asking him to complete them every day. It's a part of growing up and being responsible. "How can you prepare for doing chores?"

"I could do it before they ask."

"That's a very intelligent answer." I watch as a smile spreads across his face. "Your parents would be very impressed if you did that. I don't think they'd bug you ever again. What if you had a chart that listed all your daily chores and you could cross them out when you completed them?"

"I don't know."

"You could keep it on the fridge and complete it when you had time. Each time you do a chore without being reminded or without a fight, you could collect points."

"Points?"

"Yes, earning a certain amount of points could award you a treat."

"Like a video game?"

"That could be an end of month reward. A weekly treat could be staying up an hour later on the weekend or—

"Or going to the trampoline place?"

"Maybe. You'd have to discuss your rewards with your parents. I'm sure there's a lot of things that you could think of for a reward."

"They don't let me play my X-Box on Sundays and that's when all my friends are on it. Playing on a Sunday could be a reward."

"That's a great idea. But what happens if you get angry or don't complete your chores? What do you think should happen?"

"I get grounded?" He frowns.

"No, that doesn't match your actions. I think that you just wouldn't collect any points that day. You'd have to make up the points by doing your chores for the rest of the week."

"No grounding?"

"Nope. However, if you don't do your chores all week, you don't get the weekly reward and will probably have to do them all on Saturday or Sunday instead of doing what you want to do."

"Oh, I guess that's ok."

"I'm going to go talk to your mom. Stay and play with the Etch-A-Sketch and I'll be right back." He reaches for it, picks it up and starts spinning the knobs.

I walk to the reception area and Mrs. Atwater comes to stand in front of me. "Brad recognizes that he gets angry and annoyed easily. We've discussed a chore schedule with rewards and consequences and he's excited to start it."

"Brad wants to do a chore schedule?" She asks disbelievingly.

"Yes, he seems to be interested. I'll give you the information. It outlines how to implement that sort of a schedule." I turn to Margie, "Can you find Mrs. Atwater the pamphlet about behaviour modification?"

"No problem," Margie opens her file cabinet and rifles through her collection of pamphlets.

"Read it over and call me if you have any questions."

"Thanks, Dr. Cousineau."

I walk to my door, "Brad, it's time to go." As he walks toward me, I say, "Make sure you create this chart with your parents and add chores that are reasonable during a week. The fun part is deciding what reward you want, Brad, but realize they can't be super expensive."

Brad doesn't even say goodbye. He's already negotiating rewards with his mom. I'm happy that he's excited to start. "Behaviour modification. It works every time," I state, watching them head down the walkway.

Margie laughs, "I should use it on my husband with gardening and lawn maintenance."

"What would you reward him with, dare I ask?"

She blushes, "Wouldn't you like to know."

31.

My last patient leaves and I start to get butterflies knowing that I'm meeting Jack and staying at his apartment for the entire weekend!

Margie and I leave the office together. "Have a wonderful weekend!" I sing.

"I already know that you will," she giggles. "Say hi to Jack for me."

I take a detour before I go home to Agent Provocateur, a luxury lingerie boutique on Bloor Street. Somehow, I've been added to their mailing list and I've received catalogues of their sensuous and cheeky collections. I've browsed, but I've never been. I need some new lingerie and Jack definitely deserves it.

After stepping foot in the door, I'm in awe of the boutique. It's a classy and sexy boudoir with black and grey lace carpets, seventies fixtures and mirrors, all giving it an art-deco feel. A couple of ladies dressed in pink housecoats are walking around and one approaches me immediately, "Can I help you?"

"Do you work here?"

"Yes," she titters. "The robes encourage a playful attitude." She opens it to show me the pink and black bra and panties that she's wearing. "This is the Fifi collection. It is made from sheer pleated tulle, overlaid with French Chantilly lace and ribbon seams."

"It's beautiful," I say, but have stopped looking at her half-naked body. "I'm looking for something like that."

I choose a nude, plunge bra overlaid with scalloped, black eyelash lace and a tiny bow adds the perfect final touch between the cups. The matching hipster briefs have a playful peekaboo lace flap that I find extremely sexy. I also choose a white barely-there tulle bra and hipster panties. The delicate floral embroidery appears to float over my breasts and hips. They're basically see-through and I think Jack will love them.

After spending an insane amount of money, I rush home to take a shower, scrubbing my entire body with a citrus-scented body wash and shaving my legs as well as other surfaces of my body. I mentally plan what I need to pack. Jack might think I'm high maintenance if I pack too much, but he already knows that I'm not. I'm overthinking! I'm excited!

After I use my hairdryer, I throw it and a bag of toiletries on all of the clothes that are already in my bag. It seems like way too much. I take a thick, fleece sweater out. That's better.

Now what to wear? I scan the racks and scrunch my nose up at everything. Why am I making this harder than it is? It's just clothes. First, I take off the tags on all of the lingerie and choose the white, sheer set to wear tonight. I look at myself in the full-length mirror from all angles, anticipating Jack's response. Then, I stand in front of my clothes, staring up at them with my hands on my hips.

Jack said it's a surprise. It's hard to decide what to wear when I don't know where I'm going! I opt for jeans, but stop. Jeans are difficult to maneuver in and out of and they wouldn't do this lingerie justice. A dress? Or a skirt? He did say that I should always wear dresses.

"Argh!" I howl.

I pull a dark gray, asymmetrical tee shirt dress from a hanger and put it on. It clings to my body in all the right places. I pair it with my gray suede boots, leaving my legs bare. Perfect.

The doorbell rings and my heart jumps. I grab my bag and run down the stairs like a school girl, heading to the door to turn off the alarm.

I throw open the door. "Hi."

"Wow! You look fantastic."

"Thanks. You're not so bad yourself. Wait!" I inspect his face. "You shaved!"

"I did."

I reach up and run his baby face, sulking. "Your scruff's all gone."

"You like the scruff?"

"Yes," I mope.

"I didn't know that." He takes me in his arms. "I shaved just for you. I'm sorry."

Standing on my tiptoes, I put my hands on his shoulders and lean into him. "That's ok. It'll grow back." I kiss his soft chin. "It's not so bad."

He makes a face. "I'm glad you approve." His face softens and he kisses me.

I reach my hands up and pull my fingers through the back of his hair. "Just don't get rid of this." I yank on it.

"A woman who loves scruff and hockey hair? You're one in a million."

"Just to be clear…I like the look on you. Only you. I wouldn't change a thing."

"Aren't you sweet?" This time his kiss is deep and urging.

I respond with equal insistence, leaning my body against his. The thin material of my dress makes it easy to feel his solid manhood. I groan into his mouth.

His hands move up my back and I feel him clutch my dress, pulling it away from my body. If he wants it off, I'm game. I kiss him hungrily to tell him he has permission, but his grip loosens and he begins to run my back lightly. He pulls away from my lips.

"We need to stop," his voice is coarse. "I have plans."

Can't we skip it all and go to bed? "What plans?"

He winks and squeezes my hand. "Is that your bag?"

"You're ignoring me?"

"I'm going to assume that this is your overnight bag." He scoops it up and throws it over his shoulder. "Are you ready to go?"

I laugh and get my long, wool coat from the closet. "I'm ready. Take me where you want and do what you want with me."

"That's dangerous." He lowers his eyes, smiling flirtatiously.

Flip flop. He's the dangerous one. I try to ignore him and set the alarm, locking up. He waits for me and takes my hand as we walk to his truck.

Inside, he leans over the console and stares at me for a second, before kissing me. "You're beautiful."

I smile small and duck my head, letting my curls hide my face.

"You're not allowed to be shy around me." He starts the truck and the five litre engine growls.

I'm never going to get used to the noise. "I'm not shy."

He pats my hand, "We'll soon see about that."

Now, I'm confused and a little nervous. "You're going to test my shyness?"

"Dinner first and then, the shyness test."

Oh no.

"You shouldn't be worried. It'll be fun."

We only drive a few blocks and he lucks out, finding a parking spot on John Street. He helps me out of the truck and holds my hand as we walk down the hectic street. There are many restaurants on this block, as well as lounges and a grand hotel. People and cars permeate the area, creating a dynamic and stimulating entertainment district. This is Toronto to me.

Jack leads me to *N'awlins Jazz Bar* where the music exuding from it sounds like a bunch of relatively random notes and seems to have no real structure or recognizable melody. That's jazz. It's a nice change.

Stepping inside, we can see that it's packed and the music is overwhelming. Black and white photos of Jazz legends, like Charlie Parker, Dizzie Gillespie and Miles Davis hang on the walls and the band is playing in the back corner of the restaurant. I smell seafood and realize that they offer a Cajun-Creole style menu, which I love. The atmosphere's boisterous and flamboyant, but it's not what I had in mind for a romantic evening.

A long-haired brunette greets us at the door and yells over the music, "We don't have any tables open right now."

"Can we sit outside?"

I look at Jack in surprise and shout close to his ear, "Isn't it too cold?"

"They have propane heaters. We could always come in or go somewhere else if it's too cold." I nod and he turns back to the girl. "Is that all right?"

"I don't see a problem with it." She grabs two menus and escorts us back outside to a table close to the door. She steps up to the heater and reaches for the knob above her head. In seconds, the heater fires up and emits warmth.

Jack pulls his chair close to mine, "This is cozy. I bet we're the only people sitting on a patio in November."

"Love it." I kiss his cheek.

He places his hand on my bare knee and rubs it carefully. "Are you sure you're warm enough?"

"Yes, I'll tell you if I get cold."

An older waiter comes up to the table, "Are you guys ok with being outside? A table just opened up inside."

"What do you think?" He asks me.

"I like it out here."

He turns back to the server, "As long as you don't mind serving out here, we'd like to stay."

"I don't mind at all. It actually cools me off. What can I get you to drink?"

"Do you want wine?"

I scrunch up my nose, "I feel like beer. Is that ok?"

"It's great. Two large draughts, please."

"Does beer convey romance?" I ask.

"It does to me." He sits back in his chair and stares at me. "How are you doing?"

"Me? I'm great. Why do you ask?"

"Just wondering."

"I've been looking forward to tonight all day and if I haven't thanked you already, I have to say that I've really enjoyed the last few days with you. Thank you for spending time with me."

"It's my pleasure. Have you talked to Steve?"

I'm taken aback by his question. "Steve? No. Why would I?"

"He hasn't called you?"

"No. Why would he?" I really don't like talking about Steve. I just want to enjoy the night and our time together.

"Just curious."

I sit back in my chair and take a deep breath. Jack must be concerned or uneasy again. I lean in towards him and put my hand on his thigh. "Steve is in my past. That part of my life is closed. I have no regrets or any feelings for him. I want to move onto the next stage of my life with you."

"You've pushed me away so many times to be with Steve. It's hard to accept that it's over between you two."

"I'm here now and I'm not leaving. You have nothing to worry about." I kiss him to cement my affirmations. "Try to remember that."

Our waiter comes back and spouts out the day's specials, but I can barely concentrate with Jack's hand sliding up my thigh. It's really distracting. Jack takes his hand away to read the menu and I get goosebumps. I'm so content. I feel so relaxed and peaceful sitting outside on the patio with Jack, without a care in the world. Steve would've been worked up at the noise levels in the restaurant or the fact that there weren't any tables. He never would've sat alone with me on the patio. He always needed people around him to make fun of or to notice him. Worst case: Steve would've sworn at the hostess and we would've left to find another restaurant. It's hard not to compare the two when Jack is the complete opposite of Steve. Jack wants to be with me and I don't think it matters where we are or who we're with.

"Do you know what you're having?"

We discuss the menu items, tell the waiter our selections and discuss last night's hockey game. During the meal, he also tells me more about his friends and some of their escapades in university. We eat at a leisurely pace and our conversation reminds me of the ones we used to have in my kitchen: Easy-going, funny and genuine. Every once in a while, he'll touch my knee, kiss me gently or rub my back. He's very affectionate and I reciprocate as much as I can. I love touching him.

The waiter takes our dirty dishes and Jack looks at his phone. "We should be going soon."

My heart starts to race. "Is this the part in the evening where you're going to test my shyness?"

"It's coming soon."

"Will we be doing this at your house?"

"That could come much later in the evening," he grins. "But no, we're going somewhere else right now."

Jack pays the bill and we exit the patio, holding hands. We walk past his truck and down the block. I try to stay tight to him, trying not to get separated by the crowd. At a red light, he steps in front of me and kisses me lightly. When he pulls back, I smile, squeezing his hand. He squeezes back. The light turns green and we continue walking, until he stops in front of a nondescript building and opens the door.

I step inside, but have no idea what I'm about to walk into. I can hear singing. Bad singing. Really bad singing.

The hallway opens up into a dim lounge with a handful of people sitting at tables. I step further inside and to my right is a stage with a woman singing into a microphone.

"Karaoke?" I panic. I can't sing.

"Don't worry." He pulls me to a table, pulling my chair out for me, but when I sit down, he leaves me to talk to a man at the bar. After a few minutes, he comes back.

"Jack, I'm a horrible singer."

"You're not horrible. I've heard you sing before."

"When?"

You sing when you're cooking and you don't think anyone's listening."

Shit. He's right. I punch him lightly in the arm. "You heard me? That's beside the point. That's at home, in private. I can't do this."

The man from the bar walks over with a tray lined with shot glasses full of a clear liquid, limes and salt.

"Tequila?" I ask, laughing.

"Liquid courage." He pays the man and offers me the salt

I've used that saying before with my Sex Project samples. I snatch it from him. "I don't know if this will help." I set up my shot.

Jack downs it without all the fixings. "I'll go first." He bends down to kiss me and walks up to the stage. I'm shocked to see how easy it is for him to go up there. I tip the shot into my mouth and chew on the lime, watching him.

A man helps him set up his music and raises the microphone to Jack's height. I hear the beginnings of a song. It's an upbeat country song.

"I only wanted to catch your attention
But you overlooked me somehow.
Besides you had too many boyfriends to mention
And I played my guitar too loud."

The lyrics are spiteful and almost bang on with what happened between me and Jack, but I don't think he chose the song for that reason. I shake that thought off and focus on his voice. He's got a great voice. It even has that country twang. I notice that he fits the part too. He's wearing a plaid button-down shirt with his jeans and the sleeves are a bit too tight over his biceps. He just needs a cowboy hat. I gape at him in appreciation.

"How do you like me now,
Now that I'm on my way?
Do you still think I'm crazy
Standin' here today?"

When he finishes, I'm the only one who applauds and cheers. I put my two fingers in my mouth and whistle loudly.

Jack comes back to the table beaming. "How was that?"

"You were unbelievable. You have such a great voice. Do you do this a lot?"

"I've come here with the guys a few times after hockey, just for fun. There's never anyone here at this time, so it's not too intimidating. It gets busy later with the drunk kids."

"I don't know if I can do this."

He pats my hand, "I'll get the song list and we can look at it together." He turns on his heels and goes up to the stage, coming back with a binder.

Still feeling wary about singing, I browse through the titles slowly, hoping a mad rush of drunk people come into the bar. A man does get up on the stage and starts singing *Living La Vida Loca*. He's horrible and it makes me more uneasy.

"We could do a song together?" He suggests.

That makes me feel a bit better. "Which one?"

"*Ebony and Ivory*?"

"Seriously?" I laugh.

"Kidding. How about *I've Got You Babe*?"

I think for a quick second, "No, it's not my favourite era." The man on stage finishes and I lightly clap out of respect, hoping he'll do the same when I sing atrociously.

"*I've Had the Time of My Life*?"

"Getting closer. Keep that one in mind." I turn a few pages and I find the perfect song. "I've got it. Can I surprise you with it?"

"What if I don't know it?"

"You'll know it." I stand up and do another shot. Jack does the same. The tequila warms my insides and makes my legs feel like rubber. The alcohol is working.

We walk up to the stage and I whisper to the man, "*Picture* by Kid Rock and Sheryl Crow."

"Got it." He hands me a second microphone.

"You ready?"

"No," I swallow.

He smiles and chuckles, "You'll do great." The music comes on and Jack recognizes it immediately. "Great choice.," he mouths. He's up first:

> '*Livin' my life in a slow hell,*
> *Different girl every night at the hotel.*
> *I ain't seen the sun shine in three damn days.*"

Jack sings it well and my butterflies act up. I take few deep, long breaths, preparing for my part.

> '*I called you last night in the hotel,*
> *Everyone knows but they won't tell.*
> *But their half-hearted smiles tell me*
> *Somethin' just ain't right.*"

I pulled it off! I don't think I faltered or sounded too bad. I avoided Jack's eyes the entire time, just to be safe.

When we sing at the same time, I look at Jack for a second and I almost start giggling out of nervousness, but I choke it down. During the last line, I stare at him intentionally as we sing together,

> *"I just called to say, I love you*
> *Come back home."*

The song's over and I hand the microphone back to the man. Jack puts his arm around me and we walk off the stage.

"You did great."

"Thanks for saying that, but you were the one that carried us."

"Whatever. You have a very sweet voice." He hugs me tightly. "Are you ready to go?" He whispers in my ear.

"Really? No more singing?" I'm so relieved.

"Do you want to do another one?"

"Hell no!"

"Then let's get out of here."

32.

Jack grabs two bottles of beer from the fridge and we head upstairs to his man cave. He places the beer on the fireplace mantle and opens up a large chest, pulling out furry-looking blankets and some pillows. He lays them out on the floor in front of the fire, turning it on with a flick of the switch.

"Instant romance."

"Are you trying to seduce me, Mr. Fraser?"

"Maybe." He grabs the beer. "Is it working?"

"A little." I take a bottle from him and we sit on the floor.

We put pillows under our bodies, trying to get comfortable and we end up half-lying on our sides, facing each other.

"I had a great time tonight. Thank you."

"You're welcome. I think we'd have fun doing anything."

"I was thinking that exact thing tonight. It wouldn't matter what we did or who we did it with. I just like being with you." I get shy all of a sudden.

"What's wrong? You can't be shy now, after singing with me."

"Nothing's wrong. I just don't know what I'm able to say to you."

"You can say anything."

"That's just it. I know I can, but I'm afraid to express anything too quick because you said you wanted to go slow. All of these feelings for you are coming to light and I want to tell you, but I don't want to scare you off or make you think that I fall in love easily."

"You're in love with me?" He asks incredulously.

"See! No, I didn't mean it that way." I don't know why I'm worried. He told me that he loved me not too long ago. "I really like you and I want you to know."

He moves over and kisses my forehead. "Colleen, telling me that you like me is not a bad thing. I feel the same way and it's nice to hear."

"Did I just blow that?"

"Not at all." He kisses me gently and places his hand on my hip.

I bite his lower lip softly and pursue his tongue with my own, nudging it and taunting it. His grip on my dress tightens and he pulls me slightly to him, but stops. "Can I take your beer from you? It's in the way."

I nod, feeling my heart in my throat. I'm so excited to be finally lying with him again, knowing and hoping that there's a chance we might make love.

When the beer is safely out of the way, he scoots closer to me and sneaks his bottom arm below the pillow that's under my head. His body is lined up with mine with only our thighs skimming against each other, but he just gazes me. I hope he can see the desire for him in my eyes. My whole body is shaking with anticipation and I can't wait any longer.

I kiss him, bringing my hand to his shoulder and pulling at him lightly. I want him to be as close to me as he can. The hand that's on my hip caresses my bottom and he slowly inches my bare leg over his hips. My dress rises further as he strokes my bare skin. The leverage I get with my thigh over his hips allows me to grind against his groin. I wrap my leg around him and hold him tight.

All of a sudden, he rolls on his back, pulling me on top of him. He brings both hands to my bottom, which is completely uncovered now, except for my sheer panties. He cups and squeezes it, as he pulls me down over the length of him. I feel every wrinkle in his jeans, as well as the hardness of his impressive erection.

Slowly rocking, I continue to kiss him, each of my hands on the pillows beside his head. My hair has fallen into his face and I try to pull it back out of the way.

"Let those curls fall, Colleen."

I let them go and they frame his face. He attacks my mouth with desperation, kissing me from all angles, making me breathless.

Jack starts to sit up, lifting me and I bring my legs around on either side of him to sit between his and face him. "Let's get those boots off." I reach for the zipper, but he brushes my hands away. "I've got this." He unzips one boot and pulls it off and then does the other one, placing them an arm's length away.

"My turn." Staring with the top button on his shirt, I undo the row, down to the bottom and slip it over his shoulders. I lean in and kiss his bare chest, running my hands down his abdominal muscles.

His hands slide up my thighs and when he finds the bottom of my dress that has bunched up around my hips, he pulls it up over my head. I raise my arms to help.

Once it's off and thrown to the side, his eyes scan my body and my new lingerie. "Wow!"

"I just bought it today. Do you like it?" I whisper, feeling demure, but sexy.

"You look absolutely amazing." He lifts me up again and closes his legs. I wrap my legs around his hips and he fingers one of my nipples overtop of the bra. "Unfortunately, it's all going to have to come off." He slides one bra strap down from my shoulder, flipping the cup open to reveal the nipple he was playing with. He devours it and I throw my head back, moaning. Reaching behind my back, I unhook my bra and it falls in his face. He gently pulls it off of my arms and tosses it away.

"Hold onto me." I feel him lift me, so I hold onto his body tightly, crossing my heels around his waist. He lays me down on the blankets and hovers over me, smiling. He kisses me once, very lightly and then moves down my body, watching me. He goes right down to my feet and sits back on his knees, lifting one of my feet up to his mouth. He kisses my toes.

I smile and shiver with delight. He's going to kiss every inch of me, like he promised. I lift my arms over my head and let them fall onto the pillows behind my head.

It's a strange and erotic feeling to have my toes licked. His mouth is warm and moist on my cold extremities. He lifts my other foot and repeats the process. I want to giggle, but it's strangely stimulating too. He places it back on the floor and kisses my ankles, calves and then crawls up further to my knees. The lightness of his lips tickles the backs of my knees. I flinch and he laughs, but continues to my upper thighs. I take a deep breath and close my eyes.

"Look at me," he whispers.

My eyes blink open and I see him above my hips, his head close to my panties. He dips his head down and I feel his hot breath on my sex. He opens my thighs and gets between them, gently pressing on my sex with his tongue. I arch my back and lift my hips up slightly, flexing my legs and bottom. A pulse of electricity shoots through my body with every nudge.

His fingers delicately lift my panties away from my sex and I feel his tongue ever-so-lightly at my opening. He licks from the bottom, upwards, lingering on my clitoris. He pauses each time he arrives at the top, staring at me. Then, he begins the descent again. It's so intense. It's a slow and careful rhythm that's bringing me to my peak already. My breath quickens and I push my hips up to meet his mouth. The feelings are swirling around and accumulating inside my body. I'm ready to explode.

Suddenly, he stops, puts my panties back in place and gets on his knees to kiss my lower stomach and hips. I lift my head up to question him, but I can see the devilish smile on his face.

"Not yet, baby."

I drop my head down on the pillows in false frustration and smile. I don't want it to end either.

He kisses my ribs and ends at my breasts, partially lying on me, while he fondles and licks my nipples. I reach down and tug on the waistband of his jeans, wriggling my legs.

"You want these off?"

"Mmhmm," I murmur.

Jack stands up and takes off his jeans. He's left wearing his black boxer briefs and I stare at the vee, where his lower abs meet his hip flexors. It disappears into his underwear, where I see a different muscle bulging.

Holding his hands out for me to take, I comply and he pulls me to stand in front of him. He takes one of my hands and raises it above my head, twirling me around.

"What are you doing?" I ask, with my back to him.

"I had to see your panties. Those are insanely hot. I can see every inch of that delicious ass." He twirls me to face him and he kisses me, backing me up. I reach up and take a hold of his neck, for balance. Without warning, he lifts me up, putting my legs around his waist again. I squeeze tight and he continues to walk toward his bedroom.

He lays me down on his bed with my legs hanging over the edge and gently pulls down my panties. I lift my bum up for greater ease. He raises my panties to his mouth and kisses them, before he flings them across the room. I smile and bite my thumbnail in anticipation of his next move.

I watch him put his thumbs in his briefs and my mouth opens slightly waiting for it. Knowing that it's going to happen. In one swoop, he has his underwear down and I give his manhood a quick glance, getting very excited. He raises my legs, steps between them and I feel his tip at my entrance, which is still wet from his salaciousness.

I keep looking into Jack's eyes, waiting for him to enter me. He's either teasing me or everything is in slow motion. Maybe he's trying to savour the moment. I'll never forget this. The smile is gone from his eyes and has been replaced with a serious look. It's resolute even. He pushes a little more and I can feel his tip surge inside me, but he pulls out quickly.

The action repeats again and again, slowly and steadily. Every time he does it, I lift my hips up to take more of him, but he withdraws. It's driving me crazy. I need him inside of me. All of him.

He must be able to read my mind. The next time he thrusts, he fills me completely with his solid length and leaves it in, unmoving. My muscles contract around it, getting used to its girth and for the marvelous sensations it conjures inside of me. I begin to grind, but can't get any leverage with my legs in his hands. He watches me and smiles slyly, retreating slowly, but not all the way. Then, just as meticulously, he pushes back in. It feels like he's re-opening me each time and I have to keep adjusting to him. It's entirely sensual and frustrating. My sex throbs with desire.

Finally, he releases my legs and I wrap them around his waist. He grabs my hips and starts plunging into me urgently, filling every inch of me. His forceful pace generates intense pleasure deep within me. I reach above my head to grip the blanket on the bed, trying to brace myself.

Jack slows down and leans over me, putting one nipple into his mouth. I cup his face with my hands and run my fingers through his hair, pulling it when I get a buzz of sensation from his nibbling.

He pulls out unexpectedly and crawls onto the bed over top of me. He grabs a pillow and throws it well beyond my head. "Move up," he mouths. I inch to the top of the bed, which is actually the side of the bed and lay back, bending my knees and planting my feet. He crawls up to meet me and I feel his hardness enter me at the same time he kisses me.

My hands maneuver all over his body, to his back, waist and I even grab his bare bottom, pulling him deeper into me. Our kissing is fierce and animalistic. I hear him groan and he starts to pumps harder and deeper. His stomach hits mine and I know he's as far as he can go.

Raw sensations wash over me and I can barely concentrate on kissing him. My moaning intensifies and my breathing escalates, bringing me to that ultimate peak. I grasp his cheeks and my body tenses up completely, with my hips as high as they can go and the orgasm takes control of me. I euphorically erupt, which generates a series of fervid convulsions throughout my entire body.

Jack pulls out as I'm still reveling in sensation and moves down between my thighs. He licks my sex and I jump slightly. It's very sensitive, but it feels wonderful. He stays down only a few minutes and comes up to lie beside me, lightly dragging his finger across my stomach.

I smile at him, jumping up to kiss him. I lick his lips and chin. "So that's what I taste like."

"You've never...?"

I shake my head.

"You taste really good."

"It's my turn." I push him onto his back and slither on top of him, kissing him lower and lower down his body. I spend some time on his abs, loving every inch of them.

When I go lower to his groin, I notice that he has a tattoo on his right hip. "Is that a dove?"

"Yup."

The mailman that delivered a package once had a dove tattoo on his neck.

"It represents—

"Steadfast love and devotion," I interrupt and outline the dove with my finger.

"How do you know?"

"I just do." My heart grows larger in my chest for this man. I almost start crying.

"Is something wrong?"

"Not at all," I choke back the tears. "I love it." I kiss it gently and continue with my plan to satisfy him.

I take his erection in both hands and marvel at the size of it. I lick it slowly from root to tip, swirling my tongue at the end. I do this continuously all around it and finish by putting the entire tip in my mouth and sucking hard as I release.

Jack moans and it encourages me to continue. I try to put all of him in my mouth and down my throat, but he's just too big, so I focus on what I can get in my mouth and stroke the rest with my hands. I get a good rhythm going and enjoy feeling the softness of it on my tongue. Jack groans loudly and pulls at my hair, so I keep going.

"Stop!" He takes a hold of my shoulders.

"What's wrong?" Am I doing it incorrectly?

"It feels too good, but I don't want to end it that way. Get up here."

That pleases me and I smile smugly as I creep up beside him.

"What are you smiling about?"

"I'm glad I can please you."

"I didn't have any doubts about that. Now, turn on your side. I want to see your perfect, little ass." I turn my back to him and he caresses my ass, pushing his hardness against it. "Open your legs a little." I do and he enters me quickly, persuading my leg back down.

Holy! It feels much bigger in this position. He's going to split me in two! I reach behind me to touch his hip and he reaches over my arm to palm my breast and pinch my nipple.

He's spiking my arousal again and I bask in it. My arm on the bed steadies me and helps me push back into him with every thrust. His hand goes back to my hip and he starts banging into me faster. I squeeze my thighs together, trying to contain him and that action brings more sensitivity to my sex. I feel a constant friction on my clitoris and I begin to go through the stimulating motions again.

The pleasure builds up just as strong as before and I listen to Jack moaning loudly. That puts me over the top. I moan in unison with him and climax with such great force that I become too weak to keep going. Luckily, Jack climaxes just after I do. He slows down slightly, but spasms into my body a few times, grunting quietly.

We lay there, catching our breath and I feel Jack running his fingertips along my arm.

"That was fantastic," he says.

"Yes it was." I feel utterly content laying here in his arms. Everything feels natural and I'm completely satisfied. I'm fulfilled? I *am* fulfilled. I get it now! I need to have feelings for the man I'm with to feel fulfillment. Not just sexually, but emotionally too.

I pull away from him and turn around to face him, kissing him hard.

"What's that for?"

"Nothing… Everything… I don't know. I'm just so happy."

"I'm glad, but why?"

"You just make me super happy."

"Well, that makes me extremely happy," he says, kissing me on the nose.

I snuggle in close to him, my forehead resting on his cheek. I can see his tattoo, so I touch it, "Why a dove?"

"I got it in university."

"Ok," I urge.

"Remember I told you about that girl I dated who broke my heart?" I nod. "I got it for her to promise her that I would be faithful to her for the rest of our lives."

"That's sweet…and sad. I'm so sorry."

He pushes me away, making me look up at him. "You're really different from other women, Colleen."

"Why do you say that?"

"Aren't you jealous or pissed about this tattoo?"

"Should I be?"

"It represents another woman."

I frown and think about it, "No… It represents you. You had it in your heart to be true to someone." I touch his face, "That says so much more about you and your character."

His blues eyes contemplate what I said and then he kisses me. "That's why you're different."

33.

Jack stirs beside me on the bed, waking me up and I rub my eyes, scooching toward him. He's lying on his back, so I carefully place my hand on his chest and slide it down his body, over his abs, pausing for a second above his groin area. I look at his face to see if he's still sleeping and then find his awaiting erection. This surprises and excites me.

I carefully get on top of him and rub my sex over his hardness. I'm wet already, which makes it easy for it to slide right in. Jack startles me by grabbing my hips as I start to grind.

"I thought you might sleep through this."

"Not a chance."

Throwing the blankets off of us, I sit up and lift and lower onto him, feeling him deep inside me. He reaches for my breasts and I lean forward, placing my hands on the headboard, so he has more access to them. I rock back and bring my hips down and forward, slowly and carefully. He groans and I continue my pace, wanting to feel that build-up again.

Jack flicks my nipples a certain way and the desire comes to the surface and escalates quickly, bringing me to the brink. I pump my hips harder and faster, feeling that wave of sensation permeate my body.

I realize that Jack is climaxing at the same time and I watch him. The yearning in his eyes is intense and it heightens my levels of emotion and sexuality. I'm breathless when it ends and I collapse on top of him. Our hearts thump against each other through our chests.

"Good morning," I breathe.

"Yes it is." He hugs me tightly and I bury my face in his neck.

"Do you have any plans today?"

"To stay in bed with you all day."

My heart soars. "Really? You don't have to work?"

"Nope. I want to lounge around, watch T.V. and enjoy this naked version of you."

Flip flop. "I'm in. Can we order Thai food later?"

He laughs, "Sounds delicious."

"Can I eat my cashew chicken in bed?" I bite his ear lobe and breathe into it.

"If you keep that up, you can do whatever you want."

"That's all it takes?"

"Pretty much. You have me by the ear, literally."

"You're too easy."

"Only with you."

I slide off of him and press my body against his, with my head in the crook of his arm It feels perfect.

"You fit perfectly right there." He kisses my forehead.

All of a sudden, the doorbell rings and Jack slides out from under me, sitting upright. "Who the hell could that be?"

I shrug.

The doorbell rings again, a few times and loud knocking ensues. He jumps out of bed all naked and sexy. "Holy fuck!" He runs to his closet and comes out hopping into his pants and putting a shirt on as he walks out of the bedroom.

Curious, I sit up with my knees against my chest and listen. I can't hear anything, so I grab the button down shirt that Jack wore last night and pull it on. I walk halfway down the stairs and listen.

"You said you'd call me," a high-pitched girl's voice echoes through the stairwell.

"Is that why you're here?"

"Well, you're not returning my calls or texts."

I bend over and see Jack run his fingers through his hair. He looks frustrated.

"I...uh..." He starts to look toward the stairs and I take a few steps up, trying to hide my feet. "Listen, I didn't mean to lead you on, but I didn't call you because I'm not interested in having a relationship with you."

That was harsh. He's cruel... I smile and wait for her expected response.

"What? But we had such a good time."

I don't want to hear any details, so I purposely stomp my feet down the stairs and as I pass by them, I pat Jack's bum, nod to the redhead and keep walking toward the kitchen. In the kitchen, I lean against the wall and listen.

"Who's that?"

"My girlfriend."

"You're an asshole. Good luck, sweetheart," she says loudly. "This one's a player!"

I assume she means me. The door slams and I hear Jack's feet walking toward the kitchen. I busy myself with the coffee maker.

"I'm so sorry about that, Colleen."

"Where do you hide the coffee?"

"Don't be mad."

"I'm not mad," I say, kissing him. "Where's the coffee?"

He opens the freezer and pulls out a brown paper bag. "Here."

"Thanks." I take it from him and put it on the counter. "Honestly, how can I be mad? It's an ex-girlfriend, right? When did you last see her?"

"About a month ago," he says sheepishly.

"At this point, I'm assuming that we're exclusive now?"

"Yes, of course."

"I suppose it'll take time to get the word out that you're not single anymore." I laugh. "I'm actually kind of glad it happened."

"Why?"

"It shows you that the past seems to pop up from time to time, but it's how you react to it that matters. You were honest with her. What more can I ask for?"

"Wow." He shakes his head. "Like I said last night, I've never met anyone like you." He pulls me toward him and kisses me. "I loved the way you strolled by us in my shirt. It was awesome."

"I was trying to help you out."

"I know. Thank you for that. You even slapped my ass!"

"I did. It's my ass."

He pulls up the shirt and discovers that I'm naked underneath. "What do we have here?" He squeezes my bottom and bends slightly to gently pull my cheeks apart. I feel the tips of his fingers at my entrance.

"You're insatiable," I moan.

"I'm pretty sure you're the one who instigated this morning's romp." He brings one hand around front and his fingers dip into my wetness.

I kiss him and bite his lower lip. "Coffee can wait."

34.

After a round that utilized the island and its surface, Jack turns on the radio and begins to make coffee.

I look in the fridge and take out eggs, butter, broccoli and cheese.

"What are you doing?"

"Making omelets."

"Yummy."

I start rummaging around looking for a cheese grater and a cutting board in the lower cupboards.

"You have to stop bending over like that."

I turn around and he's sat down at the island, with his chin in his hands, watching me. "Keep your mind occupied on something else and chop up this broccoli." I shove it towards him, smiling.

"Yes, ma'am."

With his help, I finish and serve Jack the first omelet and start making the second one. "Is it good?"

"I'm waiting for you."

"No, go ahead. Yours will get cold." I turn to look at him and see that he's inverted my plate over his eggs. "You're sweet. I'll be done in a few minutes."

A song finishes on the radio and the news comes on:

"Three more women came forward to tell stories of sexual assault and harassment they'd received at the hands of Kevin MacLean. He is alleged to have sexually assaulted four women between March 2011 and March 2015 at his office on Charles Street in Toronto, where they were seeing MacLean for sex therapy. MacLean's attorney, Gerald P. Boyle, said his client denies anything sexual happened while he was treating the women and they intend to fight the allegations. MacLean's scheduled to appear at a Brampton courthouse on November 15th."

"Hey! You're burning your eggs!" He takes the spatula from and starts flipping my omelet.

My heart is racing. I still can't believe I wasn't able to see the kind of man Kinky Kevin really was and actually slept with him. He hid it well. I shudder.

"Are you ok?"

"Sorry. Yeah, I'm fine. I spaced out." I force a laugh and grab my plate, helping him slide the omelet onto it.

Jack pours us some orange juice, brings over the toast and we begin to eat. "This is great. Thank you."

"My pleasure."

"You've had a lot of pleasure lately."

I hold my glass up, "Here's to a lot more pleasure."

"I'll drink to that." He clinks my glass.

Jack watches me take a bite and says, "You seem so relaxed and happy."

"I am." I reach for his thigh, rubbing it. "Why do you say that?"

"This is the Colleen that I know. The Colleen that I loved to talk to in your kitchen. I haven't seen you in a while."

"A lot has happened. Mr. Baker messed me up and so did Steve."

"I'm glad you're back."

"Me too." I sip some orange juice and watch Jack gobble up his omelet. "You know, I think I'm a better version of myself."

"Why's that?" He takes his last bite of toast and wipes his hands on a napkin.

"I've learned so much about myself in the last few months. I couldn't have done that if I was still with Steve or if Mr. Baker didn't exist."

"Pain makes you grow."

I look at him, impressed. "Yes, it does."

He kisses me. "I'll never hurt you. I'll always keep you safe."

Tears well up in my eyes. "I believe that."

"Baby," he reaches for me. "Come here." I put my glass down and climb onto his lap. He holds me tight and I rest my head on his shoulder. "Why are you crying?"

"I'm just so happy to be with you."

"That shouldn't make you cry," he laughs.

I smile and look up at him. "I know, but it's been a long road to get here."

"Are you finished your breakfast?"

"Yes, let's clean up."

"Nope." He scoops me up in his arms and carries me out of the kitchen. I squeal with amusement and hold onto his neck. "We're going to take a shower and snuggle under some blankets in my love cave."

"Love cave?"

He starts up the stairs. "We can't call it a man cave anymore. You're in my life now. I'm going to have to share it with you."

I squeeze him tight and absorb the comfort and affection he's providing me. I feel so special and so…loved? Is that too soon?

He puts me down on my feet in the bathroom. "Do you need any privacy first, before we hit the shower?"

"No, I see my over-weekend bag. I have everything I need." I smile, hoping he gets the double meaning. "Are you going to shower with me?"

"I wasn't sure, but I'd love to." He opens the glass door and turns the water on. It's one of those extreme showers with a large head on the ceiling and three more on the sides.

"Good." I crouch down and get my shampoo and conditioner and put it on the shower floor. "Nice shower."

"Remember, it was my mom and the decorator, but this is one thing in the house that I do enjoy."

I start unbuttoning my shirt and Jack eyes me lustfully. "Stop staring at me like that. I don't know if I can handle any more sex."

"I'll be good. I promise."

He takes off his shirt and my libido awakens. I can't get over his physique. With his blonde unkempt hair, he looks like a Hemsworth. Which brother played Thor in the movie? I think it was Liam. Damn! My boyfriend looks like Liam Hemsworth.

I drop the shirt and walk to him naked, putting my hands on his chest and nudging him with my breasts.

"I thought you couldn't handle any more sex?"

"I was wrong." I grab his bottom playfully and walk into the shower, with Jack following close behind.

35.

Later in the evening, we're spooning on the couch in his love cave, watching the Avengers, surprisingly enough. I was right. Jack does look like Thor. We had a long, lazy day and a lot of sex. My body is slightly achy and I'm tender between my legs, but I'm completely content. I don't think I've ever been his happy.

Jack's behind me with his arms around me, holding me like I've never been before. I'm sure Steve was a lot more affectionate when we first got together, but I can't remember at all. It must've disappeared quickly.

When the movie ends, we stretch a little and I turn to face him. "I'm hungry."

"I'm hungry."

We say it in unison and start laughing.

"You said something about Thai?" Jack asks.

"There's a place close by. Want to get fresh air or do you want it delivered?"

"We'd have to get dressed." He lifts up the blanket. I'm wearing his tee shirt and he's bare-chested, wearing just his plaid pants.

"So, order in then?"

"No, let's get out of here."

We walk into his room and I keep going into the bathroom, to rummage through my bag. I pull out a pair of black leggings and a long tee shirt. Do I wear my running shoes or my grey, suede boots that I wore last night? I really don't want to wear my boots. I'll wait to see what Jack's wearing.

In the mirror, I see that I'm flushed and my lips are swollen and red. It must be from all the kissing. My hair is unruly and I start to pat it down, but remember what I did yesterday. I bend over, shake my head and throw it back when I stand up. Wild curls. Not bad.

Jack walks in when I'm squeezing toothpaste onto my toothbrush and I see that he's wearing a hoodie and warm-up pants. "You're not dressing up, are you?"

"I have running shoes," I say, relieved and pleased that we're on the same page.

He nods and we start brushing our teeth. It's not an awkward silence, but it's a silence that I'm not used to. It's a silence that only a couple can share. He's never seen me brush my teeth before or get ready to go out. This is the beginning of a relationship. Flip flop.

I bend over and spit quietly, rinsing my mouth and toothbrush. I look over at Jack and he winks at me, spitting too.

"Does this feel weird to you?" Jack asks.

"I was just thinking that, but not weird. More like intimate."

"Just so you know, you're the first woman who's brushed her teeth in my bathroom."

"Really?" Why does that mean something to me?

"I've dated, as you know, but I never did relationships. After two or three dates, I'd never call them again. I'm that jerk that doesn't call."

"The redhead said you're a player," I swat him, joking. "Get it right!" But then I grit my teeth and frown.

"Hey!" He takes my hand. "I told you what I want with you. I'm not going anywhere." He leans down and kisses me. "Going for Thai makes this our ninth date and I still want to see you."

"Ninth? How do you figure?"

We leave his house and discuss how many dates we've actually had as we walk down the street, holding hands. It's cold out and the wind is blowing against us. I'm glad Jack made me wear his sweatshirt, even if it is five sizes too big. I never should've taken that sweatshirt out of my bag.

Jack counts running together and running into each other at the deli as dates. "I've even added our Dundas Square date."

"That was pivotal for me. Even though I was so stuck on trying to get back with Steve, you stayed in the back of my mind after that night."

"You didn't just decide to go for me when it didn't work out with Steve?"

"Do you think that?"

"A little, but I'm just happy that you came to your senses."

He doesn't sound believable. I stop him on the sidewalk and face him. "Since dancing and holding hands at Dundas Square, you've been lingering in my mind. I compared you to other men, I thought of you at random times, dreamt about you and I was extremely jealous that you went on a date with my best friend!" I punch him in the shoulder.

"Ouch! Hey! Nothing happened!"

"I know." I rub his shoulder. "I'm just trying to tell you that my feelings for you started to grow and I tried to squash them, but they got stronger and stronger. Deep down, I know that a main reason why it didn't work out with Steve was because of you." I grab his hoodie with both hands, "I lo…" Shit! I look down embarrassed that I almost proclaimed my love for him.

He tips up my chin, "I know." He kisses me. "Me too."

Flip flop. I stare up at him at a loss for words.

He kisses me softly again and he tugs at my hand to start walking. This time, we're both deep in thought. Did he say what I almost said? He wasn't afraid to say it in my kitchen before I met with Steve. Are we still taking things slow?

"Is this the place?" He points to a small sign that reads, 'Bangkok Café'.

"Yup, they have the best cashew chicken."

He opens the door for me, "I'd eat anything right about now." As I pass by him to walk into the restaurant he whispers, "That includes you."

I giggle and pull at the sweatshirt I'm wearing. "I look super sexy in this balloon."

"Nothing could make you look bad." He grabs at my bum.

We order food and decide to eat it in the tiny restaurant. The food would probably be cold by the time we brought it back to his house. There are only two tables and one's taken by two older gentlemen, so we sit at the other one by the window.

"I'm going to take your word about the food because I would've never eaten here. This place is a dive." He lifts his hand from the table and looks at it. "The table's sticky."

"That's what I thought when I first came here with Christine, but you'll be blown away, I promise."

A few minutes later, an older Asian woman places our heaping plates of food in front of us. She nods and leaves.

"Wow! That's a lot of food." He ordered drunken chicken, which is a bit spicy and had wider, flat rice noodles and his meal sits in a mound about five inches high off his plate. I watch him twist the noodles around his fork and take a big bite. "Mmm…" He closes his eyes. "Better than sex."

"What?"

"Never! This is the best Thai I've ever had."

Pleased, I dig into my rice and chicken. It's delicious.

We eat quietly for a while, watching the different people come in to order. The place is constantly busy. The older Asian lady takes the orders and the younger Asian man cooks all of the food. He works at a rapid pace and the bags filled with takeout containers line the counter.

I manage one more bite and put my fork down. "I'm stuffed."

"You barely ate half." He looks at me, concerned, but I just shrug. "You're a tiny, little thing. I can't expect you to eat the entire plate. I guess I can always eat it for a midnight snack," he says.

"I've been meaning to ask you this… When do you work out? I mean, you can't have that body without doing something?"

"What does that mean?"

I tilt my head and scowl at him, "You're going to make me say it?" He stares blankly at me and I roll my eyes at him. "Babe, you have the hottest body that I've ever seen."

He ducks his head shyly. "Whatever."

"Oh, don't you get shy on me." I poke his hand with my fork. "When do you make the time to work out?"

"You're silly. I have a gym in the basement."

"There's a basement? What other secret rooms do you have in that house?"

He laughs, "Yes, there's a basement, but no other secret rooms. I have weights, a bench and a treadmill."

"When's the last time you worked out?"

"Friday morning at five a.m."

"Do you normally workout on the weekend?" I'm interrogating him.

"Yeah, but I'd rather spend all my time with you."

I smile, "That's sweet, but I don't want to take you away from your normal routine."

"It's only one day and you're worth it."

"You're going to get flabby," I tease. He has to maintain the Thor image. He starts chuckling, but a figure passes by the window that takes my attention away. I panic. "Mr. Baker?" I point.

"What? Did you see him?" He stands up and heads for the door.

"Don't go! I'm not sure if it was him."

Jack opens the restaurant door and steps outside. I can see him from the window, looking down the street. He suddenly takes off running.

"Oh my God!" I don't know what to do. I didn't bring my wallet or my phone. I can't pay the bill or call the cops. I go to the door and open it, ready to go after him.

The Asian woman yells at me, "You no pay! You no pay!"

"I'm not leaving, I promise." I close the door and go back to the table, peering out the window frantically. The older gentlemen are staring at me curiously.

What can Jack do? Will he beat him up? Then he'll get charged with assault! Dammit, Jack! I pace in front of the window, fiddling with the extra-long sleeves of the sweatshirt I'm wearing. My heart continues to race.

After about twenty-five minutes, the restaurant door opens and Jack walks in, searching for me. I run into his arms.

"It was him. It was Mr. Baker. I ran after him and tackled him on someone's front yard, but he threw me off him and I landed on a shovel or a rake, right in my back. It knocked the wind out of me and while I was down, he kicked me hard in the ribs and took off."

"Are you ok? Does it hurt?"

"I'm fine. For a big guy, he's pretty strong and agile. I'm mad at myself. I could've had him."

"And he could've had a knife, Jack. It could've been way worse. Don't do this to me." I hug him tightly.

He kisses my forehead. "I'm sorry, but I just want him back behind bars."

"When he called me that day you came home from Niagara Falls, he asked me where my boyfriend was. I'm pretty sure he meant you." I look up at him. "If he's been watching me, you're the only man who comes to my house on a regular basis."

"Why does he want me?"

"Maybe he thinks you're my boyfriend because you rescued me…" I look down and think it through, "Maybe he's pissed that you foiled the abduction… Maybe he's been after you and not me?"

Jack shakes his head, "He had his chance right there. I was down and he only kicked me once. If he wanted me, he could've done much worse. He can come get me any time."

"Don't provoke him."

"Colleen, he's a fucking psychopath. He's obviously following you and me both. He doesn't need to be provoked. He's got his own agenda."

"Do you think he's going to do something again?" My stomach turns, thinking the worst.

"I don't think he's done with us yet."

36.

After brushing our teeth like a couple who's been together for years, we walk to opposite sides of the bed and begin taking our clothes off. I place his bulky sweater on the chair, along with my other clothes and stand waiting for him to see my other new lingerie set.

Jack takes off everything, but his boxer briefs. They're blue this time. He puts his knee on the bed, but stops looking at me. "What are you waiting...? Oh! More new lingerie for me to rip off in two seconds? He dives into bed and holds his arms out. "Get over here, you sexy girl." He keeps the blankets lifted as I climb in.

"You like?" I turn my back toward him so he can see my peekaboo bottoms.

"Very much." He cups my bottom. "Before I get too excited, turn around and kiss me." I flip over and kiss him gently. He pulls back and stares at me. "Are you ok?"

The walk home was pretty solemn. I think we're both shaken up about Mr. Baker and how he isn't going away. There's always going to be some sort of threat, that's why Jack was trying to handle it himself. I'm scared that Mr. Baker's next move will be just as bad as the abduction. I take a deep breath and let it out slowly. "I'm fine. I was really worried about you."

"I didn't mean to scare you. I wouldn't have left you alone if you weren't safe. I would never let anything happen to you."

"How? You can't be with me all the time and for the rest of my life."

"I can try... And for the record, I want to be with you for the rest of your life, if you let me."

Flip flop. I didn't expect him to say that. Is he asking for a commitment from me?

"You're quiet. Did I say something wrong?"

"Not at all. You keep surprising me by showing me what a decent man you are."

"Decent?" He laughs, tickling me. "I have never been called that. You heard that woman this morning. I'm an asshole."

"Be serious!" I push him away slightly, but he springs back toward me. "You're honest and caring..." I feel him slide his hand down my belly and dip underneath the edge of my panties. "And I'm going to stop talking now because you're not listening."

He presses his fingers into me. "I'm listening. You're turning me on with all your talk about decency." His fingers plunge deeper.

"Well...I...can't...concentrate...anymore." I say with each push and kiss him hard, urging my tongue into his mouth.

Jack continues to manipulate me, purposely cupping and pressing on my clitoris with his palm. The pressure is gratifying and sends powerful impulses throughout my body. I lift my leg overtop of his to allow for his complete seizure and he locks my ankle with his leg. He leans me back slightly and bites at my nipple through my bra, while continuing the tortuous handiwork.

Suddenly, he stops and gets up on his knees, pulling my panties down. He pulls off his briefs and gets on top of me, between my legs. I feel the tip of his hardness at the opening of my sex and I open my legs wider, wanting him inside me.

He looks at me with great desire in his eyes and enters me fast and hard. It takes my breath away. I grab his bottom and pull him toward me, with every lunge. His eyes are closed and his forehead furrowed in concentration. I love the fierceness of his rhythm. He's taken control of me. I'm his. I want him to fulfill his primal needs. I want to be his release.

I reach up and grab behind his neck, tugging his hair and his eyes snap open. He grabs one of my hands, pinning it above my head and then takes my other hand, bringing it up too. Both of my hands are captured by his one and he keeps driving into me. He's completely dominated me. The provocative and aggressive nature of his actions stimulates my desire. I'm on the fringe of an orgasm.

He stares at me lustfully, but unexpectedly smiles and slows his rhythm. He pulls out almost entirely and then slowly slides into me, pushing the last inch in with great force. I gasp and moan during the first cycle and the familiar sensations begin to stir deep inside me. He withdraws slowly and does it again, watching me the entire time.

I try to lift my hips up to make him enter me quicker, but he has all of the control. The escalation begins and I pant, trying to keep up with the waves of pleasure he creates with that strong push. I want more intensity.

"Baby, go faster!"

"Like this?" He picks up his pace slightly.

"More!"

He complies, but it's not enough.

"Fuck me hard, baby!"

He releases my hands and I grab his hips, pulling him into me as we move to a new, animalistic rhythm. The impact of our union makes a slapping noise that heightens the carnality of it all. I topple over the edge with unbelievable intensity. We orgasm together and Jack collapses on top of me.

After a few minutes, Jack starts making a weird noise, like a rumbling and then I feel him shaking on top of me.

"Are you laughing or having an attack of some sort?"

"I'm laughing." He pulls out and sits up on his elbow, smiling at me. "You surprised me this time."

"How?" Are we talking about being decent again? Or how much we've had sex?

"You told me what you wanted, actually you demanded it."

"I don't understand."

"Don't make me say it."

"You mean... Oh my God!" I stuff my face in a pillow, groaning with mortification. He tries to push me on my side, but I fight him. I can't let him see my face. I've really expanded my sexual repertoire, but 'fuck me hard'? I groan again.

"No! Don't be embarrassed. I loved it." He rubs my back.

I lift my head away from the pillow marginally, just enough to still muffle, "Really?"

"Baby, don't get me wrong. It was amazing. I love that it was in the moment."

I face him, uncertain of his genuineness. "It wasn't too much?"

Jack smiles and pulls me toward him. "Never, it was hot!"

All the research I did really paid off. But did I learn to say something like that? It's not like I practiced it or thought about it before I said it. Jack was right when he said it was in the moment. It just spewed out of me naturally. Naturally? I never even thought about dirty talk with Steve. That wasn't even an option. So, somewhere in my psyche, I felt comfortable and confident enough to say what I did to Jack. He's really brought out the sex fiend in me. I didn't know it existed.

37.

"Good morning, baby."

I stretch and roll onto my back, slowly opening my eyes. Jack's standing above me, holding a coffee mug. The thing I notice most is that he's shirtless and glistening with sweat. His biceps look very vascular and swollen. They bulge as he holds my coffee. He must've worked out. "Yummy," I say. "And I'm not talking about the coffee."

"Oh, I'm sweaty and I'm pretty sure I stink."

"Don't you know anything about pheromones?" He shakes his head and I sit up, propping a pillow behind me and keeping the blanket around my naked body. "Pheromones are chemicals that are secreted in your sweat and are believed to influence the behavior of the opposite sex, like triggering sexual interest and excitement."

"Is your sexual interest triggered?" He hands me the coffee.

"Most definitely. Thanks for the coffee." When I take it from him, I notice a bruise on his ribcage. "Is that from your fight with Mr. Baker, baby?" I put the coffee down and reach for it, touching it lightly.

"It's nothing I can't handle."

"That's awful,"

"I'm fine. Do you want to join me in the shower?"

I ponder this, knowing that my womanly parts are somewhat bruised from last night, actually from the whole weekend. "I think I need a short sex break."

"Are you ok?" He sits down on the bed beside me, looking concerned.

"Oh, it's nothing I can't handle," I smirk. "I'm just a little tender."

He smiles and touches my knee, "I'm sorry. I'll give you a little break."

"Don't be sorry. It's been amazing."

"I'll be back soon." He kisses my forehead and stands up. "I'm making my famous waffles this morning."

"Good, I'm starving."

I nestle back into the pillows and pull my knees into my chest. I'm flooded with happiness, excitement and hope. I'm looking forward to the future with Jack. Everything just seems so much optimistic with him, even the problems with Mr. Baker. I can endure his shit because I have Jack.

These last few days have been more jammed-packed with emotion and utter satisfaction than my entire relationship with Steve. How can Jack have such a substantial effect on me?

Maybe it's me? I've changed quite a bit from that logical, organized robot that Steve called me. I'm open to new things and have learned a few tricks myself. I cringe slightly about last night's dirty talk, but shake it off. Jack liked it and he likes me. I hug my knees into my chest. Maybe I will take that shower with him.

Naked, I walk into the bathroom and peek my head in. The shower's not on, so he must be out already. I knock on the door.

"Come on in."

I walk in boldly and find him standing in a towel wrapped around his waist, putting on deodorant. He puts the deodorant down when he sees me and turns his back to the mirror, half-sitting on the counter, to watch me.

Inside, I smile proudly at my self-confidence. I walk to the shower and lean in to turn it on.

"You, my naked girlfriend, are absolutely beautiful."

I step up to him and pull on his towel. "You, my partially naked boyfriend, are extremely hot."

He takes me in his arms. "I could be completely naked too. Say the word." I can feel the bulge through his towel at my stomach.

I tilt my head up and kiss his chin. "Let me shower and after breakfast I should be good to go."

"Baby, it's not going to kill me to wait. I'm just teasing." He kisses my nose. "I'm very happy just being with you."

"That's good to know, but trust me, I want you."

"If it's as much as I want you, I believe it." He slaps my bum. "Hurry up! Waffles will be ready soon."

I do hurry and I make it downstairs within twenty minutes, with my hair still damp.

"Perfect timing, my dear. The first batch is almost done." He's still shirtless, but wearing his red, plaid pants again. They must be his favourite.

"You're not calling me trouble anymore. I miss it."

"Oh, you're still trouble, trust me. I have to endure you prancing around my house naked or nearly naked," he points at me.

I'm wearing one of his tee shirts again. "It's a Leafs shirt. I had to wear it and I might take it home with me."

Jack frowns, "I still have you all day today, right?"

My stomach drops. "Yes! And for the record, I don't want to leave you either."

He gets busy with the waffle iron and when he turns back to me, he hands me a plate with a fluffy waffle on it. "There you go, trouble."

"Thank you. It smells delicious. I've never been this hungry before or eaten so much in one weekend."

He leans toward me, across the island, with his elbows on it. "It's all the great sex."

I tilt my head and smirk, "You're probably right."

"Eat up! You need to restore your energy because the weekend's not done." He sits beside me with a plate of waffles for himself.

Laughing, I take my first bite. "Mmm…so good."

"I thought we could go to the St. Lawrence Market today. I need some fresh fruit and veggies. Is that something you'd like to do?"

"Yes, I love that market."

"We could stock up on grapes, cheese and prosciutto and have a Sunday afternoon picnic in our love cave later. This time with a little wine, instead of beer."

He's being very romantic and sweet. "Sounds wonderful."

We finish our breakfast, change into more appropriate clothes and drive to the market. It's a beautiful building, interesting on the outside with its 1800s architecture and on the inside with cultural food, exotic meats and homemade natural products, like honey and baked goods. Jack holds my hand, pointing out the chicken feet, pig snouts and other animal parts, making me laugh. We go overboard and buy of all kinds of produce and deli goods. It's so much fun to shop with him. Our connection is growing.

Back at the house, we put away the groceries and make a plate of nibbles. I carry that upstairs with Jack trailing behind, carrying a bottle of white wine and two glasses. After pouring the wine, we cuddle on the couch under a blanket.

"Do you want to watch T.V.?"

"Not really, unless you want to," I say, not wanting to control him.

"I like the quiet."

"Me too." I rest my legs over his, turning sideways and sit back into the arm of the couch.

"Have you travelled anywhere in the world?"

"No, never. I've always wanted to go to Europe or even the Caribbean, but I was always in school and St…" I stop myself, not wanting to bring up Steve. "I never got the chance. Have you been anywhere?"

"I've been to most of Europe. I back-packed through Italy, France and Germany the summer after high school. It was a phenomenal experience."

"I bet. I'm so jealous."

"I'd like to take you somewhere and not just to Coburg, Ontario," he laughs. "I want to take you wherever you want to go."

"You would?" My heart screams with delight. "Actually," I pause, not sure if what I'm going to say is appropriate. "I have a week booked in Mexico in December."

"You do?"

"The thing is that it was supposed to be an anniversary present to Steve. He told me he didn't want to go after I had booked it."

"Oh."

Is it too soon to ask him? I hint further, "If I cancel it, I can't get a refund."

"That's too bad."

I take a deep breath and blurt it out, "Would you go with me?"

"Are you asking me to go to Mexico to enjoy your ex-husband's anniversary present?"

"I know, I know. I'm sorry. That was in poor taste." I shake my head, feeling stupid.

He touches my hand, "No, Colleen, I'd love to go."

"Really? You don't think it's weird?"

"I'd love to go with you. And it's not weird. I believe that you want to be with me, right?"

"Of course I do."

"And it's not like you'll be in Mexico wishing it was Steve with you."

I make a face, "Never!"

"Then I see no problem with it. If you're inviting me and I'm accepting."

"Thank you!" I lean over and kiss him.

"No," he reaches for my face and looks me straight in the eyes. "Thank you." He kisses me tenderly.

"I'm so excited now."

"Me too." He's not talking about the trip anymore. He takes my hand and places it on his lap, moving it up to his awaiting hardness. "Stand up."

He reaches for my shirt as he stands up and pulls it over my head. He also pulls my leggings down and goes for my bra and panties. I stand there naked, poised and calm while he takes off his clothes. I can be confident and please him.

Taking my hand, he leads me to our blankets that are still on the ground from yesterday. "Lie down," he commands. I do and I watch him lie down too, but reversed. It confuses me. His head is close to my knees and my head is at his upper thighs. I don't know what to do, so I wait anxiously for the next instructions.

"Move closer, baby."

Again, I comply, but I don't know what to do.

Jack guides my hips by tapping them, "Straddle my face."

Flip flop. What comes after 69? I can do this. Shakily, I put my knees on either side of his head, looking down at him. He lifts his head off the ground, licking my sex.

I whimper, closing my eyes and enjoy the softness of his tongue. He's so good at it. I really like how he does it with such tenderness and…proficiency. After a minute or so, I suddenly realize why I'm in this position and look down toward his hips. His erection is close to my face and I'm sure Jack's waiting for me to indulge and gratify him.

It's hard to concentrate when he's swirling his tongue about and making me shudder with pleasure, but I manage to handle his manhood with one hand while licking and mouthing it. I focus on his dove tattoo and hope I'm pleasing him in this crazy position.

Jack finds a good spot and an even better rhythm and I momentarily forget what I'm doing, ceding to his expertise. I moan loudly and feel my hips and inner thighs tense up, but my upper body becomes shaky.

He must feel my stability or my imminent orgasm, as he stops completely and taps my thigh, motioning for me to release him from my sex trap. I lift my thigh and after he moves out of the way, I place my knee back down, ready to lie down again.

"Stay in that position. You look incredible." He drags over a padded foot stool, "Put this under your hips."

I hug the stool and Jack gets on his knees behind me, entering me slowly, with his hands grasping my hips. I grip the padding with both hands, bracing myself, but Jack keeps a slow pace.

"Look at yourself."

I look back and around. I don't know where to look?

"In the fireplace."

The reflection of the glass on the fireplace is pretty clear. I can see Jack watching himself enter and withdraw from me. He looks sexy. His arms are flexing and I can see a dimple on his bum.

"You look hot," he says.

I keep staring and I feel like I'm intruding on the couple in the glass. It doesn't look like me. The girl in the reflection has a wild, mass of curls and looks extremely sensual bent over the stool. I can't believe it's me. The position is so foreign to me, compared with what I did with Steve. It's a turn-on that Jack finds me sexy this way. I try to arch my back more and move my arm to show my breasts.

Jack moans and starts pumping faster. Did I do that to him? God, I love that I can turn him on. I fondle my breasts, making sure he can see.

"Please yourself, baby," he grumbles.

He likes it! I push off the stool and lean slightly forward, cupping both of my breasts. He's still able to drive into me, but at a different angle inside me, that hits a different part of my inner walls. It feels good.

"You like touching yourself?"

"Yeah," I whisper.

"What do you want me to do to you?"

I don't know what to say. I like what he's doing. "Turn me around" I murmur.

He pulls out and I turn around, sitting on the stool now. I open my knees wide and hold my arms out, "Come to me."

He grabs a pillow and sticks it under his knees, close to the stool. I reach for his hardness, guiding him inside me and I pull his hips toward me. He begins to thrust into me and I wrap my legs around his waist, leaning back to grip the stool. The fantastic sensations begin to accumulate inside me and cause me reel and throw my head back, panting.

"Kiss me," he says, with a fiery look in his beautiful blue eyes.

I throw my arms around his neck and kiss him deeply. The kissing seems to intensify everything we're feeling. I squeeze my legs tightly together and he grabs a hold of my bottom, squeezing gently. That does it for me. I let out a long, loud moan forcefully and the electricity hit every party of my body, pulsating mainly deep within my core.

"Come for me, baby."

"Yes," I cry. I feel my sex contract repeatedly and my breath gets away from me.

Then, Jack comes. He makes a short, grunting sound and jolts into me a few times, finally relaxing in my arms. We stay still, with our foreheads touching and eyes closed. Our breathing rate starts to slow down.

"Damn, baby. That was unbelievable."

"Yes it was."

He kisses me lightly, picks me up and he shuffles on his knees to the blanket. He lays me down on it and lies beside me, covering us both up with a blanket. "You're the most amazing woman I know."

"Thank you, but you're the amazing one. I just want to be able to please you. I hope I'm doing everything right."

"Are you kidding me? Of course you're doing everything right. Why would you say that?"

I shrug, "I don't know."

"Is it because some jerk told you that you were bad in bed?"

"I guess..."

He tilts my face to make me look at him. "Listen to me. You're fantastic. You always have been, I'm sure. It's just that you didn't have a secure or solid connection. You know what I mean? Don't you see how well we connect?"

"I see it."

"You're sexy and completely capable of satisfying me," he laughs. "Trust me, I'm satisfied and maybe even slightly spoiled by you this weekend."

"I'm glad. I mean, I wasn't exactly nervous to be with you. I was looking forward to it, but now that we're getting more comfortable with each other and trying new things, I—

"New things?"

"Uh…yeah…That crazy position you just put me in…reverse…whatever." I don't want to say '69'.

"That's new to you?" He seems surprised.

"Yes," I duck my head down, embarrassed. "I never did that before."

"Baby," he hugs me and rubs my arm. "You need to tell me these things. I don't want to make you feel uncomfortable."

"But I wasn't uncomfortable. I was up for the challenge," I smile at him. "Did I do ok?"

"Better than ok." He kisses my forehead. "I love being this intimate with you, but please, talk to me about what makes you nervous or if something's new." He makes me look at him, "Ok?"

"For sure." We kiss tenderly and my heart soars. I embrace my new sexuality and the fact that Jack has accepted me and cares about me in every way.

38.

We trudge slowly up to my front porch and I unlock the door. I'm dreading the moment I'll have to say goodbye to Jack for the night. We've decided to sleep at our own homes tonight, so we can get rest up completely for work tomorrow. I fought the decision, knowing that I'll probably lay awake thinking about him and missing him, but my well-being presided over my 'sappy girly emotions'. I had smacked him playfully for that comment and agreed to disagree.

"Do you want to order pizza before you go home?" Anything to keep him here longer.

"Sure, I'm starving. I'll order it and pick it up."

I'm excited that he said yes. "I'll put my stuff away and make a salad while you're gone."

"Sounds good." He kisses me goodbye and heads out the door. "I'll set your alarm." I told him the code, so that he was able to come and go as he pleased.

I head upstairs with my overnight bag and as I walk into my room, I bang my bag on the doorway and it falls off my shoulder. I catch it, but I feel my fingernail catch on the strap. I inspect it and see that it tore at the side.

Dropping my bag on my bed, I go to the bathroom, searching for nail clippers and a file. I find the clippers in a drawer and cut the breakage, but I can't find a file. I know my bedside table should have one, so I open it and find one under my Sex Project notebook. I sit on my bed, put the notebook on my lap and file my broken nail.

When it's shaped and smooth, I throw the file back in the drawer and open the notebook, skimming the pages. I giggle to myself and grab a pen from the drawer. I'm going to write about Jack. He beat all of these guys hands down.

Data Collection

Final Sample

<u>Seek persons who understand study & are willing to express inner feelings & experiences</u>

- *Man, aged 34, Physiotherapist.*
- *Blonde, unruly hair, scruff, phenomenal, muscular body. Gorgeous!*
- *Man of my dreams!*

- *Perfection!*

Describe experiences of phenomenon
- *Known him for years as a friend and then something developed between us.*
- *We had a few dates and then our relationship went to the next level.*
- *Our connection is unreal. I've never experienced anything like it.*
- *The "phenomenon" lasted all weekend: different positions, fellatio, cunnilingus, dirty talk and even 69! Many times and multiple times a day!*

Direct observation
- *What is needed to be more sexual: A secure and emotional relationship; trust, honesty, friendship, hope for the future.*
- *Future goals: Anything and everything!*

Audio or videotape? n/a
- *This could definitely be a future goal.*

Data analysis

Classify & rank data
- *Out-ranks everyone I have ever been with. There's no comparison whatsoever.*

Sense of wholeness
- *I feel adored and sexy. He makes me feel special and I want to make him know that he's the only man for me.*
- *I'm completely content and satisfied.*

Examine experiences beyond human awareness/ or cannot be communicated
- *My sexuality has reached new heights and I'm proud and lucky to be able to be intimate with this man.*
- *I think I love him.*

"I'm back!" I hear Jack yell.

"I'll be down in a minute!" I throw the notebook in the drawer and go to the bathroom to freshen up.

I wash my face and hands, drying off and close the drawer that I found the clippers in. Something catches my eye before it closes and I open it quickly, my stomach dropping.

It's an empty pack of birth control pills. I had finished it when Steve left me and I never bothered to get a refill. What was the point? I was too devastated and depressed.

I carefully sit down on the edge of the tub, holding the empty pack, contemplating the extent of my mistake. I'm not on birth control and I've been having sex with Jack all weekend without any protection.

How could I be so irresponsible? You'd think all of those samples would've taught me something about safe sex! I'm so stupid! How could I just forget like that?

Dropping my face in my hands, I unintentionally slap my forehead, but do it again frustrated. Fuck! I assume it was all the excitement and eagerness of being with Jack that made me forget. I got lost in the moment. But there were so many moments! How am I going to explain this to him? He'll think I'm an idiot! I'm a grown woman!

I'm going to have to tell him. I put the pack on the counter beside me and stand up, frozen and afraid. *Come on, Colleen!* He'll be fine with it. We'll figure it out. He cares about me. He may even love me. It'll be ok.

I open the door and am startled by Jack sitting on my bed, with a bouquet of flowers beside him and a notebook in his hands. I look at the open drawer of my bedside table and nausea washes over me. He has my Sex Project notebook and he's reading the pages. He doesn't even look up.

"What are you doing with that?"

"What is this?"

"It's nothing." I try to take it from him, but he pulls it away avoiding my eyes.

"No, it's not nothing. You wrote about who you fucked?"

This has to be another bad dream. There's no way my nightmare came true. "No, it's not like that."

"Oh no? What does this mean then? *'Foreplay consisted of kissing, foot massaging and breast manipulation, heavy petting. He performed cunnilingus on me and I climaxed. Then we had intercourse (with a condom) and I climaxed again*'," he reads from my notebook.

"It was something I did." How do I explain it?

"And this: *'I was attracted to his mind and creative genius first. He is intelligent, laid-back, and relaxed. I initiated foreplay; kissing and fondling over his jeans. In his bedroom, I performed fellatio and he ejaculated in my mouth; I swallowed'*. Holy fuck, Colleen!" He yells, staring at me angrily, but only for a second.

"Jack, I can explain everything. Please calm down."

He stands up and explodes, "Calm down? *'He sold me my new car, had dinner together and had sex in his sales office'*. You fucked the car salesman! You lied to me!"

I cringe. This isn't good. "You don't understand."

"I understand just fine. You lied about what you did with Steve too." He flips a few pages and I reach for the notebook, feeling the bile rise in my throat. "No, please. *Let me read: 'Met him at his apartment. I tried to seduce him and performed fellatio, but was interrupted by a football game on TV.'* It's such a shame that you didn't get to fuck him too."

"I didn't want to. Didn't you read it all? I learned that I don't want him and—"

"It gets even better. You took the time to write about me. Did you write it today? You must've written it while I was gone…while I was getting you these fucking flowers." He picks them up off the bed and rifles them across the room. Gerbera daisy petals scatter all over the floor like confetti.

"Did you read it? It's all good. You're—

"I don't fucking care! You wrote about all your fucking sex partners and you added me to it. Am I just another fuck to add to your list?" He stares at me now, his face seeping with disgust. "You've been fucking busy."

"It's not like that!" I cry, tears streaming down my face. "Let me explain."

"I fucking believed that you were inexperienced, when the whole time you…" he looks at the notebook and throws it down on the floor. "The whole time you weren't. Was it all just an act?"

"No, Jack. Please listen to me. Sit down," I try to speak calmly.

He walks toward the doorway. "No, I'm done here." He heads down the stairs and I chase after him.

"You don't understand what that notebook means."

"I really don't want to know." He shakes his head and looks away, opening the front door. "How could you do this?"

"Jack, don't leave. I love you."

He pauses in the threshold, but keeps his head down. Then, without a word, he leaves closing the door behind him.

"No!" I fall to the floor crying, unable to catch my breath as the sobs consume me. I feel like my heart is breaking into a million pieces.

39.

At eight-thirty the next morning, my cell phone rings and I fumble with it to see if it's Jack. It's Margie. She's expecting me to be at work by now. I'm lying on the couch, covered in a blanket. I've been there all night.

"Hello?"

"Colleen, where are you?"

"I can't… I can't come to work." I manage to say through my tears. I haven't really stopped crying. Just when I'd get calm, I'd think of my weekend with Jack and start all over again.

"Are you ok?"

"No," I wail.

"I'll handle your appointments and be right over." She hangs up before I can say anything.

Great. Margie doesn't know anything about my Sex Project. What the hell? I might as well explain it to her too. Tell everyone how foolish I was. That stupid notebook! I should've burned it.

I look at my phone for the millionth time to see if Jack called. He hasn't, but the phone's almost dead. It needs to be charged, in case he calls. I called him throughout the night, but he didn't answer, so I left him a number of messages, begging him to call me back. I even texted him my regrets, but nothing more than a few words. I don't want to explain the Sex Project via text or voicemail.

No matter how I word it, it won't sound any better that what it is. I wrote about my casual sex encounters. How can that sound good? He's never going to understand.

I shuffle to the kitchen with the blanket still wrapped around me and plug my phone in to the charger. It rings at that exact moment.

"Hello?"

"Ci-Ci, Margie called me. What's going on?"

"Christine…he found out…" I start bawling.

"He found out what? Never mind. I'll be right over."

I drop the phone on the counter and slide down to the floor, banging my head against the cupboard a few times. I'm so stupid! I bury my face in my hands, over top of my knees and sob heavily.

Time passes and there's a knock at my door. "Jack?" I quickly get up and open it.

"Ci-Ci, what's going on? You look awful." Christine and Margie rush in and hug me.

I release them and grab some tissues to blow my nose. "It's Jack." I take a deep breath and exhale slowly. "He found out about my Sex Project." I look at Margie and she looks confused.

"How did he find out?"

"He read my notes," I say sheepishly.

"You made notes?" She cries. "Oh, Ci-Ci, that wasn't too smart, but I get it. That's how you do things."

"He left me! He won't talk to me!"

"Last time I talked to you, you were going on a date with him. What else has happened since then?"

"Oh, I think I'm in love with him!"

We go to my living room, sit on the couch and first, I tell Margie about my Sex Project. She seems shocked and almost appalled, but it leads to understanding when I remind her that Steve left me after calling me a boring robot in bed. Then, I tell them about our weekend together. I describe some of details of the sex we had and the abundance of emotions I'm feeling, as well as the connection I think we've developed so quickly.

"You've got it bad, honey," Margie says.

I nod excessively at her, "What do I do?"

Margie pats my hand, "You give him time. He'll come around."

"What if he doesn't?"

Christine pipes up, "Then he's a hypocrite. All you did was write everything down. I'm sure he's had just as many experiences, if not more. It's not fair that you're not allowed to have a past."

"I don't want to lose him."

"If everything you say did happen this past weekend and he's reciprocated your feelings, then you won't lose him."

"How do you know?" I look at both of them for an answer.

"We don't, but you're a smart woman, Ci-Ci and you're an amazing person all around. He's not going to let you go. He'd be an idiot."

Margie nods in agreement, "He seems like a good person, Colleen. He'll do the right thing."

Christine stands up, "Do you want some tea?"

"Yes, please."

She makes a pot of tea and we sit on the couch for the rest of the day, talking and trying to figure out how a man's mind works.

40.

Margie arranged my schedule today so that I don't have to go into work until eleven. I finally did fall asleep last night around two a.m., so the extra hours of sleep in the morning helped tremendously. However, I still wake up exhausted and groggy. I'm sure my eyes are still swollen from crying. I feel puffy.

In the shower, the water feels comforting and I stay in for twenty minutes, letting the water wash over my head and down my neck and back. I'm back to taking long showers trying to combat stress. How did I end up here again?

I dress slowly and try to put on makeup to hide the dark circles under my eyes. I stand back to look at my reflection and I still look worn out and spent. The makeup doesn't hide a thing.

When I get to work and park in front of my office, I look down the street toward the café. I want to go, to see if Jack's there, but he needs time and I can't really confront him about our problems in public. I miss him.

"Good morning, Colleen. Are you feeling better today?"

"Not really, but I have work to do." I rush right into my office. Her sympathetic stare is going to make me cry. "Let my first appointment in anytime." I sit at my desk waiting and breathing deeply to calm my mind. I'm no good to my patients if I'm stressed out.

Charlotte walks in and my blood pressure rises. She's my sixteen-year-old mini me. She gets high grades, does a lot of extracurricular activities, but had a total meltdown when she didn't get perfect on a test. Two weeks ago when we met, her attitude toward me was unpleasant and somewhat hostile. She didn't like my ideas or techniques. I know what she's going through, but like me when I was her age, I didn't want to be told how to live my life.

"Hi, Charlotte."

"Hi."

I open up her file and pretend to scan my notes. "Last time you were here, we talked about improving your physical health to reduce stress and improve your overall health. Am I right?"

"Sure."

"I asked you to fit two exercise classes a week, into your busy schedule. Did you do it?"

"No."

My blood boils and I take a deep breath. "Why not?"

"I looked, but I was too busy with an essay that was due, a, upcoming test and an event that I was coordinating. Like I said before, I don't have time."

"It seems like you don't want to make time."

"True. I don't need to exercise." She looks at her nails, picking at her cuticles.

"Do you understand that if you don't do what I ask or try to help yourself, you're going to have to keep coming here?"

"I don't need help!" She yells at me, standing up.

"Why are you getting angry?"

"I don't have time for this! I have to study for another test. If I…don't ace it…my average…will drop!" She seems to have trouble talking and stumbles across the room to grip the back of a chair. She holds her chest and her breathing is shallow and fast.

"Are you ok?" I stand up, walking to her.

"I can't…breathe and the room….is spinning….I think…I'm going to….vomit."

"Sit down," I lead her to the couch. "You can get through this."

She sits down and I place my hand on her back, urging her forward. "Try to slow your breaths. Inhale for the count of three…one…two…three…and now exhale for three…one…two…three…" I repeat this sequence a couple of times and then I ask her to inhale and exhale for a longer count. It seems to be working.

"Sit up now and raise one arm over your head." She complies and I instruct, "Put that arm down and raise the other one." Again, she responds and her breathing is almost back to normal. "Do you feel better?"

She nods.

"What you were feeling is scary, but it's not dangerous. You had a panic attack. Have you had any before?"

"No." She starts to cry. "What's wrong with me?"

"Charlotte, you're putting a lot of stress on yourself and it's not healthy." I rub her back gently. There's little reason to worry about this one panic attack, as panic attacks are treatable. There are many effective treatments and coping strategies you can use to deal with the symptoms."

I talk to Charlotte about deep breathing and relaxation techniques, and stress the importance of taking care of herself. We get on the floor and I show her a few yoga poses and how to breathe through them.

In child's pose she says, "I like this one. I can feel the stretch in my shoulders. Do you know one for the neck? I always have aches in my neck."

We sit cross-legged and I show her how to stretch her neck. "There's a yoga studio, not far from here that has beginner yoga classes. I know there's one at night that's only forty-five minutes."

She thinks about it, "Sure. I think I need it."

I smile and stand up. "Good for you. I'll get you the information and ask Margie to book you another appointment in one week."

When she leaves, I feel better about my situation with Jack. It's not the end of the world. I do have strong feelings for him and I know that if I had the chance to explain things to him, he'd understand. If he doesn't, it'll hurt, but I'll be fine. I know I'm lying to myself. I look at my phone to see if he called and throw it bitterly into my purse when I see that he didn't. It hurts a lot.

After a few more appointments and saying good night to Margie, I consider going to Tuesday night volleyball. Just like Charlotte's situation, I know it'll do me some good, but I don't know if I have the energy or the focus. Dammit! *Just go!* I march out of my office and head home to change quickly.

At the university, I park and sit in my car watching people head into the gym. I feel weak and dejected and… Blah. I feel blah. I don't want to mingle with the mediocre volleyball players. I want to hide at home in my bed. I can't do this.

There's a knock at my window as I reach for the keys in the ignition and it startles me. I look and see Ryan standing there. I open my car window, "Hey, Ryan."

"Are you coming?"

"I don't think so. I've had a bad couple of days and thought this would help, but I changed my mind."

"Are you ok?"

"Not really."

"Do you want to talk about it? We could go for a drink."

Ugh. "I don't think so."

"Do you like hockey? There's a Leafs game on. We could go to Hoops."

I can handle that, I guess. "Sure, that sounds good. Want to come in my car?"

He nods and heads to the other side of the car, getting in. "Volleyball wouldn't be the same without you. Everyone else sucks."

I laugh faintly in agreement, "I know."

At Hoops, we sit in front of the massive 126-inch infinite plasma T.V. and the same petite waitress from when Ryan and I were here on our first date serves us. Again, she can't take her eyes off of Ryan. I understand that he's a great looking guy, but pull yourself together.

Ryan orders two pints and she stares at him for an extra few seconds before she leaves. We sit back and watch the opening ceremonies.

"What did you do this weekend?" He asks.

"Not much," I lie, not wanting to get into it. "You?"

"I went on a date with this airhead flight attendant."

"Oh yeah? It didn't go so well?"

"To say the least. We met at a coffee shop and decided to flip through pictures on each other's phones and she stopped at a picture of my sister and broke into hysterics. I glanced at the photo and saw it was a candid shot of Gabby. My date asked me who she was, I told her she was my sister and she called her fugly."

"Fugly?"

"It's a combined word meaning fucking ugly."

"I know what it means. I just can't believe she used that word. How old was this flight attendant?"

"Late twenties. Anyway, I tried to take my phone from her, but she kept flipping and stopped on a picture of Belinda, laughing and said that she was fuglier."

"Your sisters are beautiful. She's crazy."

"That doesn't even matter. Who says something like that? I grabbed my phone back and told her that I didn't want to talk about my fugly family anymore. Know what she said?"

"What?"

She told me not to feel bad and that I wasn't fugly, but the fugly gene really slammed the women in my family."

"She actually said that?"

"There's more. She said that my daughters will probably be fugly because I'm a carrier of fugliness."

"No! She didn't."

"Yup. I excused myself to the bathroom and snuck out."

"I would've done that too. That's hysterical."

The waitress comes back with our beer and actually leans over our table almost bumping Ryan with her breasts, to put my beer in front of me. I don't bother saying thank you. She's too focused on Ryan. He takes a sip and yells at the T.V. screen about a goal the Leafs missed.

"The waitress likes you."

"Oh yeah?" He stares at me. "I'm not interested."

"She's cute."

"You're cuter."

"Ryan," I warn.

"Don't worry, I'm not going to hit on you. You've made it clear that you don't want to date me and I've made peace with that. I think you're great and love that we're here watching a game together."

"Really?"

"I'd rather be your friend." He makes a face and laughs, "I'm fucking lying. I'm hoping that you'll change your mind."

Laughing, I whack him on the arm, "You're incorrigible."

"That's why I'm a great lawyer. Now, do you want to talk about your bad couple of days?"

I cringe, "No, I don't think so."

"Why? You can tell me anything."

"It might piss you off."

"Is it about another guy?"

I duck my head, "Yes."

He nods and looks up at the T.V. "I see."

"I'm sorry, Ryan."

"Don't be sorry. You're a gorgeous and intelligent woman. I was stupid to think that someone hasn't snapped you up."

"To be honest, he's been a long-time friend and it just happened."

He shrugs, "So, what's the problem? Is he treating you badly? Do I have to kick his ass?"

"No, nothing like that. I don't think I should get into this with you."

"Why not? Maybe I can help you see his point of view and I could tell you if he's right or wrong."

"You'd do that?"

"Sure."

I hesitate and try to find my words. "Let's say I had a diary and let's say that I wrote about my sexual experiences in it."

"All of them?" He points to himself.

"Yes, all of them and the guy I'm dating read my diary."

"First, he shouldn't have read it."

"I know, but I did leave it out accidentally."

"That doesn't make a difference. It's an invasion of privacy. Unless you specifically gave him permission to do so, he had no right to read it."

"That's the lawyer in you talking. I didn't even think about that, but I'm not mad at him for reading it. I'm not angry at all. He's the one who won't talk to me. He's upset about my past relationships."

"You have a past and so does he. It doesn't and shouldn't matter what went on before your relationship if you are both committed to each other and have the same standards now. Give him some time to process and if he still won't talk to you, then it wasn't meant to be."

I frown and look down at my hands.

"I know it's not what you wanted to hear, but that's the reality of it. He has a choice to forgive you and to trust you. Forgiving you means realizing you have a past, but accepting at face value your present feelings for him. It means believing that you have chosen him and that you want to be with him and not with any of your exes."

"I get it. I've told myself the same thing and so have my friends. I guess I'll wait for him to come around."

"Don't wait too long. He seems pretty insecure and not worth all the heartache," he smirks.

I shake my head, smiling, "You were doing so well with your advice. Was all of it a sham?"

"No, I meant what I said, but I had to be the devil's advocate too. So, uh, you wrote about me? What did you write?"

"Never mind," I have another sip of beer.

"It was all good, wasn't it?" He teases.

"Ryan, stop it." I get that he's joking, but I don't want to rehash my one night stand with him.

"You don't have to tell me. I know it was fantastic."

"Thanks for the beer. I should be going now." I start to stand up.

He pulls on my hand, "Come on, I'm kidding. Stay and watch the game."

"I'll stay to watch the game, but that's it."

"Understood."

41.

After I drive Ryan back to the university and give him a quick hug, I head home. When I pull into the driveway, I see a police car parked at my front curb. I haven't been home all weekend to see them, so it surprises me. Were they here last night?

I park and walk to the cruiser. "Hi, Officers. I didn't know that you were still patrolling my house."

"Jack Fraser called us yesterday and made sure that we would still be here. He told us that Martin Baker was following you, so we want to be extra precautious," Officer Nicholls smiles.

Jack still cares about me, but doesn't want me. "Yes, Mr. Baker followed us the other night."

"Mr. Fraser told us that too. We'll be here as much as we can."

"Thanks, but I have the alarm. I'm pretty safe in my house."

"It's no problem. Mr. Fraser was adamant about us being here," Officer Leeds says, not looking too happy.

"Well, thank you. I do appreciate it. I feel safer when you're here."

Officer Nicholls nods, "You're welcome." Officer Leeds looks straight ahead.

"Have a good night."

Inside my house, I reset the alarm and pull out my cell phone to text Jack:

"Thanks for getting the police to watch my house. I appreciate the extra security."

I put my phone on the counter and rifle through my mail. It's mostly pizza flyers and credit card applications, so I recycle them and look towards the phone.

No response yet.

I put the dirty plates and cups in the dishwasher and wipe the counters, walking by the phone.

Nothing.

I head upstairs and change into comfortable sweatpants and a tee shirt, carefully hanging up my work clothes. I walk downstairs slowly and check my phone again.

Still nothing.

Dammit! He's so frustrating! I wander aimlessly around my house, fluffing up pillows, rearranging candles and knickknacks on shelves and straightening the dish towel on the oven door. I walk back to my phone.

Nothing!

That's it! I've had it:

"I can't believe that you're going to give up what we shared this past weekend just because of what you read. It's my past. It's in the past. You probably have a past worse than mine and I don't care. I don't care if you slept with a hundred women. You showed me a side of you this past weekend that made me believe you wanted to be with me and I'm pretty sure I showed you how I felt about you. If you can't get over my past, then you aren't the man I thought you were and I'm glad I found out now, rather than years from now. Please give me the courtesy of a phone call or text, so that we can hash this out like adults."

It's a bit long and not how I would've liked to handle the situation, but I don't have an alternative at this point. I hit 'send' so hard, that the phone drops from my hands and onto the floor, bouncing and sliding across the kitchen floor.

"Shit!" I pick it up and see that the screen is shattered and black. It won't turn on! "Lovely!" I throw it on the counter and head to my room, falling into bed and snuggling under my comforter.

I'm so full of energy and anger that I don't think I'm going to sleep, but I close my eyes and try. Images of Jack fill my head and thoughts of how I would talk to him when I see him next. Different scenarios play out where I yell at him or he pulls me into his arms and kisses me. All of the fantasies end up differently and I can't stop them from entering my mind.

At the café the next morning, I purposely keep my eyes straight ahead and avoid looking at anyone. I don't care to see Jack. I want to remain indifferent if he's here. I don't want him to think I'm pining away for him. The café scenes that I played out in my mind last night all ended up differently. I decided to play the aloof scenario with the hope that I wouldn't appear needy.

The barista says my name and I grab my vanilla latte from her, heading for the door. I can't help myself. I do a quick sweep of the café as I walk out the door and I don't see Jack. I shrug. It's for the best.

Work is busy. Most of the appointments are forty-five minutes to make up for missing Monday. I engage with each patient, giving them my undivided attention.

The day runs smoothly and I feel I'm back to my old self. I'm organized and precise, but my pencils don't have to be pre-sharpened and put in my holder a certain way. When I take a few minutes to peruse a psychology journal, I don't worry if the spines align with the other journals on my desk or care if they're in chronological order.

After using play dough with a patient, I laugh at myself, realizing that I have most definitely changed. I squished the red and blue dough together, making an inseparable mess and stuffed it back in the can when we were done. I didn't panic or throw it out. I just put it back on the shelf without a worry.

I feel liberated! Who cares about Jack? I can endure and survive without him in my life. I don't need a man. I don't need anyone. I'm a strong, resilient woman. I repeat those words to myself all the way home, thinking that I may start to believe it.

My landline rings, as I enter my house and I rush to answer it.

"Don't you answer your cell phone anymore?" Christine barks at me.

"I dropped it last night. It's broken."

"That sucks. Want to go out tonight?"

"Yes." I don't want to be alone.

"Really? I thought I was going to have to beg or bribe you."

"Nope, I'm game. Where are we going?"

"Not sure yet. I'll pick you up in half an hour."

The clock on the stove reads 7:00 p.m. "Perfect. See you then."

I take the stairs two at a time and go straight to my closet, taking off my clothes. I choose jeans and a baby blue sweater to change into and go to the bathroom to put on some makeup.

My reflection shows a confident, good looking woman, but I'm only pretending. I don't want to go out. I want lie in my bed and cry, but I did that after the abduction and it didn't do anything positive for me.

A car horn honks outside, so I quickly lace up a pair of black, leather boots, go downstairs and run out the door. I hear my landline ring again, but I ignore it and head to Christine's car.

"Hey, Ci-Ci. Did Jack call you yet?"

"No and I don't want to talk about it."

"Ok…. So, we're going to the Blue Iguana. Is that ok?"

"Sure." That's the bar where I decided to start my Sex Project, beginning with Steve the orthodontist.

"Good. There's a hot co-worker who said he was going to be there."

"I though you didn't do co-workers?"

"He's getting fired." She laughs, "He doesn't know it yet."

"Good news for you." I shake my head, "You're crazy."

"Yes I am."

"Thanks for calling me and taking me out."

"I'm here for you, Ci-Ci."

We park across the street from the Blue Iguana and run across to greet the bouncers out front.

"Looking good, Christine," the six foot, two hundred and fifty pound bouncer says. "Go right on in."

"Thanks, Bubba." She kisses his cheek and he opens the door for us.

The place is already starting to get busy and loud. The music is blaring. "It's Wednesday! Why is it so packed?" I yell over the music.

"There's an Ultimate Fighting Championship fight on tonight."

That's when I notice that all the T.V's are tuned into the pay-per-view channel and muscular, half-naked men are being interviewed. I've never seen a UFC fight before.

Christine takes me to the bar and gets the attention of the bartender immediately. When she gets our beer, a bell clangs loudly. She always gives great tips.

We walk over to a table full of her co-workers and squeeze in beside them on the bench seat. Christine begins talking animatedly, introducing me to everyone. I recognize a few from 'Chill', but I still smile and shake a few hands, not remembering anyone's name.

An attractive man steps up to the table and eyes me, but leans in to talk to someone else. He has brown hair, brown eyes and a dimple in his chin. He's very cute. He catches my eye again, so I turn away and try to listen to what Christine's saying, but it's way too noisy. I think she's gossiping about work anyways.

"Who are you?"

I look to my right and see the man with the dimple in his chin. "I'm Christine's friend."

"Hi, Christine's friend."

"I'm Colleen."

"Hi, Christine's friend Colleen. I'm Jaden. I work with Christine."

"Nice to meet you." He shakes my hand.

"You look bored."

"I'm not. I'm having fun."

"You like UFC?"

"I've never seen a fight before."

"You're in for a treat."

I'm not sure about that. "Ok."

"What do you know about UFC?"

"Men fighting in their underwear, lots of blood and basically, no holds barred."

Jaden laughs, "That's all correct, but it's somewhat more technical than that." He pulls up a chair. "The competitors fight MMA style, which is mixed martial arts. It's combines boxing, Brazilian jiu-jitsu, Sambo, wrestling, Muay Thai, karate, and Judo." He gets excited and goes into detail about the fouls, "They aren't allowed to bite, spit, hair pull or head butt. There are actually a lot of rules."

I nod and smile, but it just doesn't interest me. I take a sip of my beer and look at Christine who's cozied up to a man. They've moved down to the crook of the booth and his arm is around her shoulders. He must be the co-worker who's about to be fired.

"The fight's about to start," Jaden elbows me.

I look up at the screen. The first fighter is Jorge Masvidal is 5', 11" and 155 pounds with twenty-nine wins and nine losses. Benson Henderson, his opponent is 5', 9" and also 155 pounds with twenty-two wins and five losses. They're evenly matched, I guess.

"My money's on Henderson. His striking offense will dominate Masvidal's defense. I don't think he'll win by a knockout, it'll probably be a win by decision."

I have no idea what he's talking about. I watch the screen and Henderson and Masvidal are tentative for the first couple of minutes, but Henderson quickly lands a crisp right hand that only grazes the top of Masvidal's head. He then follows up with a vicious shot to the head.

The bar goes crazy. Jaden stands up and yells, "Hit him again!"

My glass is empty, so I grab the next server who walks by, pointing to my glass. She nods and walks back to the bar. I look up at the television and the fighters are in their corners. Is that the term? They're drinking water and Masvidal has a bloody eye that they're fixing up. The server comes back quickly and I pay her, taking a big swig. I feel tense and the beer is helping.

The next two rounds proceed rapidly, as does my beer. Jaden is completely enthralled by the screen, but I don't care to watch. It's barbaric like the gladiator games of the Roman Empire. The only difference is that death is not an expected part of a UFC fight. The extreme combat and brutal bloodbath is relatively similar and I'm not too keen on it, but I'm out and not at home pining away for Jack. I'll leave after my next beer, which the server suddenly places in front of me.

I look at her questioningly. She points down the table to Christine, who smiles at me while her date nuzzles her neck. I wink and hold the beer up to her. Looking at them, I recognize that I need to live my life more like Christine. She's so carefree and social. She lives her life day-to-day, but respectfully and intelligently. Why should I settle down again right away? Do I really want to get married again? I should just focus on me and have fun.

"Isn't this great?" Jaden says to me. "It'll be over this next round, I'm sure. Henderson's got him beat, like I said."

"Great. I'm going to the ladies room. I'll be right back."

Halfway there, I notice that he's following me. Maybe he has to use the facilities too. I put my hand on the bathroom door, but he abruptly shoves me past the door and pushes me against the wall, kissing me forcefully and stuffing his tongue down my throat. I move my head from side to side and he doesn't let up. His hand thrusts between my legs and I use all my strength to push him away.

"What are you doing?"

He puts all of his body weight against my body and grabs at my breast. "Come on, you want it."

"No, I never said I wanted this." I powerfully heave him backward and he topples only slightly.

"Don't be a tease."

I start to walk back into the bar, but he grabs my hand and pulls me back, slamming me into a wall. My knee automatically comes up right between his legs as he steps closer to me. The impact scares me. I know I did some damage, especially when he yelps loudly and doubles over.

"You fucking bitch."

I run into the bar and straight to Christine. "Your co-worker, Jaden just attacked me by the bathroom."

"What? Are you ok?"

"Yeah, I gave him a knee in the groin."

"Come with me." She takes my hand and leads me to the front door. "Bubba? Where's Bubba?" Christine asks a server who points to the door.

Bubba appears from outside. "What's up?"

She leans into Bubba's ear and points to me and the bathroom.

"Where is he now?" His deep voice booms over the crowd.

I look around and after a few minutes, I see Jaden walking towards us. "He's right there."

Bubba barrels through the crowd, knocking people away like bowling pins, and grabs Jaden by his shirt, lifting him off the ground. He drags Jaden to the front door.

Jaden points at me, "You fucking tease!"

With that, Bubba looks at Jaden, pushes the door open with Jaden's body and charges forward. Christine and I follow to watch what ensues, sticking our head out the door.

Bubba tosses Jaden like a piece of trash to the sidewalk and he stumbles back, falling on his bottom. "Don't come back! Ever!" Bubba yells.

"Fuck you!" Jaden screams.

Bubba rushes toward him, but Jaden jumps to his feet and runs across the street.

Christine starts laughing and puts her arm around him. "Thanks, Bubba."

"Anytime."

"I'm going home now, Christine," I tell her.

"Really?"

"Yeah, I'll take a cab."

"I'm sorry that happened. I'll fire him tomorrow."

"You can do that?"

"I was promoted to Senior Project Manager."

"Congratulations!"

"No big deal. I can just fire people now and at a higher rate of pay."

"That's great. I'm so proud of you." I hug her and when she releases me, she smiles and walks over to Bubba, whispering in his ear.

Bubba walks out onto the street and lifts up his arm in the air, hailing a cab for me.

"See you later, Christine."

"Bye, Ci-Ci."

I walk to the cab and Bubba opens the door for me. "Thanks, Bubba."

"Not all men are like that. Go home and sleep it off. It'll be better in the morning."

42.

The phone rings loudly over and over again, waking me up from my deep sleep.

"Hello?" It's 5:15 a.m.

"Colleen, it's Margie. Sorry to wake you up."

I prop myself up on one elbow, "What's wrong?" She never calls me at home this early.

"I'm taking Jerry to the hospital."

"Oh no!"

"I think it's a bad bout of food poisoning. He's been vomiting and on the toilet all night and he's not getting any better."

"Go! Take care of him. I can handle today without you."

"I know you can. Remember that we have tomorrow off too. I'm supposed to go away this weekend, but I'm sure that won't happen now."

"That's right." I was supposed to go away with Jack too. "Try to have a good weekend. I hope Jerry gets better soon so you can still go away."

"Thanks. Do something for yourself this weekend."

"I'll try. Take care."

If last night didn't test my strength enough, these next couple of days will. What am I going to do all weekend? My absurd decision to start living a life like Christine's got tossed in the trash, like Jaden's butt down the street. I can't go out night after night and risk my personal safety, hoping that I meet a guy that's nice to me. Never mind beginning a relationship with one. Do I start joining all those clubs again?

Instead of wallowing in bed, I take a long shower, considering my options: yoga, running, a good book, a movie… I can keep myself busy. I can't let the disappointment of a failed relationship ruin my weekend or my life for that matter. *Move on, Colleen!*

I purposely pick out one of my favourite dresses. The blue wraparound one that makes my eyes sparkle. I feel pretty in it. I turn around in the mirror and look at myself from all angles. Perfect.

There's enough time to make breakfast, so I take out some eggs and scramble them. I also make toast and pour some orange juice, sitting down to eat in silence.

At first, I enjoy the peace in my own niche that I've carved out. My house is exactly the way I want it and I'll be off to work at the practice I've established. My life is great, isn't it? That nagging feeling that I've been trying to forget resurfaces. It'll take time to get over it and forget. I push my partially eaten breakfast across the table and leave my house sluggishly, trying to pump myself up for the day.

A chai latte would make me happy. I travel a couple blocks out of my way to a drive-through coffee shop. It's quicker and I avoid any potential encounter with Jack, along with the unpleasant feelings that I'm trying to escape from.

The young man who serves me hangs out of the window, "Your order's almost ready. Would you like a muffin with it?"

"No, thank you."

"It's on me," he winks.

I smile at his flirtatiousness, "I had breakfast already."

"How about your phone number?"

How sweet and utterly bizarre. The guy has to be ten to fifteen years younger than me. "I'm flattered, but no."

"I had to ask." He disappears for a minute and comes back, "Here's your latte. I hope you have a wonderful day."

"Thanks, you too." He definitely improved my day.

I smile all the way to work and into my office, stopping at Margie's desk to look at my schedule. "Monique Dominion is first and then Sarah Everest, Justin Harris and Jennifer Smith. Got it." I pull all of their files and head into my office, sitting down at my desk. I open Monique's file and remind myself about her case. When that's done, I re-familiarize myself with the other files.

Where is Monique? She's fifteen minutes late. I walk back to Margie's desk and look at her message book. Nothing's written on it about Monique. I check the voicemail messages next. There's a message from Mrs. Harris about rebooking Justin's appointment and one from Mrs. Smith, wanting the same thing for Jennifer, but nothing about Monique. Why did everyone cancel today?

Monique's twenty-five minutes late now. Patients have been known to cancel or forget before. I'll just call her later to reschedule. I brush it off and take the time to review my afternoon appointments on Margie's computer and then go online to read the Toronto Sun.

An article about Zach the pilot catches my eye:

"The CEO of The Bank of Canada has been accused of rape and a long list of other offenses against a former employee, The Canadian Press reported.

Bank of Canada employee Dana Peterson alleges in a lawsuit filed in Ontario Superior Court that CEO Zachary Brown 'threw her on her desk, ripped her pants off, abused and raped her while holding her down, hurting her, and bruising her arm.'

Ms. Peterson claims in the lawsuit that she was 'deathly afraid' of Mr. Brown who allegedly harassed and abused her between June 2012 and February of this year, raping her, putting her in multiple chokeholds and 'likely' giving her a vaginal infection.

When confronted about the infection, Mr. Brown allegedly told Ms. Peterson the following:

'Don't threaten me. I don't care if you got an infection. I don't even care if I got you pregnant. I'm not getting treated for any infection and if I got you pregnant, you will have an abortion. I can't have you waddling around the office for nine months

pregnant with my child. It would ruin my personal and professional life. Clean up my messes like you always do and keep your mouth shut.'

Ms. Peterson's lawsuit claims that Mr. Brown *'flaunted the law,' 'changed documentation', 'lied' and 'fraudulently reported data to an insurance carrier to reduce expenses'*, among a slew of other non-sexual allegations.

Ms. Peterson seeks lost wages and benefits, future wages and benefits, and punitive damages for sexual harassment/failure to prevent harassment.

The Bank of Canada provided the Canadian Press with the following statement:

'The Bank of Canada is committed to providing a workplace free of harassment and discrimination and in accordance with the law. It is the company's policy not to comment on litigation and we have every intention to aggressively fight this matter. We are confident that the facts of the case will reveal that these allegations are completely without merit and this is nothing more than a frivolous lawsuit."

Chills run through my body. Zach is a rapist and I had a date with him. God! It was more than a date. I was intimate with him. I knew what happened between us was terrible, but from the sounds of it, it could've turned out way worse. I close my eyes and lean back in the chair. There's another reason why I shouldn't embrace Christine's lifestyle. I don't know how she does it.

The clock at the bottom corner of the computer monitor reads 8:40 a.m. and Sarah should definitely be here by now. I walk to the window and look down the street. I don't see her or her parents.

I grab the phone and look up Sarah's phone number. After a few rings, Mrs. Everest answers. "Hi, Mrs. Everest. This is Dr. Cousineau."

"Hi, Dr. Cousineau."

"Are you coming in for Sarah's appointment today?"

There's a pause, "What? No, I thought you cancelled it."

"I did?"

"Well, not you. Someone called me yesterday and cancelled it. They said that you weren't coming into work today. You had a personal issue that you had to deal with."

"Was it Margie?"

"No, it was a man. He said he was filling in for Margie."

"What?" I gasp, completely mystified. "I'll call you—

The line goes dead.

"Mrs. Everest? Mrs. Everest, are you there?"

I hang up the phone. A man called her? I walk into my office trembling. Something's not right. I pick up my phone to call Margie, but stop when I hear the front door open.

"Hello?" Maybe it's another appointment. I walk out of my office to see who it is.

Suddenly, I'm hit hard on the head and everything goes black.

43.

Oh, my head hurts. I wince and lift my hand to rub it, but my hands are stuck behind my back. I can't move them. I blink my eyes open. Why am I on the office floor? What happened? Are my hands tied together? My fingertips feel tape. It's duct tape. I see it around my ankles. I open my mouth to speak, but the tape's on my mouth too.

I hear footsteps and look around. Lying on my stomach makes it extremely difficult to see. Instantly, large, steel-toe boots come into view and walk toward me. Then I look further up to see blue work pants and a rather large, familiar torso. It's Mr. Baker. Terror strikes and floods my entire body and it paralyzes me. The tightness in my chest makes it hard to breathe and my legs start to shake uncontrollably. Even the hair on the back of my neck stands on end. What's this monster going to do?

"It's about time, you stupid shrink. We don't have all day. We have to get you home," his familiar, cruel voice creates more fear.

He's taking me home? His foot is inches from my head and I know he could crush me whenever he wants. I can't think of anything else. My brain has seized up with panic.

"I'm going to take the tape off your mouth and if you scream, I'm going kill you." He pulls out a gun from his waistband and bends down over me.

He's progressed to a gun. I'm completely terrified. I've never seen a gun so close before. His finger is on the trigger. Tears spring to my eyes and one runs down my cheek. I wish I could brush it away. I don't want him to see how petrified I am.

"Don't scream," he whispers and I can smell booze on his breath. "Do you understand?"

I nod profusely. I understand. The adrenaline pumps through my veins so fast I think I'm going to vomit. I can't seem to think logically. What can I do to get out of this situation? Do I run or fight?

He rips the tape off my mouth in one motion. I rub my mouth and ask, "You're taking me home?" I can't control the tremor in my voice.

He holds the gun up, "Shut up! You need to listen and do what I say. I don't need your fucking mouth asking questions."

I nod again. I have to obey him. Going to my house is better than driving to Windsor or sneaking across the United States border, but why *my* house?

"I'm going to take the tape off your legs and hands and we're going to walk to your car. You're not going to make a scene. You're going to get in and drive us to your house."

My mind reels. I have to talk some sense into him, "Are you sure you want to do this? You're already in a lot of trouble. This could—

"Shut up, shrink!" He roars, shoving his knee into my back. "I don't need your psycho mumbo jumbo. Just fucking listen to me." He puts the tip of the gun to my cheek.

My heart thumps out of my throat and I can't catch my breath. "Ok. Ok. Ok," I repeat, terrified.

"That's better." He goes down to my feet, keeping the gun in one hand and he starts to unwrap my feet. "Don't do anything stupid."

What can I do? I try to rack my brain and figure out how to manipulate him, but the gun shining in my face makes it extremely difficult. He undoes my hands and I roll over and sit up abruptly, moving away from him. I pull my dress over my knees and stare at him while stretching my arms and rotating my wrists. I give the back of my head a rub, too. Did he hit me with the gun? I feel a large bump just over my ear.

"Let's go!" He yanks me up by my elbow and my shoulder pops. "This gun's going to be at your back the entire time."

I rub my shoulder and nod. He's so strong. There's no way that I can overpower him and take the gun. I don't even want to chance it.

He pulls me to the front door and peeks outside. It looks like I wasn't unconscious for very long. It still seems like it's the morning. I'm guessing my afternoon patients aren't coming. Mr. Baker has to be the one who cancelled all of my appointments… He also cut the phone line… Did he poison Jerry too? I'm piecing it all together and I realize with dread that Mr. Baker worked painstakingly hard to plan this. But what's his ultimate goal? Why is he doing this?

Mr. Baker opens the door and pushes me outside. I stumble a bit, but he holds my arm tightly and we head down the walkway. I hear my car door unlock and he takes me to the driver side, opening the door for me.

"Get in and put your hands on the wheel," he hisses.

There are two people walking down the street. I stare at them as I put my hands on the wheel. Mr. Baker closes the door. I could honk the horn and call attention to myself or maybe get out and run down the street. I'm supposed to make as much noise as possible. What am I supposed to yell? Back off? That won't help here.

Mr. Baker gets in the passenger side and I lose my chance to do anything. He holds the gun down low on his lap, pointing it at me. "Drive home." He hands me the keys and our fingers touch. My skin crawls and I pull my hand away quickly, rubbing them on my dress.

I start the car and pull out. I have to stop thinking so much and just go for it. I have to save myself. What's going to happen once we get to my house? I might never get another chance. Should I crash the car on purpose or drive super slow. Either way, the police would come. I don't have anything to lose this time, Connie's not in the backseat. Connie!

"Connie misses you. She told me that during our visit last week." I try to reach out to his softer side. His daughter must evoke some type of tender feelings. Why would he be doing all of this?

He doesn't say anything.

I continue, "She wants you to visit her."

"Turn here," he says.

"Don't you want to see Connie?"

"Shut up!"

I shudder, but urge on, "I'm just telling you what she told me. She misses you so much…"

He pokes the gun into my ribs. "Shut up now."

My body starts to tremble and all I can concentrate on is the gun at my ribs. My imagination begins to paint scenarios of me being found in various positions with blood gushing out of my body. I try to remain strong, but I just want to crumple into a ball. The car lurches when we go over a bump and the gun jabs sharply into me. I try not to look down at it, but the lure of the smooth, steel barrel is intriguing. This small man-made contraption can kill me. I can't wrap my brain around it. The situation I'm in seems like a very bad dream. This can't be happening.

My house comes into view and I pull into my driveway, stopping near the sidewalk.

"Pull all the way up, close to the house."

When I brake at the top of my driveway, he takes the keys out of the ignition, without waiting for me to put it in park.

"Stay there." He gets out of the car and comes to my side, opening the door. The sun reflects off the gun into my eyes. "Inside. Now." He pushes me up the walk, to my porch and he gives me the keys. "Open it."

I do and look at my alarm briefly. Curtis told me how to turn it off in case of a break-in, so that the police are notified without an actual alarm sounding, but I wasn't listening! Fuck!

Mr. Baker follows me and closes the door, taking the keys from me. "Turn off your alarm."

What if I enter the wrong code? What would happen? I press my four-digit code, but change the last number. Three quick beeps sound and that's it.

"Enter the right code," he pokes the gun into my back.

I move closer to the key pad, so I don't feel the gun anymore and type in the code. It turns off and I lose more hope of ever escaping.

"Sit down," he points to a kitchen chair. As I sit down, he pulls duct tape out of his backpack. "Put your hands behind your back."

If I do this, I won't be able to get away. I slowly put my hands behind my back, but when he touches my wrists, I wriggle away and turn around.

"Don't be stupid. I'll shoot you and still get what I came for."

"What do you want?" I let him tape my wrists together and he doesn't answer me.

"Lay on the floor." He uses the gun to motion to the floor.

I get off the chair and lower down to my knees and then to my bottom. I could lie on my stomach, but that seems too submissive, so I lie on my side, watching him.

Mr. Baker shoves me onto my stomach and moves to my feet, taking off my shoes and taping my ankles together. "One last thing." He rips off a piece of tape and places it over my mouth. When he gets up, he puts his hands under my armpits and pulls me up to standing. He's so strong!

He drags me to the front door and opens the closet door. Without warning, he heaves me inside and I fall through the coats and down to the ground awkwardly. I land on my side and my head bangs against the wall. It's the same side of my head where he hit me before, when he knocked me out. That can't be good. He closes the door and I can't see a thing, except for a thin line of light at the bottom of the door. I listen to figure out what he's doing.

I hear his footsteps walk away from the closet and then come toward me. Something crashes against the closet door scaring me. There are more footsteps around the house and after a few minutes, the front door opens and closes. Then nothing.

Did he leave? I wait a few seconds, listening. I still don't hear anything, so I wriggle around the shoes, getting on my bum and raise my legs, feet toward the door. I pause and then kick the door. I listen. Nothing happens, so I kick it again with both feet a little harder. Nothing still, so I brace myself against the back wall of the closet and kick the door over and over again as hard as I can. The door buckles and the noise rumbles throughout the tiny closet, but it doesn't budge.

Where did he go?

Suddenly, I hear the front door open and close again. I freeze, waiting to see what he does. The closet door swings open and I squint at the light. Mr. Baker grabs me and stands me up. He puts his arm around my waist and drags me to the living room, dropping me on the floor. I roll onto my side and struggle to sit up, putting my back against the wall.

All of my curtains are closed, the lights are off and a blanket is stuffed into the curtain rod on the front door. No one can see inside my house. I stare at him, thoroughly stunned. He's really planned and thought about everything.

He lies down on the couch, places the gun on the side table and pulls out his flask, taking a long drink. The alcoholic, wife-beating son of a bitch has proven to be a cold, calculating criminal.

44.

Mr. Baker tilts his head all the way back and takes the last drop of whatever liquor was in his flask. My guess is whiskey. He taps the spout on his tongue and snarls, putting the tarnished container back into his coat pocket. He throws his feet on the ground, gets up and disappears into the kitchen with his gun. Frantically, I look around to see what I can get to help me rip off this tape and jump when I hear a cupboard door bang shut.

"Aha!" He exclaims from the kitchen.

He comes back to the living room carrying an unopened bottle of rye that Steve had gotten for Christmas from one of his clients. I'm surprised that it's still in the house.

"You were hiding the good stuff." He puts his gun back on the table, unscrews the cap and brings it up to his nose, smelling deeply. He stares at me and takes a big gulp. He closes his eyes, "That's good stuff."

In no time at all, he guzzles half the bottle and he staggers toward me, crouching down beside me. He rips the tape off my mouth. "You've been a busy lady," he seethes. His breath is rank and I turn my head away slightly. He puts his elbow against the wall and inches down it, sitting beside me.

His leg touches me, so I shift over and I don't say anything. I don't want to provoke him. His close proximity repulses me. My stomach turns with disgust and alarm. Why is he sitting beside me?

"You're a busy woman. A busy, busy woman. I've followed you everywhere and watched you pick up and go home with a lot of men," he sneers, pointing the bottle at me. Some liquor spills out onto my arm and drips down to the floor.

I take a sharp intake of breath and my eyes open wide. How does he know that?

"You like fucking, don't you? You little shrink whore." He pushes my shoulder and I fall onto my side, but I quickly get myself up again, not liking how my bottom is facing him. He laughs and pokes my knee. "Not going to say anything? That's ok. I was thinking that I might lay the wood in you, but you're not my type."

I swallow the vomit rising in my throat and shiver as my skin crawls. I clench my teeth and tense up my shoulders. This man is sickening.

"It took me awhile to figure out who took me away from my Connie. I had a plan. I had it all figured out. You were going to help me get over the border with my baby girl and then I was going to get rid of you," he glares at me. "That was going to be the fun part."

He was going to kill me. I knew deep down that it was a possibility, but I couldn't fathom it. My whole body shudders with fear. Mr. Baker is capable of murder.

"Anyway, I knew you'd eventually lead me to the asshole who fucked up my plan in Windsor."

Jack? He does want to get even with Jack!

"I followed you to your stupid yoga class and watched you go home with some hippie weirdo. Not once, but twice. He must've been a good lay, but I knew right away that he wasn't the guy who saved you."

It really was him that night, walking home from Mark the doctor's. I wasn't crazy! He's been following me since I got back from Windsor.

"Then, there was that guy down the street from your office. You know, the sex doctor. He was probably a great fuck, eh? Who becomes a fucking sex doctor? What a loser!" He explodes with laughter. "When I went to see him the next morning in his office, I knew it wasn't the fuck head that barged into the hotel room."

He went to see Kevin? I remember Ryan told me that Mr. Baker went to his office. Did he seek out all of my samples?

"I had to laugh when you took a self-defense course." He gets up slowly and sways a little before walking to the couch. He plops himself down and puts his feet up on the table. "You fucked your instructor!" He cackles coldly and cruelly, throwing a pillow at me. I duck, but it still hits me in the head. "You're such a dirty girl."

I feel so sick. He knows so much about me... It's revolting.

"That night in the parking garage really scared you, eh?" He laughs. "You and that young guy got it on his hotel room. Hold old was he anyway? Was he a student? You fucked a student. You like them all ages, don't you?" He looks at the bottle in his hands and his eyes close. The bottle starts to tip over, but his eyes snap open and he recovers. "I thought it was that lawyer guy, Mr. Big Shot. You saw him a couple of times, but you didn't go home with him. You didn't like his ego either? I wanted to wipe that smug look off his face."

Oh my God! How much did he see? Did he have cameras? How come I didn't catch him spying on me?

"It wasn't until you disappeared on the weekend that I figured out who the asshole is." He puts his feet down and leans forward with his elbows on his knees, staring at me. "Mr. Jack Fraser, asshole of the year," he chuckles to himself. "I followed you two to his house on Hazelton. What a nice house he has. What a nice life he has." His eyes darken and he throws the bottle across the room, and it smashes against the far wall.

I bury my face in my knees. This man's psychotic.

"If I can't be with my daughter, Mr. Jack Fraser can't live." He stands up and walks toward me, lifting me up in his arms and then throwing me on the recliner in the corner. He finds the tape and wraps the tape around me and the chair five or six times. I can't move.

"Stay there," he laughs sadistically. He lies down on the couch and closes his eyes. "I'm going to take a little cat nap before you call Jack."

Call Jack? He's going to kill him here? At my house? I wriggle my shoulders around and rock back and forth, but I'm unable to get free. I have to wait for him to wake up? And then what?

What did I learn in the self-defense course? I use the time to recall anything that Darren and the other instructor taught me. Effective strikes can be made with the outer edge of your hand, a palm strike or a knuckle blow. Go for the nose, eyes, ears, groin, knee and legs. They cause the most pain. I visualize myself gouging his eyes, scratching him and striking up under his nose with my palm over and over again.

The phone rings and I look at Mr. Baker. He opens his eyes, but doesn't move. After five rings, it stops and he closes his eyes again. I wonder who that was. Margie? Christine? Jack? No one knows I'm here, but they'd see my car in the driveway if they came by.

I go back to my self-defense moves. Elbow strikes and kicks were easy. I imagine striking him from all angles of attack including diagonal, horizontal and vertical. I would have to be very close to him to pull it off.

About an hour later, the phone rings again, but stops after one ring. Mr. Baker sits up with a bit of trouble. Then, it happens again. The phone rings once only. He stands up, steadying himself by holding onto the arm of the couch and heads to the kitchen. I stare at the gun he left on the table. If only I could get it.

The phone rings one more time and I hear him pick it up, "Yeah... Tonight... Ok." A few seconds later, he comes out of the kitchen, holding the cordless phone. He heads straight toward me. "Here's what's going to happen. You're going to call your lover boy and tell him to come over." He rips the tape off of my mouth

"We broke up. He doesn't want anything to with me."

"Tell him you're scared of the big, bad Martin Baker."

"No, it won't work."

He walks backward to the table and picks up the gun, his eyes on me the whole time. Getting close to me, he points the gun at my chest. "It'd better work, for your sake."

I can't do this to Jack, but what other choice do I have?

"Do you understand?" He jams the tip of the gun into my chest.

My heart pounds uncontrollably. "Yes, I understand."

He pulls a piece of paper from his pocket and looks at it, while dialing the phone. "Don't tip him off, just invite him over. Tell him you're scared because you saw me at your work again." He pushes the last number and holds it up, so we can both listen. The line rings

Please don't pick up. Please don't pick up. Please don't pick up.

"Hello?"

I clear my throat, "Hi, Jack. It's Colleen." I hope he hears the shakiness in my voice.

"Colleen, where have you been? I've been trying to get a hold of you," he seems so worried.

"I'm at home."

"I was just there. Your car's not in the driveway. Are you ok?"

Where's my car? I look at Mr. Baker and he presses the gun into my ribs. "Yes, I'm ok. Could you come over? I think I saw Martin at my office again. I'm scared."

"I'll be right over. I need to talk to you anyways. I need to apologize."

Mr. Baker rotates the gun, telling me to wrap it up. "Ok, I'll see you soon." He hits the off button.

"Let's get you ready to answer the door." He pulls a knife out of his boot and cuts the tape away from me and the chair. Then, he cuts the tape off my feet and hands. "Rip it off your clothes." He waits while I pull the tape off my dress and proceeds to pull me toward the door.

He pulls the towel away from the door to look out of the window and I can see that it's still light outside. It's mid-day. He's probably trying to get everything done before the police park outside my house again. He must've been monitoring my house. He has to know that the police come every night. It's still a lot of time before they come... How is he going to kill Jack and get away with it? Will he kill me too?

"When he knocks, you open it from here." He steps to the right of the door. "When you open it, you step back, leading him inside."

"How can you kill him?"

"He made me lose my little girl."

"You don't have to kill him! You can just leave and we won't bother you ever again!"

He whacks me with the gun on my upper back and the wind is knocked out of me. I lean against the door, crying and trying to catch my breath.

"Stand up! Stop your fucking crying!"

I stand up and gasp for air, wiping the tears away. Mr. Baker has the gun pointed at me, as he looks out the window. Can I grab the gun from him? I have to choose the hand that's clutching the gun and go for the wrist. It removes the danger of the gun, but I have to be ready for Mr. Baker to fight back. I can do this. I take a step toward him, reaching for his wrist.

"Stay where you are," he bellows. His finger's on the trigger.

I step back, disheartened.

Within a few minutes, I hear Jack's truck humming down the street and Mr. Baker says, "He's here. I'll kill you and him, and I'll even kill your stupid secretary and your friend Christine, if you don't do what I said."

My heart beats quickly and the anxiety builds in my chest. He knows all of the important people in my life. How did this happen? My hand shakes on the doorknob. I have to warn Jack. I have to fight.

Jack knocks and Mr. Baker nods slowly at me. I carefully open the door and see Jack's handsome face and his concerned, blue eyes looking at me. He puts his hand on the door to open it wider, but stops. Time stands still. Jack stares at me and his face changes slowly to alarm and then to defense mode. He must see the terror in my eyes.

Jack uses both hands and forces the door open. I watch the door hit Mr. Baker and I step backwards to get out of the way.

Mr. Baker stumbles backward, but recovers quickly, slamming the door shut and facing Jack. Jack moves quickly and goes for the gun. He grabs Mr. Baker's wrist and his entire arm, including the gun, drives upwards. Mr. Baker punches Jack in the ribs, but Jack doesn't budge. He retaliates with an uppercut to Mr. Baker's chin. Mr. Baker shakes it off and gets his knee up, plunging his foot into Jack's knee. Jack lurches back and Mr. Baker charges forward, kicking him again. Jack trips and tries to get his footing, but Mr. Baker attacks, jumping on top of him.

"Jack!" I scream.

Mr. Baker's on top of Jack's chest, pinning his arms with his knees. Jack struggles, but Mr. Baker is immovable. I see the gun in Mr. Baker's hand lift high into the air and come down hard on the side of Jack's head with a loud thump. Jack collapses and lays on the floor lifeless.

"No!" I run to Jack and touch his face. "Jack, wake up! Jack!"

"You!" Mr. Baker bellows, pointing the gun at me. "Sit down there."

I sit back in the chair, crying and feeling completely helpless.

Huffing, Mr. Baker grabs the duct tape, rolls him onto his stomach and binds Jack's extremities. He does the same to me.

We're fucked.

45.

An hour later, Jack regains consciousness. I see him blink his eyes open a few times. I whisper to him, "Jack, are you ok?"

He looks around and finds me. "I'm fine. What about you? Are you hurt?"

"No. I'm so sorry."

Mr. Baker walks directly from the kitchen to Jack and he struggles to get away, but Mr. Baker sits on him and slaps tape on his mouth. He comes to me next and pulls me off the chair, throwing me to the floor. I cringe and try to sit up, moving away from Mr. Baker. Jack looks at me, his eyes desperate.

But Mr. Baker isn't done. He lugs Jack up and throws him onto the chair that I was sitting on. Jack struggles, but Mr. Baker punches him in the stomach. I hear Jack let out a sharp groan and he doubles over. Mr. Baker pushes him back in the chair and rolls duct tape around him, like he did with me.

I can see Jack breathing hard through the tape on his mouth. "Take the tape off his mouth! He can't breathe," I beg.

"Shut up!"

I look at Jack and we just stare at each other. Why didn't he kill Jack? What's he waiting for? What can we do?

"I'm hungry," Mr. Baker says, unexpectedly.

"We can order pizza?" Somehow, I could get a message to the delivery guy.

"No, you can make me spaghetti."

No one would ever predict this. "How? I'm taped up."

He gets his knife out and rips the tape off once again, leading me to the kitchen, with the gun in my back. I watch him put the knife on the table and give Jack a frightened glance.

"What are you going to do to us?"

"I'm going to kill you."

My stomach drops. I didn't expect that response, but I get angry. "Why don't you just do it?" I demand overwhelmingly.

"Don't worry. Your time will come. I'm waiting for my buddy to get here. He's good at disposing bodies. Now make me spaghetti." He leans against the front door, so he can see me and Jack at the same time.

Disposing bodies? This is it! The last meal I'll ever make is spaghetti. Tears form in my eyes and I brush them away. No! I need to be strong. I open a lower cabinet and bend down to get a pot, searching for something to hit him with. I push by the thin, stainless steel pots and grab my cast iron sauce pot. I rotate the pot handle in my hand. Maybe...

I take a deep breath, "I love spaghetti. My aunt used to make it three times a week for me and I'd always eat it the night before a big game," I start to babble, trying to calm his nerves, so I can catch him off-guard. I fill the pot up with water and bring it to the stove, turning the burner on. "Spaghetti's one of those foods you can never get sick of and it's great to load up on carbs if you compete in any kind of cardiovascular event."

The spaghetti is hard to reach, so I get my little step stool and use it to get to the top cupboard, grabbing a new package of noodles. "Do you want spaghetti or linguine noodles?" I look at him and he's staring into the living room, presumably at Jack.

"Spaghetti," he says.

"I like spaghetti better too, unless it's with cream sauce. I can make fettuccine alfredo if you want."

"Spaghetti's fine." He tilts his head back against the door, not looking at either of us.

"No problem." I stand with my hands on the counter, waiting for the water to boil. It's my move. I have to do something or Jack and I are both dead.

The water takes its time to boil and I tap my fingers impatiently. The water starts to bubble and steam, so I place the noodles into the pot, stirring them around, until they're all covered by the water. Decide to fight or defend. If I go for him, he has a chance to defend himself, but I have the element of surprise. I need to be ready for anything.

I need him to get closer to me. I need him in the kitchen, away from the front door. I wait until the noodles are almost done. "Do you like cheese on your spaghetti?"

"Sure."

"What kind? Parmesan or cheddar?"

"Both."

"Could you please get it out of the fridge for me?" He just stares at me, not moving. "Come on, I need to strain these noodles." I start to bend down, still looking at him. He looks at Jack and back to me. "The cheddar's in the drawer."

He finally moves and I watch him out of the corner of my eye. He opens the fridge and finds the cheddar. "Where's the parmesan?"

I stand up and put the strainer in the sink, moving to the pot. "It's on the door, red lid."

He looks at the gun and at me. I look away quickly and stir the noodles. Out of the corner of my eye, I watch him put the gun down the back of his pants and grab the parmesan with his free hand.

"Thank you, you can put it right there," I point to the counter beside me and take a deep breath.

As he puts the cheese down, I grab the handle of the pot with two hands, pick it up and throw the boiling water and noodles at his face. He yelps in pain and holds his face, bending down. I quickly bring the pot over my head and hammer it down onto his head. He hollers again, but I don't stop. My next wallop makes him drop to the floor with a heavy-sounding thump. He doesn't move, but I hit him again as hard as I can. I hear a sickening, crunching sound. I think I crushed his head into the floor.

I wait a few seconds to see if he moves, but he doesn't. I throw the pot on the floor and take the gun out of the back of his pants, running to Jack. I put the gun on his lap and rip the tape off his mouth

"What did you do?"

"I bashed him in the head with a pot, after I scalded him with boiling water." I can't get the tape off his wrists. My hands are shaking so badly.

"Good girl. The knife. Get the knife, Colleen."

I turn and run to the table and come back, slicing the tape off of Jack's hands and chest. "I don't know if I killed him. I hit him a few times, even after he stopped moving." I start to cry and can barely see where I'm cutting.

"Give me the knife, Colleen. I can do the rest."

I crumple to the floor and minutes later, I feel Jack sit down next to me, putting his arm around me. That's when I fall to pieces, sobbing and quivering.

"It's ok, baby. You did great." He kisses my forehead. "You saved us."

"I'm so sorry. He made me call you! He was going to kill me."

"Baby, we're alive."

All of a sudden, Mr. Baker charges full-force into the living room, coming straight for us. Blood is trickling down the side of his face and his eyes are blacker than night. He's livid and wants to finish the deed he began.

Jack lifts his arm and I see the gun in his hand. He aims and fires at Mr. Baker, hitting him in the shoulder. The force of the bullet drives his shoulder back, but it only stops him momentarily. The echo of the ear-splitting gunshot lingers in my ears, as Mr. Baker keeps coming. I think I scream, but I'm momentarily deaf and most likely in shock. Time is moving agonizingly slow.

"Fuck!" Jack grumbles and quickly shoots again. I see the bullet penetrate Mr. Baker's chest. He lurches back with the impact and blood immediately drizzles out of him, slowly at first and then with each pump of his heart it flows continuously. I plug my ears and hide behind Jack. Mr. Baker hasn't fallen yet. He's still in motion, coming toward us with vengeance in his eyes.

Jack fires one more time and Mr. Baker collapses, just three feet from us.

46.

Outside my house, Jack and I sit on the tailgate of his truck huddled under a blanket, as the police examine the crime scene and take Martin Baker's dead body out of my house. It's late, and we've been here waiting for hours. They wanted to split us up to get our stories, but Jack wouldn't leave my side, so we told the detectives everything together.

"Can we leave now?" Jack asks Officer Leeds

"We really need to finish processing the crime scene and get your individual statements."

"You already swabbed my hands for gunshot residue, you took pictures of our ligature marks and the bump on the side of my head and we already told the detective our stories. You don't need us anymore."

Officer Leeds puts up his finger to tell us to wait and he leaves to find to the detective. Jack grunts in frustration. They meet at the door and we watch them talk to each other. The detective looks at us and nods. Officer Leeds comes back, "You can leave, but where will you both be?"

Jack gives him his address and phone number, jumps down onto the driveway and turns to me, "Come on, let's go to my house." He helps me down from his truck and opens the passenger door for me. "Do you need me to get anything for you?"

"No, I'm fine." I climb in, not sure I want to go with him.

"Don't worry. I'll take care of you." He closes the door and goes to the driver side, getting in.

Is he just being nice because I'm a basket case? He doesn't need to take care of me. "Jack, you can drop me off at Christine's. I don't want to burden you. I'm sorry that you were involved in this, but you don't have to worry about me. I'll be fine."

"Colleen, I want to be here for you. I want to take care of you."

"That's not what you said the other day."

"I know. Listen, I came over tonight to apologize to you." He sighs softly. "Please come to my house and I'll explain everything. I don't want to do it here," he points at all of the police cars and officers walking around.

I don't know what to say to him. He wants to apologize? Does that mean he wants to apologize for judging me or does he want to be with me? I don't need any more disappointment or drama.

"Colleen, will you come to my house?"

"Fine." I don't want to wake Christine at this hour anyway.

He pats my knee, "Thank you." He pulls out of my driveway and skirts through the maze of police cars. "Are you hungry? We can stop somewhere."

"That's my car," I point as we pass by a couple streets away from my house.

"What?"

"Mr. Baker moved my car. We just passed it."

He slows down, "Do you want to take care of it?"

"I don't know where the keys are."

"I'm sure we'll find them in the morning. Do you want me to stop and get you some fast food?"

"No, thank you. I'm not hungry." I lean against the door and close my eyes. The hum of his muffler is rather soothing. It drowns out any thought in my head. I listen and try to match my breathing to the constant revving.

A few minutes later, Jack parks his truck and helps me down from my seat. We walk up to his front door and he opens it for me. His hand lingers on my lower back and I'm getting annoyed.

"Come on, let's get you upstairs. Do you want to take a shower or a bath?"

"A bath would be great."

He leads me upstairs to his bathroom and turns on the water to the massive tub. He rummages through a cabinet under the sink and pulls out a bottle. He looks at it, opens the cap and smells it. "It's lavender-scented. Is that ok?"

"That's fine. I'm fine, Jack."

"I'll just put it here on the edge of the tub and you can put as much in as you want. I'll leave now and give you your privacy," he's talking fast. "There's a bathrobe on the back of the door if you don't want to put your clothes back on."

I stare at him. Why is he acting so strange? He left me! I should be the one acting strange. I'm surprisingly calm.

"Or put your clothes back on," he hurries. "Do whatever you want. I'll check on you later." He leaves quickly, stubbing his toe before closing the door. I can hear him cursing in the next room.

The bubble bath comes out in a purple stream, right into the running water and I check the temperature with my hand. It's good. I can smell the lavender. I know lavender helps to treat anxiety, depression and nervous tension. Just what I need, I suppose.

I take off my clothes and place them on the counter. My favourite blue dress will now be known as the Mr. Baker death dress. I should just throw it out. I shake my head in disgust and step carefully into the tub. I sit down slowly, adjusting to the hot temperature with every inch that I submerge. Lying back, I watch the water come out of the faucet and run my fingertips through it, as it fills up the tub entirely.

When my body is completely covered up to my chin, I turn it off and close my eyes. The hot water swathes my body and instantly relaxes my tired muscles. I take a deep breath and my body lifts off the bottom of the tub and as I release the breath slowly, I drop back down. I love the sensation of being weightless. It relieves my body of the effects of gravity and the pressure on my joints, muscles and bones magically disappears.

The smell of lavender is pleasant and provides a calming atmosphere for me. I immediately feel my stress melt away, if only temporarily. The memory of everything that happened today will fade and I know that I won't let affect me as much as I did before, but I still feel so empty.

I take a deep breath, holding it and completely submerge myself under the water. Everything seems louder and subdued at the same time. I hear a loud humming that I recognize as the bathroom fan. I move my hands and feet around and hear the swishing and bubbles that I wouldn't normally hear.

Suddenly, I hear a loud bang, some thumps and a muffled voice. Then, a hand grabs my arm and pulls me up out of the water.

"Colleen! What are you doing?"

I wipe the water out of my eyes and sputter, "I'm taking a bath! What are you doing?"

"I thought… I thought…"

"You thought what? That I was drowning myself?" I gape at him. How ridiculous!

He doesn't say anything.

"Hand me a towel, please."

"Sure." He grabs a fresh one from the counter and gives it to me. "I'll wait for you outside." He leaves without looking at me.

What's wrong with him? I stand up and step out of the tub, drying off my legs and then wrap the towel around me. I stare at myself in the mirror, watching the water from my hair drip down my shoulders. What do I do? If I leave the bathroom, he's going to bombard me with emotions that I just don't want to deal with right now, but I can't stay here. I don't want to talk to Jack. I want to sleep. I close my eyes for a minute, wishing I was in my own bed. Yes, I want to sleep.

I take the robe off the hook and put it on, loosening my towel and letting it fall to the floor. I pick it up and wrap my wet hair in it. Finally, I take a deep breath and turn the door handle.

Jack jumps off the bed when I come out of the bathroom. "I'm so sorry about that. I didn't mean to disturb you in there. I went in to check on you and you were underwater. I just assumed—"

"Stop talking. I'm not going to kill myself over Mr. Baker. I'm tired, Jack. I'd like to go to sleep. I'll stay in your guest room."

"No, you stay here. I'll sleep in my man cave."

I guess it's not love cave anymore. "Thanks."

"Do you want to talk?"

"Not really."

"Oh," he looks unhappy.

"We can talk tomorrow. It's been a long day."

"Sounds good." He pulls back the blanket on the bed. "Good night, Colleen."

"Good night." I don't give him a second look. I crawl into bed wearing the robe and the towel, not caring. I'm exhausted. I don't know when he leaves of turns off the light, I'm asleep in minutes.

In the middle of the night, the bathrobe feels picky on my skin and hot. Very hot. I toss the towel on the floor and wriggle out of the robe. I push the robe out of the bed and turn over onto my stomach. I stare at the light coming from the bottom of the double doors of the man cave. Is Jack still awake? I look at the clock. 3:05 a.m. He has to be asleep.

I turn over onto my side and close my eyes. Nope, not happening. I'm awake and very thirsty. I throw off the blankets and creep quietly out of the bedroom, heading downstairs to the kitchen. Everything echoes louder at night. My footsteps sound like rocks dropping into water. I hope Jack doesn't wake up.

The fridge squeaks when I open it and I curse under my breath. I opened it so carefully! I pause, listening for Jack. I don't hear anything. I grab the carton of orange juice and drink straight from the spout. It tastes so good. I finish off the carton and place it on the counter. I look in the fridge for something to eat. I grab the only container of vanilla yogurt and close the fridge.

Jack's standing there and it frightens me, making me jump. I scream out loud and I drop the yogurt. It splatters all over the cabinets and floor.

He's surprised too, but he's also eyeing me provocatively. I cover myself up with my hands, "Turn around!" Obviously, he's seen me naked, but we aren't dating now.

He pivots on the spot, laughing softly. "I didn't mean to startle you. I'm sorry. Here, take my shirt." He takes off his Dr. Pepper tee shirt and blindly hands it to me.

I pull it on and grab some paper towels, starting to clean up the mess. "It's not funny. You scared me."

Jack bends down and stops my hands. "Leave it. I can do it in the morning. Do you want another yogurt?" He looks at me, our faces are close together.

Flip flop. "That was the last one." I hastily stand up and put the paper towels in the garbage. I shouldn't get butterflies. I'm mad at him…even though he does look sexy shirtless.

"I can make you eggs or a tuna sandwich," he suggests.

"I'm fine."

"Are you sure?"

"Yes, I'm not hungry anymore. Thanks for offering." I start walking out of the kitchen and he follows me.

"Couldn't sleep?"

"I just woke up and couldn't fall back asleep." I head up the stairs, holding his tee shirt tightly around my bottom.

"Do you want to watch T.V. with me? There's not much on, but it might make you sleepy."

"Sure."

We walk into his man cave and I take a seat at one end of the couch, using a furry blanket to cover up my bottom half. I really wish I was wearing underwear.

He sits down at the other end of the couch and I hurry to tuck my feet in underneath me. He furrows his brow and picks up the T.V. remote, flipping through channels. I watch him from the corner of my eye and his scruff has filled in again. He's so handsome, but he looks tired. He took a beating today. I really should talk to him about it and ask him if he's ok, but I don't know where to start.

"Do you see anything you want to watch?"

"Not really."

"Hey! Look! It's Braveheart." He smiles and looks at me. "I love this movie." He sits back and brings his feet up, tucking them under my blanket.

I scrunch down lower and put my head on the arm of the couch, keeping my feet away from his. I watch the screen and vaguely remember what the movie's about. There's torture, hackings, stabbings, throat-slitting, and death by arrows and spears. I seem to remember that William Wallace is brave and noble, but vengeful and absolutely uncompromising. My eyes get heavy during a fight scene and I allow myself to close them and eventually fall asleep to the Scots chanting for William Wallace.

Seconds later, Mr. Baker has a gun to my temple. His black eyes and looming figure scare me to the core and I start screaming, "No! No! No!"

"Colleen, it's ok. You're safe." Jack's voice says from far away.

"What?" I blink open my eyes and I'm still on the couch, but it's dark in his man cave. The television is off and Jack is kneeling in front of me, caressing my cheek.

"Baby, you're at my house. It's ok."

It was just a bad dream. I rub my eyes and sit up. "I'm sorry. I didn't mean to interrupt your movie."

"Honey, you've been asleep for a couple of hours. I've been watching you sleep."

"Why? Listen, I'm fine. Do you want me to go back to your room or sleep here? It doesn't matter to me. I don't want to bother you." I pull the blanket around me and put my feet on the ground getting ready to stand up.

"Colleen, I love you."

I freeze and look at him cautiously. What did he say? Did I hear him correctly?

"I've wanted to tell you that for a couple of days now. The plan was to tell you three days ago, but my dad had complications with his surgery, so I had to go to Niagara Falls for almost two days and then Mr. Baker happened." He gets up off the floor and sits down beside me, taking my hand, "I'm so sorry that I judged you and got mad at you for basically what I've done myself."

I can't figure out what's happening. It's too much.

"Christine talked to me about your Sex Project."

"Oh my God," I'm so embarrassed. I pull my hand from his and hide my face.

He pulls at me, but I don't budge. "Colleen, I understand why you did it. I understand the note-taking. I understand your need to be better. Steve made you believe that you were undesirable and deflated your self-confidence."

"I don't think that anymore!" I stand up and take a few steps away from him. "I was wrong to think all of those things. I was a great person and I still am. Don't feel sorry for me."

"You're taking what I'm saying all wrong. I think what you did…your project is a part of everyone's life. Everyone experiments and has relationships." He comes up behind me, "I was stupid to get angry about it. I just didn't understand it."

"You left me." I face him, feeling angry. "You walked away from me and wouldn't let me explain."

"I know and I'm so sorry I did that. I have you on this high pedestal. To me, you can do no wrong. You're strong, successful, sexy and sweet. To actually find out about your sex life and the men you've been with… Well, it floored me, but that's not fair to you."

"How am I supposed to live up to your high standards after that? You can't forget about what you read. My sex life will be instilled in your mind forever." I throw the blanket off of me and put my hands on my hips, frowning at him.

"No, you're wrong. I can let it go because I didn't let it change the way I think about you. You're still up there. You're still on that pedestal. Your past created the person you are today and I love everything about you. How can I hold your past against you?"

"What happens if something pisses you off in the future? Are you going to walk away and desert me again? I'd never do that to you." I look down at my hands.

"I can't guarantee that I'm going to handle things the right way or say the right things all the time, but I promise that I'll never walk away from you again." He stands up and walks to me, putting his hands on my shoulders and sliding them down to my wrists.

"You were so mad," my anger dissipates with his touch. I place my hands on his bare chest and his hands go to my waist. Flip flop.

Jack puts his arms around my body and holds me close. "I'm sorry. You didn't deserve that."

"I should be calling you trouble from now on," I joke.

"No, you still hold that title. What were you thinking going to the kitchen naked?"

I laugh, "I thought you were asleep."

"Sure you did," he teases. "Everyone drinks out of the orange juice carton when they're buck naked." He raises the back of my shirt and grabs my bare bottom.

"What do you think you're doing?"

"Trying to have make up sex. I hear it's amazing."

"Oh yeah?" I jump up and wrap my legs around his waist. "Show me how it's done."

He holds me by my bottom and kisses me deeply. I wrap my arms around his shoulders and kiss him back, breathless in a matter of seconds. While we kiss, he walks toward his bedroom and unexpectedly drops me onto his bed.

"Really?" I laugh. "Are you trying to start another fight?"

He pulls down his red, plaid pants and his erection springs free. "Maybe."

I pull off the tee shirt I'm wearing. "Bring it on."

He gets on top of me, bracing himself with his elbows on either side of my head and slides it inside me, powerfully. The feeling is exquisite. He fills me completely and I encircle my arms and legs around his body, trying to keep him inside me.

Watching me, he moves his hips up and into me, without pulling out and it rubs against my clitoris deliciously. Electricity shoots throughout my body and I stiffen up, stretching my neck and arching my back, wanting to climax, but not wanting it to end. He kisses my neck and reduces the pressure, but propels into me again slowly.

I breathe into his ear, "Keep it up and I'm going to come."

"Please do. I promise you many more orgasms." He keeps at it and bites my ear. "Come for me, baby," he whispers.

That does it. I moan loudly with every forceful push into me and I clamp onto his body, not letting go as the climax takes control of my body. My heart beats with every convulsing throb, until the pleasure subsides, leaving me panting.

Before my breathing slows back down, he lifts me up, turns around and sits on the edge of the bed. I wrap my legs around him, resting my feet behind him. He has my bottom in his hands still and he squeezes it, lifting it up off of his lap and releasing to come down hard onto his solid manhood. I dig my feet into the bed and help in the up-phase of a squat, using my quads to lift my body up, while holding onto his shoulders. My breasts thrust into his face and every once in a while he takes a bite at a nipple.

Then, he starts to lie back, so I put my feet on either side of him, with my knees bent. He puts his arms above his head looking very relaxed, but I'm still sitting upright on top of him like he's a stool. I start to walk my hands up his chest and start sliding my legs backwards to get onto my knees, but he stops me by holding onto my feet.

"Stay like that. I want to watch you."

I sit straight up again and place my hands behind me to hold onto his upper thighs for support. I cautiously lift and lower off of him at first. This position allows me to take him in entirely and I feel obscenely engorged. Every little movement sends lusty aches to my very core. I speed up slightly and swivel my hips forward. He moans loudly and his eyes shut tightly for a second. I'm in control and doing all the work, but I love it. His face shows pure ecstasy as he watches me and the carnal engagement that occurs at our apexes.

"Baby, stop! I'm about to explode."

"Please do. I promise you many more orgasms." I smile, repeating his words exactly. "Come for me, baby," I whisper and increase my pace.

"Oh!" He groans, pumping his hips up to meet my sex, ferociously. He brings his arms back down and puts his hands on my hips, bringing me down harder onto him.

The extreme, brute force and the look on his face initiate the reeling sensations for me again and we climax together, our moans and breaths in sync with each other.

I collapse on top of him, nuzzling my face in his neck. He smells so good. His hands eventually come up to my back and then down to my bottom. He squeezes gently and palms each cheek.

"Your ass is sweet."

I laugh and bite his ear. "It's all yours. You can have it."

He carefully flips me off of him and we crawl up to the pillows and lie facing each other. "Really, you're giving me your ass?"

"The rest of me goes along with it though."

"Hmmmm," he pretends to think and I swat him. "That's a great deal. I'll take you."

"And there are no returns or exchanges. I'm yours forever."

"Is there some type of warranty? Can I return you if you're faulty?" He teases

"I will never be faulty. You'll never have a problem with me." I pause and look into his eyes, "I love you."

He gets up on his elbow and hovers over me, looking surprised, but happy. "Baby, I love you too." He inches down and kisses me gently.

My heart feels so full. I reach up and touch his cheek, stroking his scruff and then reach back to tug his hair. "I'm so lucky."

"I'm the lucky one," he murmurs. He pulls me in close and puts his leg over mine. He playfully flicks my nipple.

"Hey, that's not nice."

"I own you. This is my body. I can do whatever I want with it."

"Very true. What are you going to do with it?"

His eyes flash and lower mischievously. He suddenly gets on top of me and I can feel his hardness between my legs.

"Already?" I'm ready and willing, not surprised at his incredible sex drive. I open my legs wider and feel him at my entrance.

"Yup. I want to test out your guarantee and see if the quality of my product meets my high standards." He slides into me slowly. "Commencing product testing number two."

We laugh only for a few seconds and concentrate on completing the thorough examination.

EPILOGUE

Jack and I lie side by side on an outdoor Bali bed, complete with a richly upholstered pleasure dome and a bamboo frame around it. The breeze from the Gulf of Mexico is light and its waves crash down in the distance. We watch a boat take off near shore and two people in harnesses attached to a tether, lift up into the air as the bright yellow parasail behind them fills with wind.

"Do you want to try that?" Jack asks.

"Not really. I'm enjoying the laziness of our day today." I look over at him and sigh. He's looks sexy in his blue and orange boardshorts. His gorgeous washboard stomach has gotten looks from the ladies on the resort, but he keeps an arm protectively around me at all times. He only has eyes for me.

It's our third day at El Dorado Maroma in Playa Del Carmen and it's the first time we ventured down to the beach. We've been in the room since day one and only left our room for dinner yesterday. Jack needed to test out my guarantee in Mexico over and over again. The fresh fruit, chocolate-dipped strawberries and the bottle of champagne that greeted us in the room sustained us for most of the first day and on the second day, we ordered room service.

It's been a whirlwind month for both of us. We didn't attend Martin Baker's funeral for a multitude of reasons, but talked to Mrs. Baker and Connie afterwards. Connie doesn't know how her dad died, only that it was an accident. She seemed fine, but more sessions with her will tell me more. Mrs. Baker hugged me, apologizing again for getting me inextricably involved in her life and Jack said that she thanked him. We didn't analyze it. We know why.

We learned that Margie's husband didn't get food poisoning. He was actually poisoned by a fruit basket that was sent to him at work. Jerry thought it was from a client and he happily ate nearly two-thirds of the chocolate-covered bananas. After vomiting all night, he complained about abdominal pain and even vertigo and went to the hospital. The doctors found arsenic in his system. The fruit basket was paid for by a stolen credit card. The police assumed it was Martin Baker who sent it to Jerry. How else would he get Margie to leave the office?

Since my living room sported copious amounts of blood on the carpet and a stray bullet hole in the wall, due to it entering and exiting Mr. Baker's shoulder, I decided that I couldn't live there anymore. At first, I was going to rent something downtown, but Jack insisted that I stay with him, until my house was thoroughly cleaned and sold. I moved in to his house immediately and our love nest gets used daily.

We always kiss goodbye in the morning, work all day, sometimes meeting for lunch or a quickie at his house. We text or call each other during the day and our nights consist of heavy lovemaking, homemade dinners, screwing around, sometimes a double date with Christine or a hockey game and a lot more sex.

I understand that we're still in the honeymoon stage of our relationship, but he bought me those flowers again just before we left for Mexico and he tells me I'm beautiful every day. He opens doors for me, helps me make dinner or pours me a glass of wine while he makes the meal and he shows me never-ending affection and love.

Will it end? I hope not, but I'm doing my part to keep the spark alive. One time, I got home before him and waited for him dressed only in a big red bow that he had to untie. I've also surprised him at his office at lunch time or between clients to give him a blow job. I know how to please him and he appreciates it.

"Aquí están sus dscquiris fresa, señor." The Mexican attendant holds two strawberry daiquiris on a tray.

"Gracias Señor," Jack says and signs the receipt, charging it to our room.

The attendant hands me my daiquiri and I put it on the table beside me.

"You don't want it?"

"I've been meaning to tell you something for the last couple of days. I don't know why I waited. Maybe I just wanted to make sure that you loved me."

"Baby, you know I love you, don't you?" He looks concerned.

"Of course I do. This is just difficult."

He puts his daiquiri and the table beside him and takes my hand, "What is it?"

"We've never been protected," I start with little information, trying to assess his reaction.

"What? What are you talking about?"

"I stopped taking the pill months ago when I became separated and we've never used condoms. We've never used protection."

His face changes from confused to awareness to shock.

Before he says anything and I lose my nerve, I start talking quickly, "I got so swept up in everything with you that I didn't realize that I wasn't on the pill and when I did, you broke up with me for that short time. I was so devastated about losing you that I forgot again and didn't remember when we got back together. Everything's been so crazy and so passionate and I didn't think… Anyway, just before we left, I finally remembered and went to my doctor to get a prescription and she made me do a pregnancy test…" I finally pause and look at him.

He's staring at me, waiting.

"I'm pregnant."

An enormous smile breaks out on his face. "You're having my baby?" I nod, smiling. "Woohoo! You're having my baby!" He pulls me in his arms and kisses me gently. He leans back to look at me, "You've made me the happiest man in the entire world. I was happy before, but this… this is incredible. I love you, Colleen."

"I love you too."

Abruptly, he gets up on his knees and closes the thick, privacy curtains around the Bali bed. "We need to celebrate," he says crawling back to me.

"Here?" I laugh, sitting on top of him when he lies on his back.

"Yes, here." He kisses me. "We can still do this, right?" He asks cautiously, caressing my stomach.

"Of course. Nothing will ever stop me from that!" I untie my bikini top, tossing it to the side.

"Good! 'Cause I'm never gonna stop!" He growls and ravages me.

THE END

Made in the USA
Charleston, SC
08 December 2015